D0812132

In the FOG

The Chronicles of Greystone Bay

Greystone Bay
Doom City
The SeaHarp Hotel
In the Fog

Recent Tor books by contributors to *In the Fog*

by Elizabeth Engstrom
Lizzie Borden
Nightmare Flower

by Charles L. Grant
Raven
Something Stirs

by Kathryn Ptacek
In Silence Sealed
Women of Darkness II (editor)

by Chelsea Quinn Yarbro
Darker Jewels
Out of the House of Life

In the FOG

The Final Chronicle of Greystone Bay

Edited by

Charles L. Grant

A Tom Doherty Associates Book
New York

IN THE FOG

This book has been printed on acid-free paper.

A Tor Book
Published by Tom Doherty Associates, Inc.
175 Fifth Avenue
New York, N.Y. 10010

Tor® is a registered trademark of Tom Doherty Associates, Inc.

Library of Congress Cataloging-in-Publication Data

In the fog: the last chronicle of Greystone Bay / edited by Charles L. Grant.
p. cm.
"A Tom Doherty Associates book."
ISBN 0-312-09703-4
1. Fog—Fiction. I. Grant, Charles L.
PS3550.A1I5 1993
813′.0873808—dc20 93-11519 CIP

First Tor edition: October 1993

Printed in the United States of America

0 9 8 7 6 5 4 3 2 1

Contents

In the FOG

INTRODUCTION

by Charles L. Grant

THE FOG, AND THE SEA, AND THE TIRED VOICE OF THE SHIP.

That's how it began, when the world was much younger, and those who came to the Bay knew less than they thought and more than they wanted; when the children grew and moved on, when the grownups moved on, and returned; when the dead were buried and the newly born were celebrated and the sun rose each morning on fresh paint and glorious flowers.

That's how it began.

The fog. And the sea.

When hotels were built and homes became boarding houses and artists thrived and shopkeepers managed and teachers somehow didn't notice what was different.

For the Bay was different, in every way imaginable, and in some ways that weren't. It didn't take long for people to notice that the sky was never, exactly, perfectly clear; that the hills were never, exactly, high enough; that the street sometimes didn't end, and sometimes went on forever; that the old-timers were too old, and the young were never young.

Still, they came, and still they left, and the stories were just stories told to the growl and thunder of the tide. And those who understood grew to love the nightly fog, and grew to fear it as well; they grew to love and know the sea, and fear it as well; they learned things, they heard things, they carried on with their lives as if their lives and the Bay were intertwined, would never end.

They were wrong.

The fog. And the sea.
That's how it began.

This is how it ends.
In the fog.
And the sea.

The Fog Knew Her Name

by Elizabeth Engstrom

AT FORTY-SEVEN AND STOCKY, Kitten Frazier wore her name like a ten-year-old girl wears premature breasts—the awkwardness of it never left her. "It must have been cute when I was a baby," she always said in apology whenever she had to meet anyone for the first time.

She knew it was the reason she never married, and the bitterness of the cruel joke her parents had played kept her mouth a firm line when it wanted to tremble, kept her back straight when it wanted to sag under the weight of her sorrow, kept her eyes bright and focused when they wanted to squint up and leak tears.

Sometime in her twenties, long after her parents were dead, Kitten dared to change her name in her mind, trying on new names and with them, new identities, fantasizing about who she could be, if only she would change her name. She liked being a Lola in her mind, but in the mirror she was more of a Clara. She longed to be a Monique in bed, but there was hardly ever a man to sleep with, and so in reality she thought of herself more as a Hester. She thought of Morgan, and Guinevere, Angelica, Scarlett, but she knew she would never have the courage to tell her friends, the community, the *public* that she had changed her name to something so fantastic. So while she assumed them in the privacy of her own mind, she gave serious thought to common, wonderful names like Alice and Margaret and Dorothy.

She considered them all, tried them all on, but remained Kitten Frazier. Changing one's name is a terrible commitment, she thought. A terrible thing. Almost as terrible as having a name that needed to be changed.

Her life peaked in her early college days, when she could still manage to be a "Kitten," but as friends married and became involved with their families, Kitten was left alone without the confidence to seek new friends.

Life continued on the course her parents had charted. She graduated from a good school and got a good job at the Liberty, Minnesota, library. Even though the name Kitten had ceased to be appropriate at her fifth birthday, the older she became, the more hideously inappropriate it became. Shy by nature, with the years, Kitten became almost reclusive, ashamed, afraid, insecure, and miserable. The most daring thing she managed after her thirty-fifth birthday was a henna rinse for her hair.

When she saw an advertisement for a new head librarian in a New England community, Kitten's breath knotted in her throat. Here was the opportunity. A new place, new friends, a new job . . . a new identity. She could be whoever she chose.

She answered the ad, signed the application *K. Frazier*, and immediately began to dream about living in New England. She fancied the soft, fuzzy coast with its severe storms, cold winters, and beachy summers filled with colorful tourists. Something brand-new. She could be new again. She could start over. She could make a lot of changes in a new environment. She'd meet a lot of people. She might even meet a man.

Yes, she thought, with a new name, she might even attract a man.

K. Frazier is how she signed her application, and K. Frazier was to whom the acceptance letter was addressed. She gave notice at the big Liberty, Minnesota, library, barely even noticing the details of leaving her job of fourteen years, her apartment of ten, as she began the serious work of finding a new name that began with *K.* Karen. Katherine. Kate. Kay. Kathy. Konstance. Kandy. Klarice. Nothing worked. Nothing.

She drove to New England, pulling a small U-Haul of carefully chosen items, mostly books, intent on finding a new name. Every word that began with a *K* was a possibility, and she found herself being a Karla, a Keysa, a Karma, a Kent, a Kentucky, a Kewpie. The closer she got to Greystone Bay, the more depressed she became.

Then she arrived, exhausted from dreaded anticipation. She found the realtor, and signed her lease with the initial *K.* Her garden apartment was spacious and airy, yet somehow not quite light enough, and her first purchases included several lamps to keep out the queer damp darkness that seeped over the floor and around into the corners.

On her first day at her new post, she admitted to her superior that her first name was Kitten, made the obligatory apology, sighed, and settled in to the new routine as if nothing at all had changed.

Nothing *had* changed. She was still fat, she was still Kitten Frazier, she was still alone.

No. Nothing had changed.

At least she noticed no change for a month, maybe two. Then she began to notice that there was a different clientele in the Greystone Bay Library. And she noticed a different type of book in the Greystone Bay Library. And then she noticed Greystone Bay.

The library in Liberty, Minnesota, had always been noisy, filled with children and their mothers, businessmen reading the newspapers and researching in the financial section, derelicts sleeping in the carrels, students asking questions, books being checked out, checked in, activity, activity, everywhere, all the time.

The library in Greystone Bay had all those same people, only they were quiet. It was as if they were all careful to preserve the atmosphere. All of them. Children never ran, they never laughed out loud; the library never had a program of puppets, or storytelling, or grade-school art on the walls. The library was subdued. Newspapers rustled gently, people whispered only when necessary, and usually, not at all. Research requests were handed to her discreetly, completely filled out and legible.

It was odd. So very odd. And it grew to be wonderful.

Kitten had a name plaque on her desk that said Miss K. Frazier, but nobody ever called her anything. Valerie, her assistant, called her "Miss Frazier." If she had no one to talk to, she thought, then no one would know her stupid name and it didn't matter. It didn't matter, she thought with thundering profundity. Her stupid name didn't matter in Greystone Bay.

How terrifyingly liberating.

While the library in Liberty had been weighted with fiction, the library in Greystone Bay had a very small fiction section. The New Releases stand in front of the door was always filled with nonfiction, mostly historic and regional, with some nature books and how-to volumes. There were no paperback racks.

The children's area was carpeted in brown, and the low,

little shelves somehow looked calm, neat and orderly, even in their profusion of colors and sizes of children's books. In Liberty, the children's area always looked like a monster mob of excited, chattering children had just blown through, but here it appeared as though the room were continually empty. Solemn. Grieving. And yet there were always children present. Subdued children. Serious children.

Greystone Bay, it would appear, was no laughing matter.

Kitten finished a paperback romance she'd been reading since Liberty, brought it in and set it on the New Releases shelf. It was white, and looked naked and shameless mixed in with the other volumes of import. She left it there, but it stared at her. Day after day, not a single person picked it up or even looked at it. She dug through her unpacked boxes of books at home, found two more dog-eared copies of silly romances and brought them in, set them alongside the first. They, too, sat in solitude, and eventually she threw them out.

People checked out serious fiction—the classics—but never popular fiction. There was one volume by John Updike, and all the rest were old. It appeared as though the buyer for the library had died in 1935. Or his taste had.

But then, she thought, surely the contents of the library must reflect the community.

If that were so, then the community was deadly serious about its history. And couldn't be bothered with frivolous romance, or thrillers, or science fiction or horror.

As Kitten's attention was drawn away from herself and into her work, she began to notice more of her new town. Summer was drawing to a close, but there were no hordes of tourists as she'd imagined. There were no bright, sunshiny days that tempted her to the beach in an outdated and undersized swimsuit. Mornings had that bright glare of sun burning through fog and glinting off the dew, but by the time she got off work, the fog had rolled in again, keeping the whole area damp, lonesome, and forlorn. Kitten loved it. She was in a small, small town, but she was obscure. No one wanted to know her; she wanted to know no one. She could be as invisible as she dared, yet surrounded by friendly people. No one at all need know her name, her history, her secrets, her poisons. Alone, yet not lonely.

Greystone Bay, she thought, you are an answer to one of my prayers.

"There's a new woman working at the library," Valerie said, and then squeezed her eyes shut tight. She hadn't meant to tell him, she didn't want to tell him, she'd promised herself she wouldn't tell him, and now . . . she'd told him. She rested her wrists on the sink and silently called herself a dummy.

"Oh? You work with her?"

"Yes."

"Nice?"

"Yes."

"What's her name?"

"I don't know. Miss Frazier, I call her."

"No first name?"

"Initial *K* is all I know."

"Where's she from?"

"Minnesota."

"Hmmm. Well. I'll have to stop by and welcome her to our little town."

Valerie winced. How had he managed to squeeze that information out of her? He seemed always on the lookout for the new women. And, it seemed, once he found them, they didn't stay in town very long. It's not that she was jealous—was she?

She turned and looked at him.

Frederick smiled at her over the top of his newspaper. He wore a green wool plaid shirt, open at the collar, to show a bright white T-shirt underneath. His hairline had receded as far as it could go, and he kept the fringes closely cut and neat. His dark-rimmed glasses gave him a studious, innocuous look, and his straight, white, even teeth bore testimony to his tidiness. His five-o'clock shadow added character to the almost little-boy-innocent face. He needed something to hide that innocence, because surely Frederick was no innocent. And yet . . .

Valerie turned back to her task of chopping vegetables. She heard Frederick rustle the newspapers as he waited for the dinner she'd promised him, but she knew that he wasn't reading, he was thinking about Miss Frazier. Damn it.

She looked through the salt-crusted window at the waves bashing themselves against the rocks. Not big surf today, just cold and ominous. The sun was setting behind the house and the overcast sky was darkening. One lone fishing boat braved the dark and the waves. Valerie rinsed her hands and went to the bedroom for a sweater.

"You okay?"

"Uh-huh. Just chilly."

"Going to be a blaster of a winter this year."

She walked back past him, pulling on her natural brown wool sweater, and he caught her arm and pulled her to him.

"Please don't, Frederick, I'm not in the mood."

He instantly released her. "I'm sorry. Something wrong?"

"No . . ." She picked up the knife and continued with the vegetables. "No."

She hated the silence that followed. "I'll make some coffee," she said. "That'll do it." Why do I have to apologize to him, or justify my feelings to him all the time? Why does he make me do those things?

Why does he make me make him dinner?

Why does he make me love him?

She filled the coffee pot, spooned in the coffee, and glanced at him out of the corner of her eye. He was reading. Or thinking. Or plotting.

I hate this.

She dried her hands and sat down at the table next to him. He put his paper down and smiled at her, his full lips soft and sensuous.

"Hi," he said, and his warm hands covered her small chilled one.

"Hi," she said, and she smiled at him in spite of herself.

"Have a rough day?"

"I don't know. Something."

"Shall I go?"

"No. Please don't." What am I saying? Yes, please go, please go, she thought. She pulled her hand away and looked at her cuticles. "No. Don't go," she said with a sigh. "I like having you here." She looked up into his dark eyes and found that she meant it.

"I like being here," he said, and leaned forward to give her a tender kiss. Very gentle. Very tender. Very undemanding, that was Frederick.

And yet . . .

After they had made love, vegetables still half-chopped and forgotten in the kitchen, Valerie moved away from him, turned on her side and looked out the bedroom window. Autumn approached. Dusk was falling, the tide was rising, and there was a greyness in her soul that blended well with the scenery.

In a moment, he'll snore, she thought. And sleep for about forty-five minutes. Then he'll wake up, be soft and shy after their slow and gentle, pleasant but somehow passionless sex, take a quick shower, dress, and leave.

To go where? To whom? Why?

She pulled her knees to her chest and her pillow down under the covers with her. She hated this, this uncertainty, this not knowing. She hated this perfectly consistent, no commitment, hassle-free relationship.

She wanted more, she wanted less. She wanted different, yet the way it was was perfect. It was perfect.

But it was so strange. She didn't know where he lived, she didn't know if he was married, she didn't know what he did for a living, where he was from, what his family was like, whether he had children . . . whether he wanted any children. . . .

And though they'd been together for almost a year now, she never seemed to find the words to ask him those questions, because whenever they were together, he was so much in control. . . .

The problem with Frederick, she decided, is that he is exactly what I want.

She bit her thumbnail, watched the clouds merge with the fog, and waited for Frederick to awaken.

The fog called her name and Kitten turned over in her sleep, restless. She heard it again, and felt her consciousness will itself to rise up through the levels of sleep. Dreams were so noisy lately, and her apartment was so silent.

Soon the anxiety in her dreams was left behind and Kitten opened her eyes to absolute silence.

A silvery slice of moon shone through the upper half of her windows, while the fog pressed close around the lower half. A wisp of fog swirled and danced on the little braided rug in her bedroom.

She'd heard her name.

Kitten, she thought. Kitten is her name, but that is not the name that she heard. No. For a moment, deep in sleep, she'd heard her real name, her *true* name.

But what was it?

It was as familiar as her hands, as comfortable as her pillow, as fitting as her skin. It reflected the all of her: her personality, her adaptability, her secrets, her fears, her attitudes and aptitudes. It was the perfect name for her, for her, for her. . . .

And someone had called it.

She raised up on one elbow and looked about the room.

The moon bleached out all the colors. The fog muffled all the sounds. The apartment was silent and stark as a shroud, and Kitten wondered for a moment if it hadn't been Death calling her name. Death would know her true name.

Heart pounding, she lay back down and pulled the covers up over her mouth. "It is not death I fear," she whispered to the edge of the blanket, and her voice sounded strange, foreign, lost in the room full of airless silence.

What *do* you fear, Kitten Frazier? she asked herself, and she pulled at the covers until they bunched up at her neck.

I'm afraid, she thought. I'm afraid that someone else will find out my real name before I do.

Stagger Lee Simpson poured a trayful of drinks, rang the tab up on the ancient register, laid the receipt on the tray between bottles of Heineken and winked at Anna. She smiled at him and whisked the tray away.

Stagger Lee checked his watch. 1:50. He limped to the far end of the bar and began wiping it down. "Last call," he said to Bernie.

"Just as well, Lee," Bernie said. He laid a ten on the countertop and made his way fairly steadily out the door.

Bernie was the only one in Greystone Bay who called him Lee. Bernie was only five foot squat, so he knew what it was like to have physical limitations and to be reminded of them every waking hour.

"Last call," Stagger said to the couple cozying up at the center of the bar. He knew they heard him, although they pretended to ignore him. Which is worse: being a friend to drunks or being a slave to them? None o' my business, he thought. I just tend bar. I just pour drinks. I just stagger around behind this damned counter filled with liquor and serve it to stupid people so they can get even more stupid. It's a job.

"Hey, Stagger Lee!" Anna was back. Her cash box was fit to bust. It'd been a good night. She checked the wall clock and tapped her foot while she waited for him to make his way down the length of the bar.

"Last call, Anna."

"I know."

He could tell that she was sorry to see the profitable night end, but he couldn't wait to get out of the smoky, boozy breath of the bar. He wanted to go outside and fill his lungs with some cold, fresh fog. Maybe a walk down by the wharf tonight, he thought. Maybe a long walk along the bay, maybe a long walk into the bay. Maybe he'd just walk right in up to his twisted knees, his faulty hips, his scrawny chicken neck, right up to his hairline. Maybe he'd take a nice deep breath of cold, fresh seawater.

He filled her order and set the drinks on the tray.

"Last call," he shouted, and those who wouldn't be caught dead closing up a bar at two A.M. swallowed their last and left.

Anna brought back a trayful of dirty glasses and ashtrays

and Lee began washing them. The lovers at the bar left, so he scooped their mess up, too.

"What you up to after work?" Lee tried to make it sound casual.

"I gotta get some rest," Anna said. "I'm on my feet since early this morning."

"Yeah," Lee said, and kept washing. One of these nights I'm just going to clean out the cash register and head on out of here. I'll be long gone before Mr. Hardy discovers the missing money, and they'll never find me.

Sure, he thought. Sure. Just until you run out of money and have to tend bar someplace. Within one week they'd be calling you Stagger Lee again and bang! you'd be found out. Just shut up, cripple, and be glad you got a job.

Anna came back with another tray filled with trash, sat at the corner stool and lit up a cigarette. "Pour me a rum Kahlua, Stagger Lee."

He poured her drink and went back to cleaning up the bar for the night. Another half hour and he'd be out of here. The last customers went out the door, and he was left alone with Anna. Anna. Lovely Anna. Crusty, hard-hearted Anna. He loved her and he hated her.

"Think I'll go for a walk down by the water tonight," he said, swishing glasses.

"You'll freeze your tiny ass," she said.

"There's no romance in your heart, Anna."

"True enough." She pulled long and deep on her cigarette, then, with cigarette still in her lips, smoke spewing out of both nostrils, she reached down and took off both shoes and threw them across the room. "Christ!" She put the cigarette in the ashtray, knocked back a slug of her drink and massaged her feet.

Lee pulled the cash drawer out of the till and began

counting bills. He wished he could just lock the place up and do this in the morning, but he'd tried that before, and could never quite make it in before Louie opened up in the morning. And that made Louie cranky, to find a bar not ready for him, and Louie's being cranky made Mr. Hardy very cranky.

"Listen, Stagger Lee?"

He looked up to see Anna leaning over the bar at him.

"Listen, I'd take that walk along the bay with you some night, but not tonight, okay? My feet are really killing me."

"Yeah, sure, no big deal," he said.

She got off the barstool and walked around, wiping down the tables in her bare feet. Her name's all wrong, Lee thought. Anna is the name for a womanly hausfrau, someone comfortable and cozy. This one is ragged and squeezed out. Someone ought to either marry her and make her soft, having babies and baking cookies, or else she should change her name to something steely.

"I'm outta here, Stagger," she said. She threw the bar towel on the bar, reached around for her purse, fetched her shoes, and swung out the door, shoulders low with fatigue.

She locked it behind her, waved without looking at him, and melted into the fog.

2:20. Stagger Lee finished counting the money, banded it up, put the excess in a canvas bag and dropped it into the floor safe. He took a last check to make sure everything was okay—the juices were low, but mornings were slow. Louie could fill the mixes and the juices.

He turned out the lights and unlocked the door. When he opened it, a blast of cold fresh air hit him in the face. It felt wonderful after the close atmosphere of the stinking bar. He waited for that moment of apprehension that always came whenever he ventured out alone into the darkness, into the Greystone fog at two-thirty in the morning, leaving the familiar bar behind him. It always came. He always said a little prayer, or something, just before he stepped into the unknown aloneness. He always felt as if he'd never find his way home, he'd never find his way back, he'd never find his way.

But tonight there was no apprehension at all. Losing his way was not a bad thought. He had no reason to pray, even a little, and he stepped out into the darkness, into the fog that for the first time welcomed him.

"Good morning, Valerie."

"Morning, Miss Frazier. Did you have a nice weekend?"

Kitten stopped in the midst of setting a stack of books on her desk. Weekend? Was it Monday? Had it been since Friday that she'd been in the library? What had she done? Had she gone to the beach? Had she eaten in a restaurant? Had she slept in? Had she read? Walked? Visited? "Yes . . . yes, a fine weekend. And you?"

"Perfect."

"That's nice. Do anything special?"

"Yeah, just played it slow and lazy. Spent a lot of time with Frederick, walking the beach . . . you know."

Kitten's breath caught in her chest a second time. Frederick. There was something familiar about that name. What was it? What *was* it? Frederick. Frederick.

"Frederick?"

"My boyfriend. I guess maybe you haven't met him yet. He'll come in to the library sometime soon, I'm sure."

"Well, I'd enjoy meeting him." Dozens of questions danced on her tongue, but suddenly unsure of herself, she dared not voice them.

The rest of the day passed, Kitten keeping herself busy, trying not to think about the weekend just passed, the weekend of no memory, the lost weekend. And when the clock finally announced quitting time, she breathed a sigh of relief. She could go home, take off her shoes and stockings and the facade of normalcy she had tried to wear all day long. She would go home and there would be a half-finished painting or puzzle or something that would remind her that she had been totally absorbed all weekend.

After the last patron left the library, Kitten locked the big wooden doors and walked down the granite steps to the street. The dark evenings of October had grown closer and closer to closing time, and soon she'd be going to work in the dark and coming home in the dark, but for now, she could walk through the after-hours streets during that strange, foggy New England twilight.

Generally, she walked home along the beach road, but today she wanted to walk among the faceless crowds, people going home from a long day at the office. She wanted to see colors, she wanted to hear snatches of conversation, she wanted to delay, at any cost, the face in the mirror at home. She didn't want to have to look at the evidence, or lack thereof, of the weekend.

So when the door to the restaurant opened and light, warmth, laughter, and music spilled out, Kitten couldn't help herself. Just one drink, she thought. It's been a long day, and so far I've seen nothing of Greystone Bay's nightlife.

She pulled the door open and stepped in. The noise of friendship surrounded her. She looked around at the wood-paneled foyer, peeked ahead to see the bar stretch before her, heard the sounds of early diners in the next room.

Then a man rose from a seat and approached her with a giant smile.

"I'm so glad you could make it tonight," he said. "Our table is waiting."

He took her coat, handed it to the maitre d', placed his fingertips at the small of her back and guided her around the corner into the dining room. She could feel his warmth, smell him as he leaned close to her ear. "You look wonderful. Your name should be Magnetica."

"It is," she said, surprised at herself.

Then they were seated next to each other in a corner booth, oversized menus on their plates, and his hand was large and warm over her small, veiny one.

Her first impulse, in the foyer, was to tell him he had made an error, but she knew he hadn't. He was so familiar, yet so unknown. This was the most thrilling thing that had ever happened to her. She patted at her hair, wished she had freshened her lipstick.

The waiter came, and the man ordered. Dry champagne. Caesar salad for two, followed by chateaubriand, rare. Coffee after. The waiter exited, and the man touched her cheek.

"I've missed you today. How was your day?"

"Busy."

"You look tired."

"I am, a little." She wasn't, though. She was energized. Will I remember this tomorrow?

He gave her hand a gentle squeeze, and smiled fondly at her.

He wore an expensive gray pinstripe suit, with white shirt and burgundy/navy striped tie. His fingernails were well manicured, and soft little black hairs grew out of the knuckles and along the backs of his hands. His hair was steely gray, his eyes sparkling blue, his lips full and soft, and she knew he had a forest of graying hair on his chest and shoulders.

She felt a tingling in her lower stomach and wondered again at her activities during the past weekend. A flush rose up her throat to her cheeks. Her ears positively burned.

"What are you thinking?" he asked with a sly smile.

"Tell me about yourself," she parried.

He frowned for a moment, and Kitten's stomach heaved as her emotions dropped down a floor. Then he smiled and she recovered.

"Not much to tell, really. Boring old story." Then he leaned closer and she smelled his warm, sexy aftershave—it smelled like her pillow this morning. He brushed his lips against her cheek, then touched her where he'd kissed.

There's nothing in the world like when a man touches your cheek, she thought.

"Let's hear about *you,*" he said. "*You're* the fascinating one at this table."

She began telling him about Minnesota, worrying only for a moment that she may have told him all this before. Their dinner arrived and she kept talking, and he listened with rapt attention, commenting when absolutely appropriate and with a delightful wit. She, warmed by the champagne and his attentions, began to relax, to feel comfortable with herself, and she put more into the stories of her family. Her stories turned out to be funny and insightful.

Over cognac and coffee, she finished by telling him of her move to Greystone Bay.

"And then, here we are," he said.

"Yes."

"I'm pleased that you're here."

"In Greystone Bay?"

"And at this table."

"So am I." Kitten broke eye contact with him and looked around. The restaurant was almost empty. "My. Look at us. We're the last ones here."

"We are among the last, that is true," he said, without taking his eyes off her. A little shiver ran through her.

"Well."

"Well. Now we shall go out into the October night for a brisk walk to another place for one more nightcap, and then I shall walk you home."

She collected her purse, the maitre d' brought her coat, her companion helped her into it, then put his arm around her as the blast of nighttime air quickened them.

They walked in comfortable silence, Kitten exhilarated and yet relaxed. The worst of the evening was not knowing his name, in case she would have to introduce him to someone. Actually, the worst was figuring out how to find out his name without being stupid about it. It was obvious they were *intimate* friends—how could she not know his name? Should she confess to him that he was a surprise to her? Where on earth did they meet?

And yet, while her mind swirled with unanswered questions, her soul was satisfied that she had an attractive man's arm around her shoulders, a man who was clearly taken with her, a romantic interest, a *love* interest, at last. At last.

He steered her toward a scarred wooden door with BAR written in stained glass over the top. They went in, the heat, humidity, and cigarette smoke hitting them hard.

Johnny Carson was on the television in the corner, and everyone seated at the bar was watching it. No one laughed at his monologue. A few couples were at tables scattered around the bar.

Kitten looked up into her escort's face. This didn't seem like the type of place he'd frequent.

"Let's sit at the bar," he said, and she was even more amazed.

The crippled bartender recognized him.

"Long time," he said.

"Hello, Lee. Two amarettos with coffee, please."

She touched his arm. He turned his eyes to her and again her spirit flew. "I'm going to freshen up."

"Hurry," he said, and kissed her hand, never taking his eyes from hers.

She saw the rest-room sign and walked over to it, conscious of his eyes on her. Inside the ladies' room, she gave in to the Big Grin and looked at herself in the mirror. She was afraid her makeup would be worn out or smudged, or her hair a tangled mess, but she looked fine. She looked just fine. And her eyes shone.

Back again at the bar, he put his arm around her. She smelled the sweet liqueur and coffee on his breath as he leaned in close. "I want you to observe very closely."

She opened her mouth to question.

"Shhh," he said. "This is important."

For a half hour, they watched the people in the bar. There was a crusty waitress, two rednecks, a Jewish gentleman, a young couple, and the crippled bartender. She watched. She concentrated. She tried to notice everything he wanted her to notice.

She saw two men drink three beers each in the half hour. They got sloppier, louder and looser, but were decidedly uninteresting.

The couple looked like they were more interested in people-watching, and found the bar an uneventful place to sightsee. They sat close together at a little table, holding hands, watching television, although they probably couldn't hear it from where they were sitting. Not at all interesting.

The cocktail waitress was a little more dramatic, a little more vocal, a little more to watch. At first Kitten thought it was this waitress she was supposed to watch. Her gentleman friend's eyes seemed glued to her.

But it was the bartender that caught Kitten's eye. He was

tall and thin and had that characteristic loping walk that spoke "polio." He was in his mid-forties, with dark hair slicked back, a ready smile, a practiced bartender's manner, but an aura of sadness surrounded him, and it had nothing to do with his physical limitations.

The waitress called him "Stagger Lee" too many times, and too loudly. Her gentleman friend had called him Lee.

He stood at the far end of the bar, washing glasses, wiping down the bar in front of the two drunks, casting glances toward her to make sure their drinks were still fresh, and every time he did, Kitten caught his eye. They had eye contact for a prolonged moment, and then Lee looked away. Several times.

The Jewish man left with a big tip and a fond farewell, and Lee swung his body over for the empty glass, and as he did so, their eyes met once again.

There was something about him, something that made Kitten's heart leap every time he looked at her.

And then she and her date finished their drinks. He left a five-dollar tip, and stood up.

They walked back to her cottage in silence. At the door, he kissed her. Softly, gently, tenderly, with tremendous feeling and controlled passion. It made her weak in the knees.

"Good night, Magnetica," he whispered, then turned and walked away.

"Wait," she said, before she could stop herself. He turned and looked at her. "What is your name?"

"What would you call me?"

Surprised, taken aback, she felt the cold seep in under her coat where his arm had been.

"Warm," she said.

"Then Warm it is. Good night."

She opened the door and went in, feeling graceful and alive.

She went to bed and dreamed of the crippled bartender.

"What is it, Valerie?"

Valerie turned over and looked at Frederick. His eyes were soft with concern for her, and she felt her own eyes fill with tears again. She'd cried when they'd made love, the shudders of orgasm turning into sobs as passion waned, and she tried to put words to the maelstrom of emotion she felt.

"I— I'm thirty-four," she finally said, then pulled the sheet over her expression of grief.

He smoothed her hair. "And you want someone to marry you."

Was that it? Sometimes Frederick could be so astute.

She hiccuped, wiped her eyes and nose on the sheet, then peered up at him. That *was* it. Trite as it may sound, time was beginning to get away from her, and she didn't want to wind up old . . . and alone . . . like Miss Frazier.

She nodded, then opened her sticky mouth. "Can it be you?" His expression told her no, and she tried to backpedal as her heart was breaking, she tried not to let it show, tried not to make him feel . . . To *hell* with his feelings, she thought. What about *my* feelings? "Oh shit!" she said. The tears came harder. "Shit!" she yelled. Frederick began to laugh. "Shit, shit, shit!" She got up on her knees and pounded on the bed, then stood up, pulling a corner of the damp sheet up with her. She bounced on the bed, feeling her flesh bounce with her. "Shit, I say," she said, laughing with him. What a sight she must be, flesh jiggling, mascara running, tears streaming, madness looming. She stopped bouncing, got off the bed.

"PMS," she said, slid into Frederick's shirt and headed for

the kitchen. She opened the refrigerator and stood there, staring in but seeing nothing.

Then she felt his hands on her waist. She turned and he enfolded her.

"God, I love you," he said, "but I'm not the one for you to marry. I'm here for you for now, just now, but when you want something permanent, something with children and forevers written in it, then it's time for me to step aside and make room for that man."

Valerie clung to him and cried. She knew it. She'd known it. She'd always known it. She loved him too, in a strangely distant yet affectionate way, but there was no way that she and Frederick could make a permanent thing of their relationship. "I'll miss you so much," she said.

He held her, closed the refrigerator door with his foot, picked her up and carried her back to the bedroom, soothed her with kisses and caresses, and made soft, sweet love to her one last time. Afterwards, they both slept, entwined.

When she awoke, he was gone.

She wandered through her house, looking out the windows, but nothing could be seen except for fog. She heard the distant moan of the foghorn, and it echoed her internal feelings.

She'd see him around town, wouldn't she?

No, she thought, she wouldn't.

He'd stop in to see her now and again, just to see how she was doing, wouldn't he? He cared for her, didn't he?

Yes, he cared, but he wouldn't stop in to see her.

He'd call?

No.

She opened the little wood-burning stove in the corner of the living room and started a fire to chase out the fog that had begun to leak in around the doors and windows. Soon flames were roaring, and the heat spread new life into the room. She brought in the pumpkin that Frederick had bought and set it on the hearth.

He was wonderful for me, she thought, and hugged herself in front of the fire. But now I'm ready for a permanent relationship, a husband and family. Frederick helped make me ready. He was perfect for me. He was a Godsend.

But I can't thank him, because—the tears began choking her again—I don't even know where he lives.

Kitten didn't hear from Warm for two days. She worried that she had offended him; she worried that something had happened to him; she worried and worried and worried. And interspersed with the tremendous worry, was exquisite joy and a profound knowledge deep inside that she would see him again. Soon.

She chewed over the details of their evening together, from that first surprise meeting in the restaurant foyer, to his calling her Magnetica, to that odd thing about observing the people in that tacky bar. And that bartender. The crippled one. How odd it all was, sometimes she just ached to tell someone, she wanted so badly to sit with Valerie, her assistant at the library and her only acquaintance in Greystone Bay, and tell her of the magic that had come into her life, but all the words she came up with, when she rehearsed it in her mind, sounded like the fanciful imaginings of an old maid.

But they weren't. Were they?

And then Valerie had come in to work looking swollen-eyed and miserable, and Kitten had, with feeling, told her that she was available to talk things over, and Valerie had said she appreciated it, and that was the end of that. But Valerie still moped. And Kitten still feared for the magic.

Warm was a fun name, but she tried to find his real name

in her mind. She couldn't forget the name Frederick, the name of Valerie's friend, and a horrible thought crossed her mind. "Valerie," she said.

Valerie looked up from her work.

"Does Frederick have gray hair?"

"Frederick is almost bald," Valerie said, "and what he does have is dark." She pouted. "At least it was the last time I saw him."

"You aren't seeing each other anymore?" As soon as Kitten said it, she was sorry. Tears brimmed up in Valerie's eyes, and Kitten fervently wished she knew Valerie well enough to go put her arms around her. But she didn't. "I'm sorry," she said, and Valerie nodded her thanks and went to the ladies' room.

He is Leonardo, Kitten thought. Leonardo and Africani and Michael. He is Moses. He is Pharaoh. He is all of these and none of these.

But what was his real name? And how was she to find it out?

But it didn't matter, really. His name was Warm to her and her name Magnetica to him. She would have it just exactly that way, if she could.

If she could. She *could.* His name mattered not at all, and neither did hers.

The door to the bar opened and Lee's insides gave a little flutter. Was it her?

He'd started out whipping around at every sound that came through that door, but disappointment attended every visitor. Now he dreaded to turn around and look, and most times he just tried to read who it was in the expression on Anna's face. Anna had her favorite customers, oh yes, she had her favorites, all right, and Lee suspected that she even hooked now and then on the side. So Anna either lit up, scowled, or raised her eyebrows every time the door opened.

Since that night, since that night the woman had come in with the familiar man, Lee had dreamed of her. More than once, sometimes two or three times in just one night. He'd wake up in his cramped little bed with its torn and dingy sheets and wonder at the night visions he'd been having of her. It was nothing sexual, at least not at first. It was more of a mysterious *knowing*; he felt he *knew* her, and he wanted her to know him.

But lying awake in his lonesome room, thinking about the first woman that had touched him inside did nothing for his peaceful celibacy, either. He stroked himself, thinking of that woman, imagining her name, wondering what she would feel like, her soft, middle-aged flesh under his fingers, her freshly showered and powdered thighs pressed tightly against his waist. Lee had only had sex three times in his life, many years ago. For years he was tortured by his forced celibacy, but when he began to shave white whiskers from his chin, he decided to give up all hopes of a girlfriend, or a wife, and he quit masturbating.

Never once did he give in to his fantasies about Anna.

But now. Now it was different. This was no pinup. This was no smudged copy of *Playboy.* This was a woman, a whole woman—his age, older maybe. These were not wild fantasies of impossible couplings, these were almost like dreams, dreams of love and life and caring . . .

"Stagger Lee!" Anna's harsh voice raked him back to the bar, the noisy, stinking bar. "Two vodkas straight up. What's with you lately, anyway? You're out in la-la land."

"Nothing," he muttered, and filled her tray.

The door opened and he didn't even look around.

I don't know which I'm looking forward to more, he thought, seeing her again, or dreaming about her tonight.

But he knew the answer. He had to see her again, just to see if there really had been a spark between them that night. If there hadn't, if it had been his imagination, he might just die. If she was not the way he'd remembered her, if it was all a trick of the moon, he'd be left alone again, in his one-room apartment, a crippled man all alone.

He wiped at the bar and looked over at Anna. She raised one eyebrow and nodded toward the door.

Lee turned, and there she stood. He cursed his limp, threw his dirty bar rag into the sink and hitched over to her.

"Hi," he said, amazed at how normal he sounded, when he had thought for sure his voice would fail him. She was exactly the same. She looked him right in the eye; she looked him right in the soul.

"Hello."

"What can I pour you?"

"Yes, a . . ." She seemed to fumble.

"White wine?"

She smiled with gratitude. "Yes, perfect, thank you."

He turned from her, walked the length of the bar, to the refrigerator where the wine was. In the mirror, he saw her settle herself on a barstool, the same stool she had sat on when she was here with him, that familiar man, that time. His heart was hammering. Settle down, cripple, he told himself. She's outta your league. He poured a glass of wine, then walked it down to her.

Her hair was shiny, a soft kind of red. Her face was carefully made-up, powdered, with the right touch of lipstick. Not overly done, not underly done. She looked her age and carried herself well. Not like that stupid tart Anna. This was not only a woman, this was a lady, and he was suddenly ashamed of himself for trying to visualize her in his bed, making love to her with his wretched body.

"Cold out?" What a stupid question, he thought.

"Yes," she said, and smiled. "Feels like Halloween."

Lee leaned against the bar, thinking his face probably reminded her of Halloween. He was bone-thin, keeping his weight between 105 and 109 in order to walk more easily. He looked down at his feet, then up again at her and said, "I love Halloween. I used to love it, anyway, when I was a kid. Now, I work, and a bar is no place to be on Halloween night."

"Oh? Why is that?"

He looked at her, and their eyes sparked at each other. She was even better than his hollow dream. She was interested in things he had to say. She was interested in *him.*

"Crazies," he said. "I've never seen crazies before like the ones that come out of the woodwork in Greystone Bay on a Halloween night."

"I'd like to see that."

"No. You stay home. Read a book."

She smiled.

"I mean it."

"I stay home anyway. I like to give out candy."

"Yeah? What kind of candy?" I can't believe I said that, he thought.

"Oh, I like the little Heath bars, and the little Snickers and the little Nestlé's Crunch. Whatever strikes my fancy at the time. I throw the leftovers in the freezer."

"Stagger Lee!"

Lee whipped around to see Anna, her hot face glaring at him.

"A little service here, please?"

He smiled an apology at the lady and walked to the end of the bar.

"Two more vodkas. Who's the broad?"

He poured the drinks, put them on her tray, and gave her a glare as good as the one she gave.

"Ohhh . . . Special stuff, eh? Hmmm." Then she whipped her tray up and away toward her customers.

And the beautiful redhead at the end of the bar was gathering her purse. She waved good-bye to him, silently mouthed the word, then turned and went out into the cold.

Her wine was untouched. And she'd left him a fiver to cover the wine and his tip.

Lee wanted to throw a beer mug at Anna.

But the redheaded lady hadn't come in with that man, and she hadn't come in to drink. That told him two things, and they both were that she had come in to see him.

He limped over, slipped the five into his pocket, wanting to remember to smell it later, to see if it smelled like her, picked up her glass and wiped the bar.

Then he poured her wine down the sink.

Kitten turned on the bedside lamp and sat on the edge of the bed to remove her stockings, her mind filled with Lee, the bartender who seemed to need her so much. His need filled the bar, and while she wanted to sit and talk with him some more, find out about him, maybe even flirt a bit, she found his presence too intense and the opportunity of escape too intensely inviting.

I will see him again, she thought, and took off the binding pantyhose.

The phone rang.

It was an eerie sound in the twilight. Kitten was just becoming comfortable before making a fire in the fireplace, and the phone jangled her nerves out of their quiet reverie.

Who knew her phone number?

No one.

Only the library.

She picked it up and felt his presence caress her cheek.

"My love," he said.

She sat down, her knees weak. His voice was rich with the experiences of a gentleman. He, too, needed her, only his need wasn't so pungent.

She wanted to say, Where have you been? but as she opened her mouth to speak, he spoke first.

"Shhh," he said. "Hold me with your thoughts."

She sat in silence, remembering him, visualizing him, smelling him, feeling him. She felt his kiss. She felt his touch on her cheek.

"Are you mine forever?"

"Yes," she breathed, all thoughts of the bartender gone.

"Dream of me," he whispered, and hung up.

Her bedroom slowly came back into focus. It was as if she had discorporified for a moment, under the caress of his words. It was as if she had ceased to be a person—a fleshly thing, a pound of fat and a stupid name—and had become something else for a moment, something ethereal, something ephemeral, something superb.

Kitten smiled. Such an odd thing. *Such* an odd thing, and yet, when it was happening, when she was with him or talking to him, it was the most normal, most wonderful love affair in the world. In spite of the fact that she knew nothing of him. . . . Not even . . . not even his name.

It was a pleasure, really, to think and feel and act in the moment, rather than worrying about mundane things.

And her mind said, *Real* things, Kitten, are not mundane. What would your mother say?

And at forty-seven years old, Kitten brushed her mother's face from her mind and thought about her lover. The lover who had no name, the lover to whom the *moment* mattered more than her name. He was perfect.

She ran her fingers through her hair, then turned on the other table lamps in the bedroom. She rubbed the shivers off her arms, slipped out of her dress and into her bathrobe, and went to the living room to make a fire.

As she passed by the door, she paused. Had she heard something? There was no one out there, was there?

Was there?

She put the chain on and opened the door, just a crack.

A tongue of fog licked her fingers.

She shivered and shut the door.

She built the fire, made a cup of tea, snuggled up in her hand-knit afghan, and thought about the dearth of men in her life, almost all her life, until now. And now she had two. Two very odd men. She thought for sure she would dream about both of them that night, and smiled softly in anticipation. She would luxuriate in anticipation for a little while longer.

The headlines had said that the chances are one in three hundred that a single woman over thirty-five would ever marry. Valerie paced her apartment with her finger crooked around the neck of a bottle of tequila.

"You fool," she told herself. "You stupid fool."

She swigged straight from the bottle and looked out at the fog that covered the landscape. Almost Halloween, she thought. I don't even need a mask. I could just go out and scare the bejesus out of little kids. Single and thirtyish. Monstrous.

She flounced into a chair and felt the tears approach. She always cried when she got drunk. She cried a lot, it seemed. How attractive.

Then she got an idea. An idea so good it made her sit up and set the half-empty bottle of booze on the rug.

"I'll go out."

She made her way to the bathroom, washed her face, put on too much makeup, brushed her hair, and slipped into a pair of tight jeans and a sweater. She grabbed her shoulder purse, threw in her cache of mad money from the underwear drawer and slammed out of the house.

She didn't feel quite as drunk anymore; she felt exhilarated.

She drove toward town, headlights splayed in the fog, until she could see the little rows of lights that lit up storefront windows and hotel entrances.

She slid into a parking spot and saw BAR spelled out in red stained glass. Perfect. She checked her makeup in the rear-view mirror and got out. She was a little unsteadier than she thought. Maybe coffee.

The warm air caught in her throat as she entered.

The place was dead. There was nothing going on—no music, no nothing. A bartender with a terrible limp walked toward her with a grin on his face. He looked skeletal, he was so thin.

"Hi," he said, and she looked around and felt trapped.

"Hi," she said.

"Getcha something?"

"Tequila shooter," she said.

He smiled, walked away, poured the drink, and brought it back with the salt shaker and a wedge of lime.

Valerie fumbled in her purse.

"On the house," he said.

"Oh?" Their eyes met. She looked down. "Thanks." She licked the web of her hand, poured salt on it, licked it off, downed half the shot of tequila, then bit the lime.

"Been in here before?"

"No."

"Didn't think so."

"I don't . . . I don't go out much. Just tonight . . ."

"It's a restless night."

"Full moon?"

"I don't know. I don't think so, but who can tell with all that fog?"

"Well," she said. "You're right. It is a restless night."

"Stagger Lee!" Anna's voice rasped across their faces. Both of them flushed.

"Jeez," Valerie said, and busied herself with her drinking ritual while the bartender swung his way to the other side of the bar. This is a stupid place, she thought. What am I doing here?

And then a few minutes later, he was back again, with another drink. "This is last call for you," he said. "From now on I buy you coffee. Okay?"

She smiled. "Okay." He was a nice enough guy. Beats pacing and foaming at the mouth at home. She leaned against the bar and watched the hard-faced waitress wiggle her butt around the tables. Hardly a soul in here, and I'll bet she brings down a lot of tips, Valerie thought. Hell, I could do that, and make a lot more money than I do at the library.

But look how hard she is. The melancholy settled over her shoulders again. I bet she isn't married, either. I bet she doesn't have any kids, or any prospects, either.

Am I like that? Am I that hard? She felt the tears well up, and then the bartender was in front of her again. She busied herself in her purse, hoping he wouldn't notice, but it was too late. He already had.

"Anything I can do?" he asked, and she looked up into his eyes and found more warmth than she had ever seen before.

But there wasn't only warmth. She saw pain and heartbreak and love and caring and loneliness. Valerie saw herself reflected in the man's eyes and for some reason, she *knew* him. She *knew* him.

In the space between question and answer, Valerie fell in love.

"Talk to me," she said.

He smiled and poured them each a cup of coffee.

"Your name is Hope," Warm said.

"Hope."

"Your name is Life."

"Life."

"Your name is Truth. Beauty. Goodness."

"And yours?"

"Whatever yours is, mine is also."

"Faith?"

"Faith."

"Wonder?"

"Wonder."

"Your name is Wonder," she said. "Your name *is* Wonder."

"Yes."

"So what are we to do?"

"Be. Laugh."

"And?"

"And teach love."

She laughed. "I know nothing . . ."

He hushed her with a caress. "You know everything," he said. "Teach wonder."

"Teach wonder," she repeated, and she felt him retreat from her. Cold air rushed into the vacuum his leaving made. It seemed to rush into her very essence. "Teach wonder," she said again, only this time she heard her voice, her real voice, coming from her mouth, and it sounded queer.

Kitten opened her eyes and looked around the dark room. The night was silent.

A coal popped in the fireplace.

She cuddled up to the flannel sheets and turned the pillow over to a cool, fresh side.

Tomorrow is Halloween, she thought.

And my name is Hope.

She smelled again the fragrance of him in her bed and closed her eyes with a soft smile. Sleep swooped her away in giant hands and deposited her outside the bedroom of the bartender. She could hear him breathing deeply, sleeping.

She moved to him. His room was small, smelled close. She touched his hair and he frowned. My mission here is to bring softness, she thought, and her hands moved gently over his face, massaging the muscles. The frown disappeared, his face gained peace. She was almost overcome at the feeling of affection she had for this man. She melted into his bed and felt drawn into his dream. She resisted at first, hands moving gently but persistently about his hard body, but his desire was too powerful.

"Who are you?" he wanted to know.

"Hope," she said.

"In what?"

"Life. Love. Softness."

Silence. Then: "There is no hope for me."

"Yes, oh yes. Recall faith. Gather wonder."

Pause. "Valerie."

"Yes."

"Will we . . . Dare I . . ."

"Dare."

He was silent.

She kissed him gently on the forehead, then slipped away again, her own dreams calling. And when she awoke it was morning. Foggy. Halloween.

She felt marvelous.

"I'm afraid," Lee thought as his eyes opened the next morning. He curled up into a ball, bunching the covers to his crotch. "I can't do it." But as the morning wore on and he could no longer stay in bed, the dreams of the night before faded to insignificance, and he began to feel normal again.

Then as the day waned and the dusk loomed, Lee dreaded the thought of the bar. Unsettledness swirled within him, but he bit it off and continued with his routine.

The bar was so familiar. Soon he was visiting with the regulars, pouring drinks and switching channels on the television set. The evening was slow, and Lee knew it was because all the crazies would be in late, dressed up. He checked the schedule. Mr. Hardy had put on another bartender, arriving at ten. Good. Lee usually needed another pair of hands on busy nights, and he wasn't good as a bouncer, either, so it would be good to have a big bartender on during Halloween.

The only good thing about Halloween in Greystone Bay is that people seemed to have fun. Once a year.

And then Valerie came in. Lee knew it as soon as she walked through the door. She took off her coat to reveal a harem-girl costume, hair wrapped up and a golden mask across her eyes, but Lee knew it was her. He smelled her.

He poured a shot of tequila, sliced a fresh lime and took it over to her.

What are you afraid of, Lee?

Nothing.

Being in love?

No.

Having to give up your stinking apartment, so a lovely fresh young girl can bring light into it? Having to give up all your cripple self-pity? Being normal and nice, and owning a house in the country with a dog and some sheep and raise some corn-fed, country-bred kids?

No. Yes. I don't know.

He set the tequila down and she smiled up at him. "Hi."

"Hi," he said.

"How did you know it was me?"

"I'd know you anywhere."

She smiled and Lee's world began to revolve again.

Kitten dressed carefully. Halloween was always the oddest day of the year, and this would certainly be no exception. She ran other Halloweens through her mind as she covered her face with white pancake makeup. One Halloween she had lost her virginity. One Halloween her little brother had been poisoned by some sicko who handed out bad candy bars. One Halloween she had gone for a horseback ride, galloping through the fields under the clear eye of a full moon, just her and a cowboy friend of her college roommate. A magical night. They jiggle-kissed, leaning to each other while their horses walked, snorting and foaming. One Halloween she had gone to see the Chippendale dancers with a wild friend of hers. At first, she was embarrassed, then slightly amused, and then, fueled by a martini or two, she got into it and truly enjoyed herself. One Halloween she had stayed by the side of the bed of her mother, who died before sunrise. One Halloween she had dressed up as a witch and frightened all the children who came trick-or-treating.

And this Halloween . . . This Halloween . . .

She finished her makeup job, dressed carefully, then adjusted the wig. Perfect. Frankenstein's Bride. A woman created for a certain purpose.

Created for one purpose.

She swirled into the black cape she'd rented and went out into the frosty night.

The bar wasn't far, and Kitten chose to walk the distance. She was warmed from within, with excitement and expectation.

The place was packed. Lee and another bartender danced around each other, serving a gaily dressed clientele standing three feet deep at the bar. Kitten came into the humidity, wondering if her pink cheeks showed through under the pancake makeup.

Someone in the corner was a little loud and obnoxious, but Kitten couldn't see where the noise was coming from. She felt slightly out of place as she walked among the tables, looking at the people, trying to discern the faces behind the faces. She couldn't.

Until she saw Valerie.

Valerie was dressed as a harem girl, and she sat all alone at a corner table, with a shot glass and a chewed up slice of lime in front of her. Kitten walked over. "Hi," she said.

"Who's that?" Valerie asked, grinning.

"Me," Kitten said, laughing.

"Miss Frazier!" The astonishment on Valerie's face was glorious. "The Bride of Frankenstein?"

They both laughed. "Sit," Valerie said. "Please."

"Are you here alone?"

Valerie nodded. "You?"

Kitten nodded.

Then Anna, dressed as a pirate with a moth-eaten parrot hanging down off one shoulder, came over. Her legs were too thick to be wearing net stockings, but wear them she did, and somehow she pulled it off.

"White wine," Kitten said, and the waitress turned away without a word, or even a glance toward Valerie.

"This is fun."

"Yeah. Listen, Miss Frazier. There's something I need to talk to you about."

"Oh?"

"I think I'm going to be leaving."

"Oh, Valerie, no. Why?"

"Well, I've met this man . . ."

"Wonderful! Tell me about him."

"Well, he's right over there . . ." And as Valerie pointed, Lee looked up through a crack in the crowd and saw them both. He smiled, and Kitten saw the love in his eyes.

"I'm thrilled for you," she said, and hard little tears brightened her vision.

"He's quite a guy."

"I'm sure."

Kitten paid for her drink and took a sip. "But why must you leave? I mean, isn't this kind of sudden?"

"I don't know. Yes. Sort of. It seems like the thing to do. Greystone Bay has been good for me, but right now, I think Lee and I want to start a new life in a new place, know what I mean?"

Kitten knew exactly what she meant. She nodded.

"You know, when Frederick left, I thought I was dead, but now I think . . . I think he prepared me for Lee. Frederick was really good for me."

Frederick.

Kitten sat back in her chair and pondered the name. Valerie sat back, too, keeping her eyes on the bar, hoping for another glimpse of her lover. The noise level in the bar had grown in the fifteen minutes Kitten had been in there, and would soon be unbearable. It might be time to go.

"Valerie? Are you going to stay here?"

Valerie nodded.

"I'm going to see what else is happening."

Valerie nodded and waved a finger at her. Then she downed her tequila shooter and held up the empty glass for Anna to see.

Kitten held her cape close around her and shouldered her way through the crowd and out into the night.

No sooner had she gotten out than she felt a hand, light, gentle, upon her elbow. She smelled him.

"See? See how well you work? See how wonderful you can make life for lovers?"

He was dressed as Robin Hood, a steely-gray-haired Robin Hood, complete with tights and tunic, covered by a full-length wool robe, and he wore a small golden mask across his eyes.

"I don't understand."

"It was *you* that brought them together."

"No, it wasn't."

He laughed. "Oh, my dear. Come. Let us be on to our next adventure." And he steered her toward the SeaHarp Hotel.

The lounge in the hotel was gently filled with adults in wonderfully ornate costumes. This was certainly a different clientele than at Lee's bar. People drank and danced to the music, but even here Greystone Bay was different. They were a people drinking too much, laughing too loudly, a people unaccustomed to gaiety.

They chose a small table on the edge of the dance floor and drank a bottle of champagne as they watched the dancers.

Kitten found her eyes irresistably drawn to Warm's

masked face, but tonight his intentions were elsewhere, and he paid little attention to her. He was searching the crowd. Searching, his eyes never still. Then,

"There. See the man, the . . . the turkey?"

She followed his look, and sure enough, a man was dressed as a turkey.

"He is a bank teller at First Federal. Watch him carefully."

"Do you know what happened the last time you told me to watch someone?"

He turned toward her. "Yes," he said.

Kitten flushed and looked down at her glass. Did he know? How did he know? Did he know about her visiting the bar again? *Did he know about the dream with Lee?*

"Watch him," he whispered. "Watch him for the moment, for soon he will be gone."

She looked up to ask why, but he silenced her with a finger on her cheek. "Please."

She watched the turkey. She watched him laugh and dance. She watched him be with his friends. And soon the whole table of people got up and left.

"Now," he said. "Now, Halloween is for us, my Bride of Frankenstein." And he ordered more champagne.

The evening passed in a flurry of wild emotion for Kitten. She was entranced, enchanted, flattered and wooed. She was wined and dined and danced and entertained until she was filled, and still he brought more delight to the evening. They walked to her house through fog so thick they had to hold each other, and she invited him in.

Soon they were in her bed, his tenderness fueling her passion. He was slow and steady, gentle and understanding, and he talked to her in a low, intimate voice, speaking the words of love she had longed to hear her whole life. She reached a shuddering climax that she thought would never end, but end it did, and he kissed the perspiration from her forehead and rocked her gently. She clung to him as she would a life raft in a treacherous sea.

"Will you do the work for the lovers?" he asked.

She smiled, nodded, and drifted off to sleep.

She dreamed of the man in the turkey costume. She saw him at home alone, taking off the ridiculous trappings of a night made for children and stolen by adults. He poured some vodka into a glass and drank it down, doing a little dance and laughing pitifully in the kitchen. Then he walked into the bedroom, lay spread-eagle on his bed, and fell asleep.

Instantly, she was drawn into his dream. She lay curled up next to him, her fingers entwined with his, and they spoke.

"Once upon a time . . ."

"I'm too old for fairy tales," he said.

"Is there no magic in your life?"

"I'm a banker. Reality is everything."

"Perceptions differ."

"Cash registers do not."

"There is magic everywhere."

"There is no such thing as magic."

"Oh yes," she said. "There is magic in your body. There is magic in your thoughts. There is magic in your creativity, in your ideas. There is magic in the way we speak, this very minute."

"I'd like to believe that, but . . ."

"Would you?"

"Well . . . yes, I would."

"Then keep your eyes open. Be aware. Be conscious, and I will see that magic and miracles are shown to you every hour of every day. But you must want it."

"I'll try."

"Good." She kissed his fingers, one by one, and dissolved away.

When she awoke, Warm was watching her.

"Good girl," he said.

"Hmmm?" She gave a sleepy stretch and snuggled up close to him. "I'm glad you're still here."

"You have the gift. The instinct. You will be wonderful."

"What do you mean?"

"The gift of giving love, of opening the doors. You and I are the only ones I know, and we have an important job."

Kitten sat up. "Wait." She looked at him, so handsome, so familiar, so at home in her bed. "What are you saying?"

"Greystone Bay is a spiritual and emotional void. Haven't you noticed?"

Kitten bit her fingernail.

"There is a certain type of person who is drawn to this kind of place. They exist in a certain harmony here, and that's as it should be. Unfortunately, Greystone Bay was one of the first settlements along this coast, and it grew to an unusual size for its purpose. Many healthy people, many right people come here for one wrong reason or another and become trapped here. They lose themselves in this void and can never get out. Our job is to save those people, reunite them with their feelings, and give them a way to leave Greystone Bay and not return."

Kitten's mouth hung open. "Is that what this"—she indicated their presence in her bed—"is about?"

"No, my darling, *this* is because I love you. But I need you to begin to do the work you were born to do."

"What work, exactly?" Kitten wished her glasses were handy, she wanted to look at this man again. Closely.

"You do it so well. You do it instinctively. You helped Lee, the bartender. He is leaving."

"With Valerie."

"Yes."

"Then *you* talked to Valerie?"

"Yes. Valerie was an unusual woman and took more time than I realized, but she's—"

"Frederick? You're *Frederick?*"

"To her, yes. To you, I'm Warm. To another, I'm . . . I'm whatever they need."

Kitten pulled the sheet and the blanket up to warm her chills. "I don't understand."

"Do you remember the dream you had tonight, about the banker?"

Kitten remembered, vaguely. She nodded.

"That was the work. Sometimes it takes more. Valerie took a whole year."

"A year!"

"We have nothing but time, Magnetica."

"How do you find these people?"

"They become obvious. Later today we shall go find our next prospects." He reached for her and cuddled her down under the covers. "But for now . . ."

Kitten turned her back to him and he snuggled up close.

"Warm?"

"Hmmm?"

"Valerie said Frederick was bald."

"He was."

"You?"

"I can be bald."

"Could I be . . . different?"

He chuckled and hugged her. Soon she could hear him snoring gently, his breath in her hair. It felt wonderful, but she barely had time to luxuriate in the feeling of a man in her bed, she was too busy thinking who she could be next. She thought she'd perhaps look for a young man, so she could recreate herself as a young woman in order to remind him of what love could really be. And she could choose her names, she could be all names. She could eventually be everyone. She need never be Kitten again.

Her heart began to pound in excitement. Could this be? Could this really be happening? To have Warm by her side, and yet a different man every night. . . .

She thought not at all about what it meant to live her life in a void.

Across town, Anna dreamed of her new lover. His name was Michael, and even though they had only known each other a short time, she knew he was everything she had ever wanted in a man. He was rough and masculine, and passionate and forceful. She loved that. He was so different from all the other guys in Greystone Bay. She'd almost forgotten that a man could be so passionate. She felt small and important when she was with him.

He called her Intrigue. And she loved that, too.

But the best part was that Michael was taking her away from Greystone Bay.

She was thrilled. And he was so excited because he'd finally, *finally* found a replacement at work. That meant he was free to leave.

In the morning, she began to pack. Maybe we'll go somewhere out West, she thought.

Warm

by Craig Shaw Gardner

DAVE HAD TO GO HOME SOMETIME. He couldn't do Amanda any good if he was too tired to think. He had been dozing in the waiting room, even with the TV going full blast. The nurses had woken him from a dream—something about Amanda and his mother—and told him to go home and get some rest. They promised to call him the moment there was any change.

You know your mother loves you. That's what his father always used to say. Funny he should think about that now.

He had to be careful as he walked out to the parking lot. The cold rain had left a thin slick of ice everywhere. There was a bitter wind off the bay, and the stuff that fell from the sky was half water, half ice. It stung his skin and drenched his hair, sufficiently painful to make him care enough to hurry out of it. It woke him up some, too—enough, he hoped, to get him home.

He hadn't seen the accident. He had never seen any accident. His parents hadn't even let him go to funerals when he was a boy. The first funeral he'd ever attended was that of his parents. They had died in a car crash, too. But he could imagine the accident. He could imagine all the accidents.

He got into his car. The old Fairlane was the only car left in the visitors' lot. The Ford's engine caught on the third try. He didn't turn on the radio. He didn't care about music or news. Even the rain didn't really matter anymore. He put the car in gear and drove out of the lot, up the hill, and onto the coast road that would lead him home.

The digital clock he had stuck on the dashboard read 3:17. A.M., he silently added—almost twenty-four hours since Amanda's early-morning crash. Her car had run off this same road on a downhill stretch. She was always out of the house before six, said she wanted to beat the rush hour. Her brakes had locked, and she had skidded across the icy pavement. The police said, with the sharp curves and the wind off the water and all, this was the most treacherous road in all of the Bay. He had slept in. Didn't have to be in to the office until nine. The two-lane highway was now as empty as the parking lot, and almost as slick with ice. The police said the old oak she had run into had totally demolished the front half of her Honda. She was lucky to still be alive. He was going home—what was downhill for her would be uphill for him. He had to be careful on these curves. He blinked.

He saw Amanda in her intensive-care bed, her skull covered by bandages, her body surrounded by tubes and lights and silver machines that monitored every life function. Beep-*beep,* her heartbeat echoed on the hardware, beep-*beep.* There wasn't a single bruise on her face. Beep-*beep.* She looked like she was sleeping, like she would open her eyes at any moment and whisper a sleepy good-morning. Beep-*beep.*

He shook his head. It was far too dangerous to let his mind wander like that, especially with the rain. He had to watch the road. The police hadn't told him the exact location of the accident; at least not so he could really place it. "The big oak across from Sherman's farmstand," they had said. He needed to rest. Where was Sherman's farmstand? A flatbed truck had hauled away the remains of the Honda. Surely there'd be some mark of the crash on the tree. He bit his lip to force himself to wakefulness.

He drove slowly, and very carefully, the wipers beating out a rapid drumbeat against the constantly falling rain. Swish-zup, swish-zup, swish-zup, swish-zup. Beep-*beep.* Couldn't let his mind wander. Couldn't go off the road. It wouldn't do to have another accident in the family.

His father. His mother. Dead in a car crash. His parents had been mangled and burned beyond recognition, the police report said. The police had identified them from their dental records, and the license plate of the car. The coffins had been closed at the funeral. He had never seen them again. Swish-zup. He held his breath and looked out at the rain. Your mother loves you very much. And now Amanda. He could simply floor the accelerator and skid across the treacherous road to crash into the sea cliffs or sink into the Bay. It didn't matter; either way, he could join Amanda in oblivion. He could join everyone in oblivion.

He could imagine the accident.

He shook his head, more to clear it than in any effort to say no. Amanda needed him. He eased off on the accelerator. He had to get home, and wait for the nurses' call. Swish-zup. Swish-zup. Swish-zup.

Beep-*beep.*

Your mother loves you very much.

He could imagine all the accidents.

Mom? Where are you? Mom? What have I done?

He woke up, frightened as a child. He was half-surprised to find himself in his own bed. He barely remembered getting home, and had no memory at all of taking off his clothes and getting under the covers.

Almost his entire day at the hospital seemed distant now. Once he had learned that Amanda wouldn't die, the adrenaline had left him. Their family doctor had told him she was in a coma. Dave had asked a dozen questions, none of which really got answered. How long would she be in a coma? Would she be normal when she came out of it? Would she come out of it at all? The doctors didn't know. They didn't seem to know much of anything. Those comas were tricky things. There were specialists in Boston that they could consult, specialists who would take a look at Amanda's EEG. Maybe they could give him better answers.

Dave had gone to wait then, for a long time by Amanda's bedside; later, when he could no longer bear to watch her sleeping face, in the waiting room outside intensive care. It was there he had slipped into a bit of a coma of his own, half waking, half dream.

He blinked, and saw his mother's face. He hadn't dreamed about his mother in a long time. Maybe it was the accident. Or maybe it was the rainy day.

Your mother loves you very much.

"Better be quiet, Davey."

He looked up at his father. "I want to go out and play."

"It's raining too much," his father had reasoned in that slightly fussy way he had. "You'll catch your death."

He had pouted. He had wanted to stamp his foot. But, even at seven, he knew that foot-stamping was not allowed.

"Sometimes, we can't do what we want," his father had said in that very reasonable voice. When he thought about it now, he realized that his father had been the peacekeeper in the family.

He had barely scuffed his Buster Brown shoe. He could see the fear in his father's face with even that show of defiance.

"Quiet now," his father cautioned in a voice barely above a whisper. "You don't want to bother your mother."

This time, though, he wouldn't obey his father. This time, he would run and shout and throw things. Even then, at seven years of age, he had known he needed to escape from inside these walls. Home was fine, as long as you didn't stay there too long.

And so seven-year-old Davey had run screaming defiance into the living room, his rebellion lasting a good half minute before he saw his mother.

She rose quickly from the couch in one wrenching motion, as if she was a puppet and someone had suddenly pulled all her strings. Her body was almost totally rigid, and yet it shook, almost imperceptibly, as if there was something inside that wanted to get out and destroy them all.

His mother said nothing. His mother only stared at him.

It was all his fault. Little Davey wanted to die.

He could imagine all the accidents.

He unclenched his fists, and looked down where his nails had made indentations in his palms. It was time to think of Amanda. When he thought of bad things too long, remembering her always helped.

He pushed himself up out of bed and walked to the bookcase, where he could look at their wedding picture. When he looked at Amanda's smile, he could hear her laugh.

She had been so different. So happy, so eager to have fun, so much the opposite of the cold house Dave had called home as a child. They had had their problems, but still—Dave sighed. He didn't want to dwell on the negative parts of their marriage. He couldn't bear to lose that relationship now.

He didn't want to see his mother anymore either, her face bone white with suppressed fury. How could a little boy cause that kind of anger? Both of his parents had been dead for a long time. Years.

Your mother loves you very much.

Amanda's parents were dead, too. Actually, that was what had led them to come to Greystone Bay. Amanda had inherited their house, a fine Victorian mansion on the North Hill. It had seemed the perfect solution. It was more than either of them could ever hope to afford closer to Boston. Amanda had to travel all over New England for her consulting work anyway, and Dave had found an opening at a local insurance firm. There had been no reason not to come here.

He walked to the window and pulled up the shade. It was daylight, but you could barely tell that from the colorless, rain-washed streets.

Come to Greystone Bay, Amanda had said. *It hardly ever snows; the ocean currents keep it warm.*

Exactly warm enough, he thought, for freezing rain.

"Dave? What's the matter?"

He turned from the window to look at Amanda. Even in the pale half-light of a Greystone Bay winter she was beautiful, her long, dark hair framing her oval face. But most beautiful of all was the concern on her face. She genuinely cared about him, and showed it in little kindnesses and moments of attention that he found constantly surprising, constantly wonderful. Her concern almost made up for this never-ending winter. Her warmth somehow endured in the middle of this numbing cold.

That warmth was the reason he stayed in Greystone Bay.

He looked down at the windswept beach and the rows of trees that glittered in their ice cocoons. Sometimes, even here, safely hidden behind glass, he felt like the wind froze his bones and the ice covered his spirit.

"This is real oatmeal weather, isn't it?" Amanda stepped up behind him and wrapped her arms around his chest. "There's no cold quite so biting as the cold beside the ocean. That's the sort of thing my mother would always say." She kissed his earlobe. "I think we're both feeling a little housebound. When I'm done with this project, let's go away for a while."

He started to protest. Could they afford it? The insurance business wasn't everything that it could be; he wasn't at all sure about his commissions.

"Hush," she replied. "We'll go someplace warm."

Warm. He didn't have to go anywhere to find that. He smiled at her, and went back to looking out the window.

There were always promises. And there were always accidents.

Come to Greystone Bay, to my parents' house.

It had been strange when they had first come here. Amanda was so different from everything he had known. He had felt it was strange, quite simply, that anyone would ever want to set foot in their parents' house again.

The phone rang. He moved to the bedside table to pick it up, hoping it would be the nurses, with some news about Amanda.

"Dave?" His hope left him as soon as he recognized the voice of Sally Potter, another insurance agent from work. "Any news?"

Dave told her no. Amanda was stable, but she hadn't regained consciousness.

"We all understand," Sally replied, her voice somehow caring and no-nonsense at the same moment. It was that voice that made her so good at the insurance business. "Take all the time you need. I'll tell Henry. And let me know if you need anything. Anything at all."

Dave could feel himself smile. Unlike some of those working at the agency, Sally genuinely cared what happened to others, and was in the business not to generate numbers, but to help people. Now she was running interference for him with the boss; that was above and beyond the call of duty.

"I don't want you getting yourself in trouble on my account," he said.

"There's nothing I can't handle," she replied with a laugh.

Dave felt himself relaxing as they talked. Sally and he had liked each other since the moment they met, when he first came to work in Greystone Bay. Kindred souls, she had said. Sometimes, when Amanda was out of town with her job, Sally and he had met for coffee after work. Amanda, for her part, was never jealous. She knew where Dave's true feelings lay.

"Dave? Are you still there?"

He blinked. "What? Sure, Sally. I guess my mind was somewhere else."

"Understood." The reassuring tone was back in her voice. "I'm so sorry for you, Dave. Like I said, if you need anything."

"Sure, Sally. I appreciate it. I'll talk to you soon."

They exchanged good-byes. He felt his good cheer leave him as he put down the phone. He had to get out of this house; the weather and the loneliness were sinking him into a sure depression. He would run some errands, maybe stop by the hospital. It wouldn't hurt to take another look in at Amanda.

A pale figure, almost completely lost beneath a dark, hooded raincoat, struggled up the hill with the aid of a cane. An old woman. As old as his mother would be, had she lived. He turned away from the sodden winter streets. The wind battered against the window, as if the rain was impatient to drench the inside of the house as well.

Dave shivered involuntarily. He always got like this in winter rain.

Little Davey hid in his room, frightened to death of the white specter he had seen in the living room.

His parents had converted the attic when they moved into this place a couple years before. "Davey should have a room to grow into," his father had said. It was colder than the rest of the house up here. There were always drafts. He had to wear a sweater. He could hear the rain beat against the shingles outside. At least it was private, and his mother didn't come up here unless she absolutely had to. This was Davey's room, and he could hide under the covers whenever he wanted to, so long as he remade the bed when it was time to leave.

He had stayed there all that afternoon, and all evening, reading the same three comic books over and over again. When it got to be six o'clock, his father brought him dinner with hardly a word. He got ready for bed by himself, and went downstairs to use the bathroom after all the lights had gone out down there. Eventually, he fell asleep.

The rain had ended by the next morning. Sun poured in through the dormer windows, making his bedroom seem like a completely different place than it had been the day before. With the sun like this, he could believe it was almost spring.

He still didn't feel like going downstairs. He wanted nothing more than to crawl back under the covers with his comic books. But it was a school day. What would his mother say if he didn't go to school?

He took a clean shirt out of the second drawer, and pulled his new khaki pants from a hanger in the closet. Wouldn't his parents be proud when he did everything by himself! He checked to see if his shirt was buttoned right, then checked a second time. Why couldn't he go downstairs?

"Davey!" his mother's voice called up. His breath caught in his throat. Did she know what he was thinking? Somehow, he felt that she always knew. "Breakfast!"

He walked as slowly as he could down the two flights of stairs. The way his stomach felt, he wasn't hungry at all.

"There you are!" His mother's voice greeted him, so full of good cheer that it sounded more like she was singing than speaking. "And it's such a beautiful day."

He looked up into his mother's face. Her smile was wonderfully warm, as if it had taken some of the glow from the sun. She smiled at him.

Davey sat down for breakfast. He smiled, too. His stomach felt much better. His mother had made pancakes. Now everything would be just fine.

Thinking about all this almost made him laugh. He had gone down to breakfast on that day, and everything was hunky-dory. Of course, neither one of his parents ever talked about his mother's reaction the day before. In his family, they never ever talked about anything. No, he got to spend years, and thousands of dollars learning to talk to a therapist.

His mother was always there. Somehow she always knew.

Dave realized, when his mother died, that he was relieved in some way. She would no longer be there, looking over his shoulder, forcing him to be quiet.

Your mother loves you very much. He had had a great

deal of guilt about that. But it also had allowed him to marry Amanda. His parents were dead. He could do what he wanted to.

Sometimes, though, he thought his mother was with him still.

He looked up and studied the cracks in the ceiling that he always meant to fix. He had to get outside. Otherwise, he'd sit and brood about the rain and his parents all day. It really was time to go back to the hospital. There wasn't anything else he could do. Still—it was like he didn't want to go downstairs.

The phone rang.

It was Sally. If he was coming into town, could he stop by the office? She hated to bother him but papers had to be signed.

Well, it would finally get him out of the house. And maybe he could get a smile out of it, too.

The car protested for a long moment before it agreed to start. It didn't seem to like the weather any more than he did.

The wipers started with the car. Swish-zup. Swish-zup. He remembered how hypnotic they had seemed the night before. He backed out of the garage, then drove into the rain.

The temperature had warmed up a few degrees, so that the driving wasn't quite so treacherous. However, the radio weather man said there was flooding on some of the low-lying roads. It looked like he should take the hilly coast highway again.

Now that he was awake, he was actually afraid he'd see where Amanda had gone off the road. He could always imagine accidents. But the visibility wasn't that much better in the daylight than it had been the night before. The trees were a grey wash on the side of the road, like a watercolor that had never sufficiently dried. He didn't see any felled trees, or great gashes caused by someone whose car had gone beyond control. He had trouble enough seeing the road. Where was that farmstand?

As he rounded the turn at the top of North Hill, he was taken by the way the rain made patterns out over the Bay. Great swashes of grey roiled across the sky. At first it looked like curtains shifting. Then it seemed as if there might be something more, like shadow figures behind the curtains, watching him and everything else that happened in the town and on the Bay.

If the weather hadn't been so dangerous, it might have seemed more breathtaking. When the elements grew this overwhelming, they took away all illusion of civilization and control. Under a sky like this, Greystone Bay and all of Massachusetts behind it could wash away. The rain was king.

Dave pulled his gaze from the shifting clouds to watch the road. But before he looked away, he could swear one pale cloud had an almost human face, and something like a hand beckoned him to leave the road and come closer.

It was noon by the time he reached the office.

It was strange to be here, after what had happened in the last day and a half. The place was unusually quiet. Four of the five desks in the front room were empty. The remaining receptionist told him that Sally was waiting back in her office. He walked quickly past his own cubicle.

Sally looked up as he reached her doorway. "Hi. Everybody's out to lunch. You don't need much of a work force in this rain."

He was surprised at how uncomfortable he felt in this place. He had only been gone for a couple of days. Why did things seem so different? "I guess I don't have to rush back to work after all," he murmured. It was supposed to be funny, but his voice cracked as he spoke.

"Oh, Dave." She took both his hands in her own. "I'm so sorry." She put her arms around him and hugged him tight.

The rough wool of her business suit made his neck itch. Somehow, he felt closer to Sally at this moment than he ever had before.

He started to cry—short, strangled sobs. *Don't cry, Davey.* He hadn't cried in years. *Your mother can't stand to see you cry.*

"Oh, don't," Sally chided gently. She took his chin in her hand and turned his face to hers. "Everything's going to be fine. You'll see."

"Sal— Sally." He could barely get her name out. Somehow he found himself kissing her. It was a long kiss, slow and gentle, and it tasted of salt from his tears.

He jerked his head back. "Im sorry. Excuse me. I don't know what I'm doing."

"Hush now." Sally refused to let him go. "You're just looking for some comfort. You're not doing anything wrong."

"Yeah, Sally. I'm sure you're right." He forced a smile. "I've got to go. All right?"

"Of course. Take care of yourself. And call me if you need anything." She kissed him on the cheek, then stepped away. "Anything at all."

He sat in the visitors' parking lot for a long moment. Now that he was so close to Amanda, he wasn't sure he wanted to face that reality of tubes and machines and bandages.

It wasn't simply what had happened to his wife. The hospital made him feel this way. He wasn't just avoiding Amanda. He couldn't cope with the nurses and doctors in intensive care. Their smiles had been very kind, and their words were all about hope and recovery, but their eyes had been very tired, as if they knew death far too intimately.

And what had they been able to tell him? Their prognosis had been vague at best, at worst not at all hopeful. He realized they were only waiting for another death.

But they were wrong. It couldn't happen to Amanda. She was too strong for that. She'd fight back when she thought she'd been wronged. She wasn't afraid of her anger.

He remembered his reaction when he had first come into the ward. He had wanted to push the doctors away, somehow take charge, make the accident never have happened, make everything all right again. How had this happened? What had he done wrong? He felt like slapping himself in the face, to somehow bring himself to his senses and end this dream forever.

He looked toward the hospital and made an effort to control his breathing. He would do none of those things. He let go of the steering wheel and flexed his fingers so that the blood would move back to his knuckles. He would go in and see Amanda.

He heard the beep of her heart monitor before he saw her face. The nursing staff didn't challenge him. They already knew who he was.

She was still asleep, and still beautiful, although her face seemed to have taken on a slight puffiness since the day before. It probably had something to do with all the fluids they were pumping into her. The same chair was by her bed. He sat down again, and leaned forward, one hand resting gently on the sheet above her arm, the other hand touching the sheet above her leg. Somehow, even this contact made him feel better.

"Mr. Tindal!" The voice snapped Dave out of his reverie.

Some time had passed. Dave had no idea how long. "I'm glad I caught you."

He looked up. It was their family doctor. Dr. Reid. Amanda had always liked him better than Dave had. There was something about the way he smiled, or the way he combed his hair, or something. He made Dave uneasy.

"I'm afraid there hasn't been any significant change. As I said yesterday, it's hard to say when she might come out of it."

Dave felt like striking out, ripping down the curtains, knocking over the monitor. He felt powerless. It was no use taking out his anger here. The doctor was doing everything he could. They were all powerless.

He turned back to his wife. He just wished there was some way he could reach Amanda.

Dr. Reid hovered behind him, as if he were unwilling to leave until he found a positive note on which to end the conversation. "Some weather we're having out there, isn't it? I swear, this rain is even worse than we're used to in Greystone Bay. You know, I actually saw lightning out there? And in the middle of February!"

Dave felt something under his hand.

Amanda's leg was moving. He looked up at Reid, who had finally turned to go.

"Doctor?"

But Dr. Reid glanced back around, then shook his head. "It's natural for some movement—"

Amanda's leg jerked from beneath Dave's hand. Her right hand spasmed up to fly across her chest, wrenching free of the IV.

The doctor took a single step outside the cubicle. "Nurse! Get over here, stet!"

"Amanda?" Dave called. Her whole body was shaking now, as if she were wracked with fever.

Amanda groaned. Her mouth moved up and down over her teeth. She seemed to be trying to pull her dry lips apart.

Dave looked up. Two nurses, a woman and a man, had stepped into the cubicle behind the doctor.

"I think she's trying to say something," he explained.

He turned back to Amanda. Her eyes shot open abruptly, as if someone had flicked a switch. Her lips parted then, the parched flesh tearing slightly where it had been stuck together by dried saliva. Her tongue moved forward tentatively, as if it had never felt those lips before.

"Do you want a drink of water?" Dave asked. He was aware of the two nurses moving to either side of the bed.

"Please, Amanda," Dr. Reid said behind him. "Don't try to move too suddenly. You've been—"

"Daay," she managed, her voice deep and thick with phlegm. Her shaking stopped as suddenly as it had begun.

"Yes, Amanda," Dave replied. There should have been something else he could say.

"You've lost your IV," the male nurse said calmly. "Hold still a minute and I'll put it back in."

But Amanda didn't seem to hear him. She continued to stare at her husband.

"Dave?" she murmured, as if she only recognized him now. "Davey?"

"Yes, it's me, Amanda."

Her lips curled up in the slightest of smiles. "What have you been doing, Davey?" Her voice was a high singsong, almost like she was a child. "Such a bad boy."

Dave frowned. Maybe she was coming out of a dream. Was she teasing him? What was she thinking?

"Davey? Come here right now." She held out her arms. Dave leaned down toward her.

The male nurse frowned, the still-unconnected IV in his hand. "Mrs. Tindal? You should be careful." He firmly grabbed her wrist and drew it toward him. "I don't know if you should—"

Amanda screamed. Her right hand grabbed the male nurse's coat, her left hand went for his face. He made a strangled sound in his throat, no longer trying to gently handle her arm, but pushing away with all his strength, trying to free himself from Amanda's grip as it snaked around his neck.

The doctor and the other nurse rushed to the man's aid.

"No one keeps me away from my Davey!" Amanda screamed a second time as they pressed down on her arms, and, as suddenly as she had begun her attack, she relaxed, falling back on the bed.

She was completely still. Her eyes were open, but she no longer seemed to see. The doctor and two nurses stared at each other, and began to talk among themselves as if Dave wasn't even there.

The male nurse massaged his throat. "What a grip."

"Some kind of hysterical strength," the other nurse murmured, more a question than a statement.

"I don't think she knew what she was doing," the male nurse ventured. "It was like she only saw her husband."

The doctor made noise about this outburst having some relation to her injury as the male nurse quickly restarted the IV and the woman checked the monitors.

"She's gone again," the female nurse whispered. She stared at the monitor. "She's slipped back into her coma."

The doctor quickly joined her at the side of the machine.

Dave could only stand there and stare at the others. He

had jumped up at his wife's final outburst. But it had hardly sounded like Amanda talking. The Amanda that he knew. She never called him Davey. And what had she meant, he was a bad boy?

One of the nurses shut Amanda's eyes again, and she looked exactly as she had before she had awoken.

He felt so helpless. What could he have done? If he had been able to move somehow, to reason with the nurses, maybe she would have stayed conscious. Somehow, he had failed her.

"Something has to be wrong here," Dr. Reid said as he held up a long paper streamer. "According to the record on the monitor, she didn't come out of her coma at all."

They had asked him to leave for a few minutes, to wait in the outer room while they performed some tests. They clearly had no idea what really had happened.

Neither did Dave. But that sudden outburst of activity from Amanda had made it impossible for him to sit still. Amanda had been so close!

Or maybe she hadn't been there at all. He looked down at his hands, and noticed that now they were shaking ever so slightly.

What could make him shake this way?

Unless it was that she had called him Davey.

His mother was all smiles.

"Oh, Davey." She laughed, a silvery sound that seemed to brighten up his bedroom. "You're your mother's perfect child. I'm going to love you forever and ever."

When she was happy, it was almost like she was playing ring-around-the-rosy or some other game. Everything was in its place, and the world was wonderful.

She grabbed his hands and swung him around. "Davey, Davey, Davey," she sang. "Fell into some gravy."

He laughed as he felt his feet catch the bedspread in flight.

She dropped him.

"Oh dear." She frowned a bit. "We'd better straighten that bedspread.

"Okay, Mom." He dutifully went to fix the rumpled bed.

He pulled up the covers, and half a dozen things fell to the floor: comic books, toy soldiers, a cat's-eye marble.

Davey stared at the toys in horror. He had meant to put them in their place. But then, when he got ready for school, he had completely forgotten about them.

He looked to his mother. Her smile was gone. Her mouth was thin and tight. She clenched her fists. She was trembling.

"I'm sorry, Mom," Davey said quickly. "I'll clean up. I'll put things away."

His mother looked at the attic ceiling. Her mouth barely moved as she spoke. "Davey, get out of here this minute!"

He ran, all the way downstairs into the kitchen. He sat huddled in the corner, listening to feet stomping, drawers slamming, and the raised voice of his mother saying words he didn't understand. It was the first time he had ever heard her yell. It was like there was a battle going on in his room. But what could his mother fight with up there? He remembered when he was younger, and would imagine that dark shapes hid in the closets or under the bed.

The banging ended, followed by a silence that seemed to go on forever. Finally, his mother came downstairs.

His mother smiled at him. "Would you like something to eat, Davey?"

He shook his head no. What had happened upstairs?

"Mother feels better now," she said. "But you should go clean up your room."

He walked slowly upstairs. When he reached his attic room, it did look like a battle had been fought. Drawers were on the floor, clothes scattered everywhere. His comic books had been torn to shreds.

He did his best to clean up the mess.

After all, it was his fault. He had failed his mother.

Davey.

That was the only time he ever remembered his mother acting out her anger. Davey. And he still felt that that had been only the slightest bit of all the fury she kept closed up inside. Davey. He was always convinced that, had she let out all of her anger, it would have been a terrible thing.

Davey. Davey. Davey.

Dave did his best to laugh. He was being silly. It wasn't as if the word had never passed Amanda's lips. Amanda had called him Davey for a short time while they were dating. But he had finally gotten up the nerve to ask her to stop. The word made him nervous. The nickname had the wrong associations.

He was far too upset. Something at the hospital made him feel all wrong. For want of something better to do, he decided to go back home through the rain.

There were no messages on the answering machine. He supposed he should go through the household files and take a look at Amanda's hospital coverage. That was the only good thing about being an account executive in the insurance business: If Amanda died, he wouldn't have to worry about money.

The doorbell rang. He went to answer it and found Sally.

She smiled brightly on the doorstep. "Dave. I hope you don't mind. I saw that your lights were on. You seemed so upset earlier today, I just wanted to—well—see if you were all right."

Dave found himself flattered. Sally lived way over on the other side of the hill. He was almost, but not quite on her way home. The roads got treacherous after dark these days. She must really be worried about him, to seek him out in this kind of weather.

What was he thinking of? She was getting drenched in the rain. "Would you like to come in for a minute?"

Her boots shifted around a small puddle that was growing on the flagstone walk. "I really shouldn't. I just wanted to make sure—" She looked down at her muddy boots. "Well . . . maybe we could go out and get a drink—if you want to talk."

"I'm afraid I don't have the energy," Dave said with as much feeling as he could muster. "Come in for a minute. I've made some coffee."

She hesitated for half a second. "Okay. But just for a minute."

She followed him into the kitchen, and sat down in silence. They had known each other for months and had never stopped talking. The effortless conversations they used to have seemed to have vanished, erased by that single kiss back at the office, as if only now did they realize that sex, or even love could be a possibility.

He pulled a pair of cups from the cupboard. He took his coffee black and so did Sally. Amanda always added cream and sugar.

"Uh, Dave," Sally said after he had turned away, "about today."

"I'm sorry about that," Dave blurted. "I was under a lot of stress."

"I have a responsibility, too," Sally objected. "You always take things so much on yourself."

God, wasn't that true. He had thought he could break through that barrier, but with everything that had happened to Amanda— A small, sorry laugh escaped from his throat.

"Here's the coffee." He picked up the cups and turned around. "Would you like anything to eat?"

She frowned down at her coffee. "Actually, I'd really like a drink."

He laughed at that, and looked down into the lower cupboard where they kept that sort of thing.

"I've got an unopened bottle of Chablis."

"Perfect," was Sally's reply.

He quickly went to work with a corkscrew, and got a pair of glasses. "Just push that nasty coffee out of the way."

Sally did as he asked, and he filled both glasses. Sally took a substantial swallow. "There's something about this weather," she ventured.

"It's like you're never going to get warm," he added.

"Exactly," she replied. They both laughed. They seemed to be back in perfect sync.

They drank for a few minutes and talked about things that didn't matter: office politics, TV shows, the rotten weather. Then she pushed her glass away and stood up.

"I just don't want to see you this unhappy."

He felt he had to stand up in turn. "What do you mean? Do you want some more wine?"

She stepped forward and took his hand before he could reach the bottle. He turned to face her.

"Oh, Dave," she said as she stepped closer. They began to kiss again. Before he knew what had happened, they had their clothes off and were on the couch.

It felt so good to have her hands on his naked back. Her

lips were soft, and seemed to fit perfectly with his. They were joined together, his hands on her buttocks, and the warmth poured from him. It encompassed both of them in waves.

The chill didn't come until it was over.

What had he done?

Sally ran her fingers through his hair. "Oh, Dave. I've wanted to do this for so long."

He kissed her forehead. He wanted to run away, to hide, to make believe this had never happened. "I guess I have, too." He rolled away from her, then sat up. "But it's the wrong time."

"With Amanda?" She paused. "Maybe I'm taking advantage of you here. Oh, Dave, I've been so lonely."

He didn't know how to answer. He looked back at the cracks on the ceiling. The never-ending moisture from the rain seemed to be making them worse.

"Maybe I'd better go," she said after a minute. She got off the couch.

"I just want to sleep," was his reply. What had he done? He could imagine all the accidents, except some of them might not be so accidental.

"Call me if you need anything," she said as she quickly put on her clothes. "I mean that."

She let herself out. Dave hugged his knees to his chest and rocked back and forth. What had he done? He hadn't felt this bad since he was a child. It was as if his mother had never left him.

The windows rattled. Night was falling, and the rain was turning to ice.

There was no way he could sleep. He didn't really imagine that he could. Maybe he would feel better if he went back to the hospital.

He went back to his car and the rain. Swish-zup. Swish-zup. He was much more aware of the wiper noise after it got dark. Maybe it was because they had to work harder against the freezing rain.

He felt hollow, like he was an empty shell. He could stop the car and step outside and fill himself up with the freezing rain and be cold and alone forever. A part of him wished that everyone would just go away. What could he do for Amanda? What could he do for Sally? What could he do for his mother?

What could he do for himself?

His foot pounded on the accelerator. No, never think about yourself. Only about your mother, or your wife, or any other woman who could keep you warm for an instant.

He turned on the radio. He needed something besides his thoughts. The Rolling Stones were singing about getting no satisfaction. God, wasn't that true. He sang along.

"I can't get no, no no no—" He sang as loud as he could. But he couldn't shut off his brain.

He thought of Amanda's expressionless face. He had a feeling she was trapped and would never be free. Would he? For a moment there, with Sally, he had felt warm and safe. But he wasn't. He could never be. His mother was too close to him.

Your mother loves you very much.

Sally. What if Amanda found out? How could he face Amanda? He would be all alone. What had he done?

He cranked the radio up until the speakers buzzed with the bass line. Swish-zup. Swish-zup. The wipers kept the beat.

The lightning had started again, showing the rolling clouds. He saw a rivulet of water running down the inside of the driver's-side window. The seals were going on this old car. Nothing was beyond the reach of the rain.

Swish. The reassuring beat was gone, like a failing heartbeat. The wipers were sticking to the ice. He glanced at the speedometer. He was going far too fast. He had to slow down, to stop and free the wipers.

The Ford reached the top of the hill and started down.

He slammed on the brakes. The back half of the Fairlane fishtailed wildly. Turn into the skid, he told himself. It was too late. Even with the ice on the windshield, he could tell the car was leaving the road.

He stopped with a jolt. He started to breathe again.

The car had skidded into the ditch. The driver's-side door was maybe six inches from an old wooden guardrail. Immediately beyond that was the cliff, and maybe a fifty-foot drop into the sea, depending on how far he had skidded down the hill.

But he was fine, unharmed—thank god for seatbelts. All he had to do was start the car up and drive on.

The wipers had stopped, frozen in place. He turned them off. He'd free them once he got himself clear of the ditch. The engine responded sluggishly when he turned the key.

Maybe the wires were wet. More likely he had flooded the engine. He'd have to give the old motor a minute and start again. Maybe he would go out and take a look under the hood. He could always prop open the choke to get the car started, if he could somehow protect the wires from the rain. That probably wasn't the best of ideas. Still, he should get out of the car and figure out the best way to get out of this ditch. He crawled over to the passenger door and tried to twist the handle. It wouldn't budge.

The door wouldn't open. It was frozen shut.

The storm outside was the worst he had ever seen it. The

rain had doubled in intensity since he had left home, and now seemed to be doubling again. The ice was forming patterns. He swore he could see a pair of eyes.

You know your mother loves you.

There were other features as well, a thin nose, tightly drawn lips.

We'll be together forever and ever.

Wind rattled the old car's windows. He felt the Ford shift slightly, and roll closer to the edge. The storm was pushing him. The rain wanted him.

He looked back at the windshield. It was all there now. It looked like the face of his mother.

"No!" he screamed as loud as he could. "Get away from me! Get away!"

But he wanted to say he was sorry. He wanted to say he would make everything all better. Please, Mommy, please. The wind rocked the car with savage force.

If she ever let out her anger, it would be a terrible thing to behold.

He turned the key in the ignition. The engine caught.

The wheels spun in the mud, causing the car to shift even closer to the edge. He couldn't panic. He applied even, firm pressure to the accelerator. The wheels found gravel. The car jerked forward, back onto the road.

You know your mother loves you. We'll be together, forever and ever.

No. The defroster had kicked in, melting the ice on the windshield. It was nothing but a random pattern, caused by the rain and the wind. It was only his imagination. Too much had happened to him. He needed to get away from all this coldness.

If only he could somehow get to his Amanda.

Swish-zup. The wipers kicked back in. Swish-zup. He

couldn't remember turning them back on. Swish-zup. The sound was reassuring. He crawled down the hillside, keeping the car as close to ten miles an hour as he could. The rain seemed to be lighter now. He even thought he saw some bright patches overhead. Maybe there'd actually be some breaks in the clouds.

Everything was going to be fine now.

He squinted out at the rain, half expecting the headlights to show an old woman climbing towards him.

There was good news at the hospital.

Amanda had woken up the moment the storm cleared.

Maybe, the doctors said, it had something to do with the change in atmospheric pressure. It was quite clear they didn't know. But they let him in to see her.

"Amanda?" he asked softly.

She opened her eyes. She smiled at him and held out her hand. It was warm to the touch. It was so nice to hold that hand again.

"It's good to see you awake," he added.

She nodded, fighting to keep her eyes open.

"Davey," was the only thing she said.

He let go of her hand and let her sleep.

They transferred her out of intensive care a few hours later. Dr. Reid explained that they would keep her in the hospital for a couple of days for observation, but there should be no problem with her being home by the weekend.

So Dave waited, and made plans. He visited Amanda the following afternoon, but she hadn't felt much like talking. It was perfectly understandable. She had been through a lot.

Sally had left a number of messages on the answering

machine. He didn't return her calls. She would be better off without him.

He left the house again on Saturday morning. Amanda was due to be released at ten. He was pleased to see that it had started to snow. Even though the air was colder, the heavy white powder made the landscape seem quite warm compared to the rain.

She was sitting up and waiting for him in a wheelchair when he got there. She smiled when she saw him, like she didn't have a care in the world.

Doctor Reid appeared from around the corner. "Hello, there!" he called. "I hate to disturb the happy couple, but I wanted to say good-bye." He patted the handle of the wheelchair. "Amanda's in remarkable shape, all things considered. She'll be a little weak for a few days, but after that she'll be able to get around just fine." He looked down at his patient. "And Amanda. If there's any problem, don't hesitate to call."

She smiled through all of this. Dave went down to get the car. Everything was going exactly as he had expected.

Amanda and the nurse were waiting for him when he reached the front door. The nurse helped her from the wheelchair into the car.

"Isn't the snow beautiful?" she said as they left the parking lot. "I never thought I'd see it again."

"It is a lot better than the rain." He headed back up the hill towards home. They drove in silence for a long moment.

"Oh, Davey," Amanda said at last. "I'm so happy to be back. I want to love you forever."

He smiled at her and floored the accelerator. They were almost to the top of the hill.

He'd get rid of his mother once and for all.

The Home

by Kathryn Ptacek

"THIS IS IT," JEANNINE SAID ALOUD. "This is my last *ever* summer in Greystone Bay."

The words sounded good, yet she knew it wouldn't be the last. The previous year she'd vowed *that* would be her last summer, and the year before that, *that* summer would have been her final one here. Only it wasn't; it never was. Somehow. Yet it would be nice if she'd find another job elsewhere, pack up her belongings, and move away from Greystone Bay and all the memories and this terrible summer.

Memories. . . .

Summer. . . .

From where she lay in bed she looked out the window and saw the humidity hanging in the trees like moist grey shawls. Birds sang disheartened songs; somewhere a cricket chirped. Beneath her the sheets were damp.

God, how she hated summers here. And winters, too.

But the summers were by far the worst. Jeannine had lived here all her life, yet had never grown accustomed to the summers with their high temperatures and high humidity, the way the air became absolutely still, until you struggled to breathe; sometimes it felt like something was sucking the air out of your very lungs.

Or the spirit out of your very soul.

No wonder Greystone Bay had such a high suicide rate. There was a saying among the natives: "If the winters don't get you, the summers will."

True enough.

Glancing at the clock, she saw it was 5:30. Almost time to begin another exciting day.

Bestill my heart, she thought and giggled aloud. The giggle turned into a choking noise and she squeezed her eyes shut. She forced herself to take a long, deep breath, to slowly release it . . . and not to think, to think, to think.

Maybe, just maybe, the problem was her attitude. If she viewed it—the summer, the heat, the humidity, her job, EVERYTHING—more optimistically, maybe it *would* be better, maybe things would work out for once, maybe she wouldn't feel this rotten all the time.

Maybe.

She didn't have to push the top sheet back to get up; that had been off her since midnight. The backs of her legs seemed to stick to the sheets and she almost expected her skin to pull away with a wet, ripping sound.

She padded into the bathroom, stared at herself in the mirror. Her blonde hair stood up at all angles; to avoid snarls, she'd had it cut to chin length. Not short enough, she mused. She yawned and wished she didn't have all the silver in her mouth. She had smudges under her eyes from the mascara she hadn't removed last night and her face gleamed from the sweat on it.

Swell.

She washed her face, brushed her teeth, then stepped into the shower stall. The curtain kept touching her—a clammy, mildewy feeling—and no matter how much she shoved it away, it clung to her. Exasperated, she jerked the curtain back on its rings. Finally, she turned off the hot water and forced herself to stay under the cold water. This morning ritual never failed to wake her up completely, and to cool her off, even if it was just for a while.

She reached for the towels hanging on a wooden rack on the opposite wall, just an arm's length away, and an earwig tumbled out. She wrinkled her nose and watched it scuttle away. The bug wasn't poisonous or anything, just disgusting. And *everyone* had seen that old *Twilight Zone* episode with Lawrence Harvey and the earwig. Or was it *Night Gallery*? *Outer Limits*?

Carl always claimed—

No.

Didn't matter; earwigs didn't crawl into your ears while you slept—all they had to do was just scuttle nearby and you were disgusted enough. Better an earwig than a centipede, although she had plenty of those in the damp weather. Damp weather. Meaning every day, every night of the year, practically. She didn't see them in the winter—maybe they went south to Florida—but she saw plenty of them other times. She hated it when she caught some movement out of the corner of her eye, and there, creeping across the carpet, would be an earwig or centipede. She'd kill it, then find another one on the wall, and after that, she'd sit back on the couch, and every time she had an itch or the hair on her arms was ruffled or *anything* just touched her, she'd think it was something crawling on her.

Disgusting, simply disgusting.

And then there were the flies and mosquitoes that buzzed around outside and—all too often—inside. She hated those, too. Sometimes, with all these creepy-crawlies around her, she wondered if she had simply died and someone had neglected to tell her.

She shook the towel, wrapped her wet hair in it. Then she reached for another towel, shook that as a precaution, and started drying herself. Only it didn't feel as if she were dry; it felt like she had simply moved the moisture from one spot to another.

Jeannine dressed, then ate a quick breakfast. She grabbed her purse and car keys, and left the ground-floor apartment. She waved to Mrs. McDonald, who waggled her fingers as she tended her roses. They didn't look too good this year; the blight had got them, as the old woman put it, but she was valiantly trying to save them. Usually the flowers were an exquisite deep red, a sunshiny yellow, a dainty pink. This year the petals all looked grey, as if they weren't getting enough sun.

She glanced overhead. That wasn't surprising since the sun was obscured by a haze. The haze had held on all month long, and she was beginning to wonder if the sky really was blue beyond that. Maybe there was nothing. . . . Maybe there was just night . . . blackness . . . waiting to swallow them.

She shivered, despite the heat, and got into her car. Although the sky was hazy, it was still bright and she fumbled to put on her sunglasses. Local weathermen had been predicting for some time—and so far, erroneously—that the area would be getting big storms one of these days. They muttered something about high-pressure systems and a buildup, the meeting of cool air and warm . . . and one of these days . . . shazam, down it would come, the heavens opening up, the possibility of tornadoes and downpours and vicious winds and baseball-sized hail and God knows what else. It's coming, it's coming, the weather forecasters said, and after a while, people started calling the radio and TV stations to say, yeah, and so's Christmas. She'd never done that, though she often thought about it. It was the sort of thing Carl would have done.

Quickly, the stab of pain and then it was gone.

Even this early she turned the car's air conditioning on, but she could still feel the trickle of sweat down the middle of her back, under her bra strap, and the skin between her thighs was already moist despite the hose.

She drove along Foster Street, past the closed-up buildings that had made their shuttered appearance this last year—their proprietors all having given up, past the tacky fast-food restaurants that seemed part of any urban blight now, past the youths hanging out on the street corners, watching her with empty eyes. She turned down Crescent with its small frame houses and tiny front yards, and followed that until she reached Port Boulevard. That was the fastest way to get to work.

From Harbor Road she swung north, taking the road over North Hill, past the elaborate houses and painstakingly tended estates—the gardeners all out despite the earliness of the day, clipping and mowing and sculpting—and all those people with all that money burning holes in their pockets, until she was in what was euphemistically referred to as "wetlands." Swamps. Northern-type swamps. No live oaks or alligators or Spanish moss here, but nonetheless it was a swamp, an area where water stood nearly hip-deep more months than not, where strange vegetation poked out of the still waters, where unusual birds and animals found some refuge.

Following the small road through the swamp, she reached the bridge. She paid her toll—absurd, she thought, in a city the size of Greystone Bay—and drove across the old bridge.

Originally, Harborview—the Greystone Bay Nursing and

Convalescent Home—hadn't been on an island, but through the years the thin spit of land that connected that area to the shoreline had eroded through storms and tides.

In years past if you had come this far out of town you could have walked, or driven your horse and buggy or old Model A on the connecting land to Harborview, or the Home, as most residents called it. Now you'd have to swim, and be an excellent swimmer because the currents and tides here were some of the roughest along the entire coast. So the city fathers, back in the thirties, or so she had read once, had reluctantly constructed the bridge. It was old and desperately in need of repair, and it was just one more thing that the city government had put off fixing.

So five years ago they'd set up the toll booth at the city end of the bridge.

The revenue from the tolls, the wise leaders dwelling in city hall had declared, would help pay for the bridge's repair. Right. What these learned leaders hadn't counted on were the cheapskates living in Greystone Bay, who had once thought it annoying enough to have to drive *all the way* out of town and across the Hill to go to Harborview, who *then* decided that paying a whole buck one way was just too much and so didn't come out as often to visit old Mom or Dad, the decrepit, or even the once-loved spouse who'd been forced there because of Alzheimer's or Huntington's or something equally incurable.

Now, thanks to the marvelous toll, the Home was nearly empty except for a few fossils, the only sound some days was the footsteps of nurses and aides, the occasional doctor who remembered he had patients out here, the cry of a sea gull, and the shuffling and hacking of the old inmates.

Inmates, she thought, negotiating across the narrow bridge, and feeling, as she always did, the wobbling of the bridge beneath her car's wheels, that's more apt than *residents.* They're patients, but more like prisoners.

Jeannine parked in the diminutive lot, and paused before going in. She sniffed the air; the smell of brine never failed to amaze her. There was no place, she thought, like the ocean and its environs. Overhead a sea gull wheeled and screeched at others posed on rocks along the shoreline. She sniffed something else in the air, but couldn't identify it. With one hand she shielded her eyes against the sun and gazed out across the dazzling water, wondering if there might be a tanker heading north to Boston or down to New York City; but she saw nothing except the ocean, not even the white triangles of sailboats. She shrugged and headed for the door.

The building was old, made of granite they'd hauled from some quarry in Vermont a century ago. The granite had darkened over the years, and in some places the stone appeared nearly black, while other places were simply dirty-sheet grey. It was three stories high, immense, although most of it was no longer used—the back wing, for instance, was used simply as storage these days.

In the old days, a century ago, when the Home had been constructed, it had served first as a hospital, then as a mental asylum, and it was as the latter that it had earned its unsavory reputation. There were gruesome tales told of the things that had gone on here decades ago; she had heard them all in nursing school. Some were obvious fabrications, but too many, she knew, were closer to the truth.

Gradually the asylum had given way to an old-people's home, but the conditions hadn't improved substantially. When she had first come there years ago as a trainee, she had seen old men and women tied down in their beds all day and night, aides beating some old patient who refused to eat his gruel, another being kicked, patients lying in sheets soaked with urine and feces, with bedsores the size of saucers on their backsides. She had protested, and was told to mind her own business; she was just a student, she was reminded.

She hadn't minded her own business, after all. She had complained to her supervisors, and when they didn't listen, she went to the hospital, and then to the hospital board, and then all the way up the ladder of authority until the scandal reached the state capitol. Butt was kicked, heads rolled, and conditions changed.

And in the end, after she'd had some years experience nursing, she was put in charge. She was the Head Administrator.

Not bad for someone this side of forty, for someone who was the first in her family to go beyond the eighth grade. Not bad at all.

It was her Home now, and she was damned proud of it. Oh yeah, it had some problems, most of which related to money (Didn't everything? she wondered), but she had a skilled staff, even though it was too small. Too bad there was such a lack of interest in the Home.

Every year they organized a summer picnic for the residents and their families, and every year they were lucky if half a dozen family members in all showed up. And there sat the old men and women, in their best short-sleeved shirts and best dresses with the bold flowers on them, with red and blue and green balloons tied to the handles of their wheelchairs, and bright paper hats jauntily set on their grey heads. And she and the other staff moved among them, and spoke to them, kneeling or crouching down so they could look at the residents eye to eye—never over them, as if the residents were somehow inferior—and she and the staff would sing songs: "You are my sunshine, my only sunshine . . ." Always the old favorites, and they would get the oldsters to clap and maybe one or two quavering voices would join in, and they would have hot dogs and hamburgers and cole slaw and some cake that some bakery had donated—Happy Birthday could still be seen in faint icing letters—and sometimes she just wanted to cry.

She tried so hard; the whole staff did. No one cared. No one.

Carl had cared, though, and he had come out as often as possible and helped. He had a marvelous singing voice, a silly grin, and told wonderful jokes, and they all loved him out here and—

No, no, no. She knew where that would lead; and today she didn't want the tears. She didn't want to feel that way. She was feeling good, feeling whole, she told herself. And that was that.

Only she knew it wasn't.

Every chance she had, she invited children's singing groups to come out and entertain the old group. Sometimes one or two kids straggled out to sing in off-key innocence. Occasionally a woman from the local library wandered in with an armload of books and proceeded to sit and read to those who listened eagerly. The holidays were worst, though, with the trappings of cheerfulness strung across the halls and walls of the commons room and the individual rooms, and the residents with their red paper hearts clutched in gnarled fingers or their Mother's-Day corsages, purchased out of her pocket money, pinned to their dresses, or the meager turkeys with slim trimmings set out on the dining tables for a Thanksgiving feast. And always, always waiting.

Mostly, though, no one came.

Mostly the old people sat in their wheelchairs parked by the windows, and they stared out over the rolling waves, mile after mile of grey nothingness, or they watched the swamp and pointed out the birds to her as she walked by. She never failed to stop to watch with them and to chat. Then she'd pat their hands and touch them on their shoulders, and more often than she liked to admit, they would simply sigh. Glad to have some human contact. Something . . . in this lonely, cold, remote building.

City fathers had been promising for some time to build a new home within the limits of Greystone Bay, but she and all those who worked here knew that wouldn't happen, not while they were still breathing. And so in the summer they simmered; the building had many windows, but not nearly enough, and some had window air conditioners in them, a bequest by someone who had felt guilty that he hadn't visited his mother enough. Of course, he'd only left enough money for five, when at the time they could have used close to forty. But it helped.

So they simply opened all the windows and hoped for some sea breezes. And usually they got it, too; the limestone was cool, and that kept the residents from overheating. Besides, most of the old people had such sluggish blood flowing through their veins that they didn't suffer until it really got hot. And most summer days it didn't get *that* bad in Greystone Bay.

Most days.

She went through the glass front doors and into the lobby. She wrinkled her nose at the faint odor. Normally all you smelled was the disinfectant and the freshly cut flowers that usually sat on the front desk. Today, though, there was something else. She tried to identify it, but couldn't. Yet it was familiar. She'd have to talk to someone about that.

Inside it was darker than she liked, but they'd had to turn out some lights; the utility bills were running too high, and, given the budget—or what there was of that—it was better to keep some rooms slightly dark than to cut back on the residents' meals. The old dinosaur was too expensive to run; it would be cost-effective in the long run to construct a new facility, but the wise town fathers couldn't see, either. Oh, how they hated that phrase "new construction." Unless, of course, it was another string of condos or high-rise corporate offices, neither of which anyone in the world, much less in Greystone Bay, needed more of.

Ah well, she told herself, another day as the Home's supervisor.

She called hello to Frances, the receptionist and telephone operator, who mostly sat idle these days; there were few visitors, even fewer phone calls. The older woman had brought in a stack of paperbacks to read at the beginning of the month, and was now nearly finished with it.

"Looks like you're going to have to restock," Jeannine said, nodding at the purple plastic bin against one wall that held the unread one. There was only a handful.

Frances looked up from the slim book about giant lizards and nodded, the roll of flesh under her chin wobbling. She was dressed, as always, in a sleeveless white top, which Jeannine swore must have been purchased thirty years before—after all, the blouse buttoned down the back.

"Yeah, there's gonna be a Friends of the Library sale next weekend, startin' early, and I'm gonna go down with a wheelbarrow. Me and Walter plan to get our next year's reading that way. They got pretty good prices—half, and even a third of the original sometimes."

"Certainly is better than tossing them out. I never could stand seeing a book in the trash."

"Yep. Me neither. And me and Walter trade them with our friends, although I gotta tell you, Miss Walker, sommet his friends got pretty bald tastes."

"Ah," Jeannine smiled. "Bald" meaning "risqué," meaning some of Walter's friends went for the sort of short novels that were churned out by publishing houses with names like Racy Tales Publishers and Hussy House.

At least, she told herself, they were reading *something.* On the other hand, did they really understand what they were reading?

What a snob, she thought as she headed down the hall. Her low heels tapped with slight echoes on the linoleum floor. Today she thought the place sounded completely empty. She stopped, listened. Nothing. Not the sound of telephones ringing or voices or even some faint throbbing of machinery. It was as if there were no one here but her, left alone in this out-of-date colossus.

She forced herself to look down at the floor and keep walking. She thought it had once been white and black, but now it looked more grey and yellow, despite the morning and night scrubbing it got from Mr. Wextner, their janitor. Or was that "custodian"? Or "custodial engineer"? Supervisor? Of what? He was the only one left in that department. He wasn't particularly young; and neither she nor he could lure any younger men out to Harborview. Better wages could be made in town. So Mr. Wextner did the window-cleaning, and the floor-polishing, and he cleaned mirrors and bathrooms and tried to maintain the grounds. It was a lot of work for a man his age, but he worked diligently, and when she could she slipped him some extra money.

She smiled to herself. Was it any wonder she was still living in the three-room apartment her mother thought a disgrace for a "person as important as yourself."

And yeah, try taking that to the bank.

Originally the ground floor had been all administrative offices; now half of it was shut down. No personnel. No funds.

The second floor was all residents, and the third floor was closed. She passed Mrs. Denilli, the nurse, who looked efficient, but who Jeannine knew had a drinking problem. She couldn't bring herself to fire the woman, at least not yet, because Mrs. Denilli still worked hard and she had never harmed a patient. And she thought the woman deserved a second chance; she had spoken with the nurse, who swore she would be going to AA soon.

She nodded to her secretary, Mrs. Gomez. The woman was just about twenty years her senior, about a foot shorter, had huge brown eyes always carefully outlined in heavy eyeliner, and had the most placid disposition of anyone she'd ever met. Nothing ruffled Mrs. Gomez; Jeannine liked that.

"Hot enough for you, Miss Walker?"

Mrs. Gomez always greeted her that way—during the summer; in the autumn and winter, it was "Cold enough for you, Miss Walker"?

They all called her "Miss," too, even though she'd tried to get them to address her as "Miz." Greystone Bay—and its residents—was not always with the times, though.

"Anything going on, Mrs. Gomez?"

The woman picked through a stack of manila folders and handed one to Jeannine. "Dr. Ranolf called a few minutes ago."

"He's up rather early. What's the matter—his conscience won't let him sleep?" She always thought of him as Ranolf the Werewolf. Why she thought that she couldn't imagine; he wasn't huge and hairy or even the least bit threatening. He was short, pudgy, wore thick glasses, and more than once she thought he bore a passing resemblance to that mad scientist on the old Muppet Show.

The secretary tried hard not to smile. "He says he won't be able to come out today."

"Oh swell, what did he do, screw up his golfing date?" Exasperated, she blew on the hair already straggling down into her eyes.

Mrs. Gomez chuckled. "He says he's not feeling well, has some sort of bug going around."

Yeah, the golfing bug. "Physician, heal thyself," she muttered.

"What?"

"Nothing. Anything else?"

"He said to tell you that he's sending a replacement out. Today. Maybe."

"Well, let's hope he gets more done than Dr. Ranolf usually does." On a weekly basis Dr. Ranolf the Werewolf was supposed to make this incredibly arduous trip out here—3.2 miles from his house; she knew because she had driven there to check the distance once—and check blood pressures, and sore throats, and slight temperatures, and some other minor complaints that had arisen during the week. More often than not, he simply "couldn't make it today." It played havoc with their scheduling at Harborview, but he didn't care. Obviously he had more important things to do—and richer patients to bill.

God, she was so cynical. When had that happened? Where had that innocent girl who went into nursing to change the world and make it a better place gone? Left. She left, long ago. But at least she was still doing something positive, even if it were in a small way. She hadn't given in to the bastards, not like Dr. Ranolf and all the other people she knew.

Years ago she had petitioned for a special van adapted to wheelchairs so that several of the staff could take the residents to the hospital for checkups, and for outings beyond the Home.

She was still waiting.

Always waiting.

"Miss Walker?" Mrs. Gomez was staring at her.

"I'm sorry. What was that last?" God, her mind had been drifting.

"I said here's a list of people you promised to call today."

She accepted the piece of paper with names and numbers neatly typed on it. The people she would be calling to ask—beg—for money. It never ended.

She went into the inner office, leaving the door open as was her habit and sat behind the old desk. Her chair squeaked as always. She set the file and paper down and pulled the phone to her and began making calls. As she listened to the phone ringing at the other end, she gazed out over the ocean and saw the darkening clouds far off in the distance. Well, maybe there would be a storm after all. Good, they could use the rain.

Some dark flashed along the floor, but when she turned around, she saw nothing.

She swung back to her desk then and concentrated on her pitch.

Later, before lunch, she made her rounds upstairs. She always made an effort to go up at least two, and sometimes three times a day to see the residents. Surely they must feel better to know she hadn't forgotten them.

"How are things going, Sandra?" she asked the floor supervisor.

The woman, pale and rather frail-looking, shrugged. "Same as ever."

Sandra wasn't much of a talker. In the years Jeannine had known her she hadn't heard more than a few sentences from the woman at any one time, but that really didn't matter; Sandra was damned good at her job, and the other women liked and respected her. She was about Jeannine's age, married with two sons and a husband who drank too much beer. But she never commented on her personal life; Jeannine heard things from the other aides.

"How are you, Mrs. Emerson?" Jeannine asked a little woman in a wheelchair at one of the tables in the commons room. Mrs. Emerson cradled a rag doll in her arms and was crooning to "her baby." Mrs. Emerson looked up and smiled, revealing a mouth bereft of teeth. For someone her age—a year or two shy of ninety—she was remarkably unwrinkled. She always smelled of lavender and rubbing alcohol.

"Just fine, sweetie. Just fine. You tell your father it's time for dinner, and he's got to set the table. You tell him now."

Jeannine patted her hand. "I will." Sometimes Mrs. Emerson would have a second doll with her, one in each hand, and the dolls would be holding conversations. It was rather unnerving, especially at night, Jeannine thought, when the only sound on the floor was the raspy whisper of Mrs. Emerson's two voices.

She greeted Mr. White next and complimented him on his new shirt.

He rubbed his dark hand against the soft blue material. He smelled of talcum powder, and he was one of her favorites. He was so even-tempered, such a gentleman; she couldn't understand why his daughter had put him in the Home. Probably because Mr. White just didn't fit into his daughter's extensive schedule, Jeannine thought bitterly.

"My daughter got this for me. 'Member she was here last week?"

"Yes, I do." Mr. White's daughter hadn't stepped into the Home since 1982. The woman, she'd explained to Jeannine in a phone call two years ago, just had SO much to do—you understand, don't you—what with PTA, and after-school activities of her four children, and her husband was a VERY important man on the town council, you know, and there was all that social entertaining to do, of course, because her husband was thinking of running for the state legislature, and surely, you know HOW important that is—

Jeannine had hung up on her.

It was Jeannine's money that had bought Mr. White his shirt, but she had signed his daughter's name to the card. She didn't want to shatter any illusions he might yet have.

She waved to some other residents, and stopped to chat with others. She glanced around the commons room. It was painted in what was supposed to be a cheerful color—a pale yellow—but sometimes, like today, when the light came from the ocean through the large windows, she thought it was rather a bilious color. Still, it was better than white. It was always kept spotless. Yet she had a feeling something wasn't quite right. She studied the player piano along one wall, the line of orange-and-yellow chairs, the tables with their paper tablecloths and little vases with straw flowers, the large-screen TV in the corner. Nothing seemed out of place.

And yet—

She shook her head. She didn't know what was wrong with her. She'd been feeling out of sorts since she got up. Must be the weather. She smiled faintly. Something else the natives here said. No matter what happened or was happening or about to happen, its source was traced back to the weather. "Must be the weather." No one seemed to want to admit that there might be something else involved, the hand of Fate or God or some cosmic jokester. No, "must be the weather." Very convenient.

She counted heads—twenty-two left. Once there'd been several hundred in the Home, but death had claimed the majority of them. Several had been taken out of the Home and moved to different nursing homes in different states where their children or other loved ones had moved.

Twenty-two. That was all. And even now she knew they waited, waited for death.

Don't we all? she wondered. A voice dragged her thoughts back.

"Say, Mrs. Pulnockski, see, lunch is here now."

Tina wheeled in the large cart, its shelves containing the trays of food.

"About time. Been waitin' all day," the woman next to Jeannine sniffed.

"Oh?"

"Yup. Hope it's not that pot roast." She leaned closer to Jeannine. "They make it terrible, and they *always* serve it to us."

"That's a shame."

"Yup."

Tina placed the tray in front of Mrs. Pulnockski and pulled off the lid. Chopped ham and mashed potatoes and a Jell-O cup and a slice of bread.

"Pot roast. Again." Mrs. Pulnockski shook her head and made a disgusted sound.

Tina and Jeannine smiled, and Jeannine helped the girl deliver the rest of the trays. Tina's duty, among many around the Home, was to help some of the residents eat; some could barely hold their forks or spoons. Others just need to be reminded that their meal had been set in front of them. A number of aides had called in sick today, so they were more shorthanded than usual, and Frances had come upstairs to help. She was delivering the trays down the hall to those few who couldn't sit in the commons room with the others; there were only a handful of them now. Mrs. Denilli was helping out, too, though this wasn't part of her nursing duties, and when Jeannine passed the nurse, she could smell the alcohol on the other's breath.

Briefly their eyes met, and then Mrs. Denilli turned away.

Jeannine helped Miss Hurlbut spread her paper napkin across her lap.

"Thank you, dear."

Miss Hurlbut was a retired schoolteacher; in fact, Jeannine had her in sixth grade and had never forgotten the woman or the lessons she taught. Miss Hurlbut had always been a good teacher, devoted to her students, and they had all loved her. No one forgot her.

And here Miss Hurlbut had ended up. Jeannine always thought the woman had deserved better, but the teacher had no family and when she had a stroke that prevented her from walking, she'd been forced to enter the Home. Miss Hurlbut was one of the more lucid residents.

"There's a storm brewing." She pointed with her fork to the back windows.

Jeannine glanced over her shoulder and saw that the sky had darkened considerably since she'd last looked out her office windows. She thought she saw a glimmer of lightning, but must have been mistaken. Well, it looked like the weathermen had finally been right.

"It sure looks like you're right, Miss Hurlbut."

"My favorite barometer told me so." She saw the other woman's puzzled look and indicated her legs. "They always ache when the weather's changing. And this one is going to be big. I saw green sky for a while. Not a good sign. If the storm had been brewing on land, I'd say we were in for a tornado. I don't know what this means. Probably just another squall."

Jeannine smiled reassuringly. "We've certainly had our share of those."

Miss Hurlbut nodded and speared a chunk of ham. She gazed at it. "I do wish the kitchen would realize that some of us still have our teeth and don't need to have everything blended to baby-food consistency."

"I'll remind them."

"I believe you already have, dear. I just think they're a little dense down there."

"I suspect so."

They chatted for a few minutes more, then Jeannine left and went downstairs.

"Any sign of the doctor?" she asked Frances, who was busy rearranging objects on her desk in the lobby.

"Nope."

Jeannine sighed and went back upstairs. She took her lunch out of the refrigerator, and was about to sit down when she saw an earwig on her chair. Wrinkling her nose, she swept it off and sat. She pulled the sandwich out of the plastic bag and paused. She thought she had heard something.

The crashing of the waves, the whistling of the wind and—There, something more. A moaning? A whispering? She checked to see if her intercom was on; no, so she couldn't be picking up anything from another office.

The sound stopped now.

Puzzled, she began eating, and was just finishing her tuna sandwich when Mrs. Gomez buzzed her that the doctor wouldn't be coming out. He was sick, too.

"Likely story," she muttered. Probably he didn't want to come out because of the storm, she thought as she swung around in her chair and surveyed the ocean. This area could be pretty bad during stormy weather, and in fact, a storm was now upon them.

The clouds had crept up on the Home and it was much darker than before; it looked like dusk, and yet sunset was hours away. She'd had to switch on her desk lamp a short time ago. The wind was blowing hard—she could hear it groaning through the cracks in the building—and when she stood and looked out the windows she could see the waves smashing against the island. The Home was set slightly upland, so they didn't have to worry about flooding.

Still . . .

The storm today made her uneasy. She glanced at her watch. Only 2:14. It was going to be a long day. She watched as a fork of lightning sprang from the clouds; a rumble of thunder a moment later, then lightning . . . flickering, flickering, flickering. . . .

She kept at her paperwork, although once in a while she looked up. Once she buzzed Mrs. Gomez. "Did you call me just now?"

"Just now?" The woman sounded clearly puzzled. "No, Miss, I didn't."

Someone, though, had called her name. She tapped her pen against the paper. "Where's Mrs. Denilli?"

"Downstairs, with Frances, I believe."

"Drinking?"

"Well . . ."

"Drinking." She sighed. "Will you call her up here, please?"

"Sure thing, Miss Walker."

She continued writing, and after half an hour, Mrs. Denilli finally showed up.

"Yeah?" Mrs. Denilli's eyes were bright, her face flushed.

"Mrs. Denilli, I know things are not going well today, but I would appreciate it if you don't drink. You know that I can fire you, and if you continue to—"

"I don't need this job; I don't need you," the woman said, leaning across the desk. Her breath was rancid. "I'm quitting.

All night my husband beats me, and then I come in and hear crap like this." She stormed out of the office.

Jeannine leaped to her feet. "Mrs. Denilli!" She hurried after her and shouted to the woman from across the parking lot, but the nurse had ripped off her cap and thrown it down where it was caught by the wind and blown across the lot, and was now climbing into her old sedan. She watched as Mrs. Denilli backed into a red car—Frances's, Jeannine believed—and nicked some paint, then slammed her car into gear and peeled out of the parking lot. Jeannine watched as Mrs. Denilli took the bridge at too fast a speed; but she made it. Jeannine breathed a sigh of relief. She would prepare her leaving papers in the morning, and her final paycheck. She had wanted to help the woman, really, but some people just didn't want to be helped. They wanted to continue living in their own private hells.

She glanced at the clouds, thought she smelled moisture, then smiled. Of course, she did; they were right by the ocean. More lightning with the thunder much louder now, much closer. She rubbed her arms and went back inside.

Slowly, she went past Frances, who was intently studying a cover of a book, and climbed the stairs and went into her office where she went back to work.

Some time after three Sandra called down to say that someone had heard a noise up on the third floor and some of the residents were agitated. The rain and wind lashed against the windows, and she wasn't sure some of the screens would last. They'd pulled down some of the windows, but it was stiflingly hot up there.

"Bring them down here. I'll be up in a minute to help." She got up and asked Mrs. Gomez to find Mr. Wextner and tell him that he was needed on the third floor.

Then Tina and Sandra and Jeannine and finally Mr. Wextner slowly brought all the residents down to the first floor on the elevator; it groaned and creaked and took its own time. Once Jeannine thought it was going to get stuck between floors, and she shuddered at the thought. Mr. Wextner or she would have had to climb out of the escape hatch, and then what? Please, let's not say we do, she thought.

Several of the patients, those in much poorer mental and physical condition and confined to their beds, were mewling, one screaming; they were brought down in their beds and settled into empty offices where the staff could keep an eye on them. Other residents wept; one man prayed, fingering his rosary, his words just audible. Miss Hurlbut's face was a little pale, but she flashed a brave smile at Jeannine. She put aside her work for the day and helped the others with the residents.

Somewhere along the way the rain had grown almost horizontal, slashing so hard against the windows that they couldn't see anything outside. The wind rose to a shriek and one or two residents clasped their hands to their ears to keep the unearthly sound out.

A little after four, Jeannine was wondering about the possibility of evacuation when the electricity went out. Someone—she thought it was Mrs. Emerson—screamed. Mr. Wextner labored for an hour to bring the electricity on with the backup generator, but that wasn't working, either.

Jeannine also found that the phone lines were down, too. They were cut off from Greystone Bay, from the world.

They all went hunting through desks and cabinets to find candles and flashlights, and Mr. Wextner produced a Coleman lantern from the basement.

"Just like a camping trip," Miss Hurlbut said, taking one of Mrs. Emerson's hands and squeezing it. "It's all right, dear. We'll just sing. Can your dollies sing?"

Mrs. Emerson, sniffling although no longer weeping, nodded.

Miss Hurlbut began to sing, her white curls bobbing as she moved her head in rhythm to the music. Mrs. Emerson joined in, and held up one of her dollies. Mr. White's quavering voice could be heard, and that of Tina and Mrs. Gomez, too. "You are my sunshine . . ."

Jeannine would have liked to sing, but she couldn't. Her throat felt paralyzed, as if she tried to open her mouth, nothing would come out, no air would come in or out, and she would suffocate, slowly, ever so slowly.

She had to do something. She stood up and took a flashlight and explained that she was going to take a look around.

She climbed the stairs up to the second floor, the singing growing fainter until she could no longer distinguish the words. She would check to see if there was anything she should bring down to the others. The hall echoed with her footsteps, and that was all she could hear besides the pummeling of the wind and rain. And yet there was a faint creaking, too. But she couldn't place the sound.

A centipede hurried across the tile, and she brought her shoe down on it.

They always liked to come inside when it was wet or humid, which meant just about year-round in Greystone Bay, she figured.

The second floor was eerie, deserted as it was, and once she thought she saw someone move in one of the rooms. She directed her flashlight there, but all she saw were two single beds, the spreads tucked neatly under the pillows, and a large number of stuffed animals arranged near the pillows. Nothing. Only the rain lashing at the window. This one had been left open, so she crossed to it and pulled it down. No need to soak everything in sight.

She checked each room. She wasn't sure why. She just knew she had to.

Slowly she took the stairs to the third floor. Here the staircase curved, and her flashlight cast strange shadows on the walls. When she reached that floor, she sneezed. Dust was fairly thick here; she had Mr. Wextner gave it a cursory cleaning at least twice a year, but still it gathered dust and cobwebs from disuse.

Heavy cloths were draped over some of the furniture, and they cast lumpish shadows in the faint light. Here she could hear more clearly the drumming of the rain on the roof. It was a good thing none of the residents were up here, she thought; that incessant sound would drive them crazy. Would drive her crazy if she had to listen to it all the time.

Something brown darted from one table to another. A rat. Mr. Wextner also sprayed for those up here, but she supposed the spray wore off after a while, and the dead rats' relatives just moved back in. She'd have to mention it to him again; they were due for a spraying.

Something crashed behind her and she whirled. Nothing. Nothing but dust and shadows and some rats. Still, she walked down the hall to take a look. She wanted to make sure no rain was getting in. That could leak down to the other floors, could get to the electrical wiring, and then they'd really be in trouble.

Something—someone—touched her cheek. She brushed at it absently.

Jeannine.

"Carl?" It had been his voice. She was sure.

No. Carl was dead these four years. Dead here in the Home. Carl.

She fought against the tears; they won, and spilled down her cheeks. She loved the Home, and she hated the Home, and yet this was the very place where her love had come to die. There had been the accident, and a wreckage of body and mind, and she had looked at him as they brought him to the Home after those long months in the hospital, and she had cried because he could no longer recognize her, because all he could do was stare off into space and drool, and she couldn't help but wonder What if his mind were undamaged?, What if his mind were trapped inside that wreck of a body? And she cried each day and each night, and for a year he lived that way, slowly worsening, the flesh receding until his skin seemed like a film pulled tautly over his bone, until his breathing grew labored, until the man she loved became a frail, pitiful creature. Until one night, with her sitting by his bed holding his limp, damp hand, he had breathed deeply and then died.

She had cried. From relief, sorrow, emotions she couldn't even put into words.

And she had come back to work because she had no other place to go.

Each day, though, brought back memories.

Carl.

Jeannine.

She followed the sound down the hall, and heard strange sounds—moaning and weeping and voices from the past. In the semidarkness she thought she saw the white-clad bodies of people from another time, a time when this was a madhouse. She heard the screams, the angry voices, the whimpering, saw the rats poking among the limp bodies on the dirty floor, saw a woman tied to a wall begging to be let loose, she would be a good girl now, saw and heard and smelled the horrible stench of unwashed bodies and vomit and feces smeared on the walls and—

The creaking noise beat a pattern, and, half-dazed, she

approached a window in a long-deserted room. The sound intensified. She glanced out and saw the bridge, the old tumbledown bridge, swaying violently from the galelike wind. Even as she watched, horrified, the bridge creaked once more and then *twisted,* and bucked upward, and buckled, and slowly, ever so slowly, crumpled into the waters below with the sound of a thousand thunders. Cable dangled from the towers on both shores and blew in the wind as if they were nothing more than threads, and in the middle . . . nothing.

She could hear shouting from below, and she ran down the hall, ran down the two flights of stairs down to the lobby.

Some of the residents were sobbing and shrieking, the employees talking in loud voices.

"Did you see it, Miss Walker? Did you?" Mr. Wextner's voice was trembling as he pointed out the front door. His hair was plastered against his forehead; his clothes soaked. Obviously he'd gone out to check on the racket. Mrs. Gomez stood behind him and was staring outside, her eyes wide.

"I saw it." She was calm now. No more ghosts. This was reality. The bridge had just collapsed, cutting them off. She had things to do. "Now, everyone be calm. That's not the end of the world, you know. Once the storm dies down, and I'm sure it'll do that sometime tonight, the hospital and authorities will be sending helicopters to help us get back to the mainland."

Francine nodded. "That's right. I read about things like this happening. Once these people were on an island for the summer and there were these wild dogs—" She saw Jeannine's expression and stopped talking.

"Now we don't know how long it's going to be, so we need everyone to cooperate. All right? Think you can do that?" Miss Hurlbut nodded as did Mr. Wextner, and Mrs. Emerson made her two dolls nod, and Mrs. Gomez said, "That's right." The others—Tina, Sandra, Mr. White—said nothing.

"Now, Mr. Wextner," she said facing him, "I know we've never discussed this before—we didn't think it would be an issue—do you think you can find an old radio in the basement? What about something you can send signals on?"

"Don't know. I'll take a look. And I'll take a look at the generator again."

"Good." She swung back to speak to Sandra, just as someone said, "I'm hungry."

Jeannine peered at her watch in the faint light—she had told them to conserve candles and flashlights, and only two candles flickered now—and realized she'd forgotten all about that.

There was a crash of thunder that seemed to shake the building. Conversation stopped, and someone whimpered.

She looked at Tina. The help in the kitchen had been long gone when the electricity went off. She hoped there'd been food deliveries yesterday or today. If not, they were screwed.

"I'll check for something to eat, Miss Walker," Tina said, jumping to her feet.

"Thanks."

She spotted another centipede, not far from Mrs. Emerson's wheelchair, and slowly she moved across and stepped on it.

One of Mrs. Emerson's dolls peeked over the arm of the chair.

"What's that?" asked a squeaky voice.

Jeannine forced a smile. "Nothing."

A few minutes later Tina came back to report that there were quite a few loaves of bread, boxes of saltines, jars and jars of jelly and peanut butter, and tons of canned soup, but no way to cook the latter.

"Nonsense," Miss Hurlbut said. "We'll cook it over the open fire for the others."

Tina and Jeannine exchanged glances.

"Open fire?" Tina asked. "I'm sorry, but I don't understand."

Miss Hurlbut pointed to a candle. "Open flame, open fire. It'll be slow, but at least the others will have some warm food."

"Of course. Are you sure you weren't a boy scout in another life?"

Miss Hurlbut shook her head. "Just camped out a lot with my father and sister when I was a child."

Mrs. Gomez and Frances went to the kitchen to help and they had lukewarm soup that night, along with a few crackers. Jeannine poked at her soup with a spoon and tried not to think of Mr. Wextner down in the basement by himself. Rats and cobwebs and earwigs, and God knows what. She left her meal and went to the basement door and called down to him.

"How's it going?" Her voice echoed.

"Guess it's all right. Didn't find a radio. Knew there were some things I should have picked up in town before this. I'm working on the generator right now. Keep your fingers crossed."

"We will."

Briefly, around eleven or so, the lights came on, and there was a ragged cheer, but just as quickly they went out, and finally, around two in the morning, Mr. Wextner climbed upstairs to say he couldn't do anything more. Jeannine thanked him, but inside she felt a dark coldness.

They had no end of beds, having brought more down from upstairs, so everyone had someplace to spend the night. Jeannine couldn't sleep, though, and listened to the rain and the thunder and watched the glimmer of the lightning. Occasionally she would go to the front door and stare out into the darkness. There were still no lights on in Greystone Bay. For a minute she wondered if it were still there. What if it had been swept away like the bridge? Not a pleasant thought.

Surely by morning the storm would die down, and the power would come back on, and someone would be contacting them from the mainland.

Surely.

She thought she saw something dart past the door, but she knew she was tired and seeing things.

Like those things upstairs? one part of her asked.

That was different; how, she didn't know. Just different.

She had taken off her shoes so that she wouldn't wake the others and now, in her stockinged feet, she padded down the hallway. She didn't know why she was so restless. She just had to be up and moving, had to be—

Jeannine.

"Oh Carl. I wish you were here, the way you were. I need comforting." She knew she sounded childish, but she didn't care. She knew he couldn't make it any better with his presence, but she didn't care. She missed him. She wanted him. She remembered all the nights she had lain awake, just wanting his arms around her, wanting the press of his body against hers.

No more. No more.

She didn't hear anything else, and returned to the lobby and her bed, and even though she lay with her eyes closed, she did not sleep.

The storm raged all night and into the new day. In the morning they all had more lukewarm soup, and for lunch they all—those who could eat it—had peanut butter sandwiches with jelly, and a bonus of cupcakes that Mrs. Gomez had found in one of the cabinets. Jeannine had brought medical supplies down from the nursing station on the second floor. Some of the older patients were not doing well, and she feared she might lose them if they didn't receive more advanced medical attention within the day.

Frances, who had been pacing back and forth along the hallway all day, kept saying they had to do something. And Miss Hurlbut kept telling her that they were trying, but that they would all have to be patient. Frances continued pacing, until finally Mrs. Pulnockski yelled at her to sit down because she was shaking the floor. Frances just stopped and stared at the woman and then went to look out a window. She hadn't spoken in over an hour.

Somewhere along five o'clock Frances said she couldn't stand it any longer, Walter was waiting, and this was getting ridiculous, and she went outside. She didn't come back in. No one knew what happened to her. Mr. Wextner went to look for her, but he couldn't see her. Her car wasn't there, either, and Jeannine bowed her head, wondering what could have possessed the woman.

That night it was more lukewarm soup. Jeannine had never been crazy about tomato soup, and now she realized she really disliked it, especially made with water and just this shade of cold. Not a gourmet meal. On the other hand, at least it was food. They had plenty of water, thank God; they had their own wells on the island, and she didn't think they were in danger of running dry any time soon.

She looked up from her plate and grimaced as she saw another earwig. She shifted her foot and crushed the insect. Surreptitiously she swept it up into her napkin and disposed of it.

Mr. Wextner looked her way. "Nothing kills them, does it? They've got the best survival system, all those bugs. Sure makes me envious."

"Me, too. If only I weren't so disgusted!"

They laughed and finished the remains of their soup. Miss Hurlbut entertained them with stories about some of her students, and they laughed, because that was the only thing they could do.

That night she and Mr. Wextner stood at the front door and stared out into the great darkness that was the Bay.

"This much rain," he said, "makes me glad I never lived in Seattle."

She chuckled, realized it sounded a little ragged. "I don't think Seattle gets this much all at once. Lucky dogs." For a while they were silent, then: "Do you have family, Mr. Wextner?"

He shook his head. "Just a sister in Canton, Ohio."

"Sounds like a nice place to be just about now."

"Sure does."

He wandered back to the others shortly after that, leaving her with the blackness outside, and the blackness inside as well.

She still couldn't sleep that night and heard the whisperings and moans and cries of those long gone, and when she raised her head from the pillow, she saw that everyone else slept. Apparently only she had heard anything. Or imagined it, she told herself.

Jeannine.

She forced herself to keep her eyes shut, and insisted that she had to sleep. Had to, had to, had . . .

The next morning she found she'd lost the first of her residents. There was nothing that could be done and so she and Mr. Wextner and Tina wheeled the body in the bed to one of the back offices. A second soon followed and ended up in the back office. They would have to wait, like all of them.

On the third day the lights in Greystone Bay came back

on, blinking on all at once so that Jeannine wondered that they hadn't overloaded the system and made the city go black again. They could just see the gleaming lights from the city and those along the harbor. The lights looked so reassuring, so warm.

Bet those people out there aren't having lukewarm tomato soup, she told herself.

"It'll be all right," Miss Hurlbut said. "You'll see." She nodded and munched a saltine, crumbs dripping onto her chest.

"Think so?" Mr. Wextner asked.

"Yes. I'm an old optimist from way back. We die hard."

It was an unfortunate choice of words, Jeannine thought.

"You don't have a family to worry about," Mrs. Gomez said tearfully. "I have a husband and a son and a daughter, and what must they be thinking?"

"I know, I know," Miss Hurlbut said, patting the other woman's hand and leaving cracker crumbs on it.

"You don't. You never married! You didn't have children."

For a moment Miss Hurlbut said nothing, then she sighed deeply, the crumbs on her chest shifting. "I may not have married, Mrs. Gomez. But I had children, dozens and dozens of them, and I felt for each one of them. I remembered each one of them."

"It's not the same," Mrs. Gomez muttered, and Jeannine looked away, feeling the ache of both women, and knowing that it wasn't the same, remembering the children she and Carl had talked about having, the children she would never have now.

Mr. Wextner brought out a pack of cards he'd found in a box down in the basement, and although they were missing the eight of diamonds and the two of spades, they played card games long into the night.

They waited in the Home, but the electricity didn't return. The phone service was still disrupted.

They waited for another day. Still no one came.

Ignoring the rain that continued to pound the island until she thought part of it might wash away, Jeannine walked out into the parking lot and stared across at the Bay. Within seconds she was drenched, and she shivered. The rain was too cold for this time of year. Mr. Wextner came out after her.

"I can swim," he said.

"No, it's too dangerous. Look at that choppy water." She pointed to the channel where the bridge had stood. White-caps smashed against the island. "Besides, you might get snagged on some of the wreckage. Plus, and I hate to say this, you're too old, Mr. Wextner."

He looked at her, his face creased into a sad smile. "I suppose you're right, but I have to try."

"Please, no."

"Someone's got to."

"No!"

But he ignored her, and all she could do was watch as he walked to the craggy shore of the island, slipped off his shoes and dived into the water. His head bobbed up, he turned and waved and struck off with sure strokes toward the far shore. She watched as he grew smaller and smaller, and then a huge wave crashed down on him, and when the wave receded, he was gone.

She watched until it was dark, but she didn't see him again.

She went inside and Mrs. Gomez found her a blanket to wrap around her shoulders, and she sat and thought of poor, brave Mr. Wextner.

"A fire," Miss Hurlbut said.

Jeannine looked up. "What?"

"You could start a signal fire. Away from the building, of course." She laughed a little nervously.

"Maybe."

"You have to, honey. It's the only thing you can do."

It was, and Jeannine knew that. She hated feeling helpless, she who had been in charge for so many years. She looked around at those left. They were waiting, depending on her. She had to act.

A signal fire to let the others in town know about them out here.

She and Sandra and Tina dragged wooden desks and chairs and curtains out into the rain while Mrs. Gomez went searching for some lighters. They set some papers afire—ones they had kept from the rain until the very last moment and then set them among the curtains. Time after time water squelched the flames. Finally, on another try, the old, dry wood caught, and they stood back as the flames roared up into the night sky. They worked feverishly to bring out more furniture. They had stripped the third floor of everything that could burn, and still the fire burned bright yellow and red against the blackness.

Jeannine watched, ash flicking onto her face and sodden blouse. She watched the fire, then turned to look at the Bay. She waited for the flashing lights that would indicate a rescue was underway.

Nothing.

Life seemed to go on as usual in the Bay.

The fire burned out and she returned to the others inside, and wrapped another blanket around herself, and no matter what she did, her teeth chattered. The cold had seeped down into her bones, her soul.

The earwigs and centipedes crawled across the floor, and

something inside the walls made scratching noises. It kept her awake.

The next night Mrs. Emerson's heart gave out and she died. They moved her body back with all the others.

The Coleman lantern burned out after that, and not long after that the candles and flashlights began flickering out one by one, until they sat in the darkness, listening to the wind and the rain and the thunder.

Miss Hurlbut tried to lead them in songs, but no one had voice, and so hers was the only sound in the night, the only sound beyond the whistling wind and pounding rain, the heartbeat thunder.

Still, through the glass doors of the Home, they could see those bright lights of Greystone Bay. They could imagine the people going out to dinner, heading to a double feature, or occasionally glancing out their windows in their warm, comfortable homes and commenting on all the rain they were getting this summer, but wouldn't it be great for the lawns and flowers?

Sandra left the Home the next day and tried to swim across the channel. A piece of steel from the bridge bobbed up and pierced her instantly. She sank below the waves.

Jeannine knew she should try. She was in charge, wasn't she? Or was she any longer? Was anyone? But what if she died? Yes, but what if she made it?

She couldn't; she didn't know how to swim.

The old ones died hour after hour after that, until only a handful of people were left in the building. The sounds of squealing and moans and whimpering were louder now, and sometimes she thought she could feel earwigs and centipedes wiggling through her chest and neck.

Jeannine.

She squeezed back the tears. Tina sat in a chair and cried

most of the time now. Mrs. Gomez tried to help Jeannine, but she could see the other's heart wasn't in it. Was anyone's?

"Sure is hot," Mr. White said and blinked at her.

"Sure is," she said with a faint smile and tried not to feel the pain. His new shirt was ruined, the sweat stains darkening it, and here and there were the darker stains of blood where he had hurt himself somehow. She brushed an earwig off his arm.

The air was close, the smell of urine overwhelming. They hadn't eaten in a while. The food was running out, but no one wanted to get up and make a meal. No one wanted to do anything.

She sighed long, and felt the hollow ache under her breastbone. Sometimes she thought she saw people moving around the room, but when she looked she saw no one. Once a hand touched her cheek, or maybe it wasn't a hand. Maybe it was a cobweb or a centipede.

Mr. White smiled at her and patted her hand. The sweat trickled down her cheeks.

She blotted away the moisture on the old man's face. Miss Hurlbut slipped her hand into Jeannine's, and Jeannine squeezed it. Mrs. Gomez said nothing, while behind her Tina sobbed, choking, and Mrs. Pulnockski lay in bed, neither dead nor alive. And they waited.

Waited for someone to come, on this summer's eve.

Waited. But she knew no one would come to help them. That wouldn't happen. She knew.

No one cared.

The Bay had forgotten them.

Jeannine.

Whiteface

by Chelsea Quinn Yarbro

It was the next-to-the-last stop for the Cotelli Traveling Carnival, coming after most of the coastal towns and one week before Kinsmans Landing: Greystone Bay. Two weeks from now and all the carnival people would be on their way to their winter destinations, some leaving earlier than others. Always one or two of the acts had left by this time, some for the winter haven of Florida, others for less usual places; Vito Cotelli found acts to fill at the end of the season every year, though even he had to admit that Simon—or Osama—Gattu, his assistant, and snow leopard, this year's pickup, were peculiar.

"I like this place, because it's almost over," Vito said to the air. It was a ritual phrase; his voice was resonant even after decades of hard use, and it filled the motor home effortlessly. He paid little attention to his nephew. Years ago Vito had been the ringmaster, before age and his fondness for sticky pastry caught up with him, turning him into a comfortable couch of a man. Now he was the chief clown and left most of the ringmastering job to his handsome thirty-two-year-old nephew Michel.

"Slow afternoon," Michele observed as he watched his uncle count stacks of one- and five-dollar bills. From where he sat, the stacks of fives were disappointing, as were the few tens and twenties.

"It's the rain; nobody likes carnivals in the rain," said Vito, pursing his lips. "I hate New England."

Michele laughed. "Pretty dour, isn't it? All that granite, or whatever the hell kind of rock it is." He smacked his hands together as if in anticipation of a treat. "Tomorrow we'll do better."

"We have to," said Vito heavily. "It's been a rotten season, Mike; and you know it as well as I do."

"Don't worry; I've got a side job to do—that'll swell the coffers." He looked toward his side of the Itasca motor home they shared.

"Who's it for?" asked Vito with apprehension.

"You sure you want me to say?" It was not quite a game with them, this steady refusal to discuss Michele's other employment. "It's in the neighborhood," he added vaguely, which meant somewhere in the state.

Vito sighed. "Probably not—not too much." He recorded the day's take in his ledger. "We aren't going to be able to keep the animals in feed, the way things are going."

"Why bother?" Michele asked. "We don't need animals. People don't stare at llamas anymore, and they couldn't care less about miniature horses, or goats turned into unicorns. We ought to sell them off and look to get some more exciting acts, maybe some gonzo jugglers, like those five guys we saw on TV, or someone who does *Swan Lake* on the high wire." He indicated the rain-streaked windows. "A couple chimps aren't going to bring anyone out in this. They can see that on the evening news. Who knows, some of those animal-rights guys might come and picket." He chuckled at the idea.

Vito nodded once again. "Still, we ought to do better on the weekend. This is only Thursday, and you know what wet Thursdays are like."

"Yeah," said Michele. "You got someone to cover for me for Saturday? I don't think I can make it back in time to start things. I should be here by three; I can do the evening show easy." He picked up a stale pastry and began to eat it. "I don't know how you stand this shit."

"I got a sweet tooth," said Vito, then considered their predicament. "Well, I guess I can find someone to take care of the announcing. So long as you're going to be gone."

"The job's fairly local," Michele conceded. "I don't suppose it would hurt to tell you that." He finished off the pastry and began to lick the sugar off his fingers.

"Greystone Bay?" asked Vito.

"A couple, three miles outside, actually," said Michele, deliberately vague. He began to look around for something to drink. "I accepted it because the money was so good, not because I wanted it near to hand."

Vito gave a swipe of his hand, indicating his submission. "I trust you to do what's best." He glanced at the microwave. "You want something more? I got some St. Honore's cake I could heat up."

"You're not supposed to eat that hot," said Michele with a gentle smile. "But it tastes good." He leaned back against the rickety bookcase where Vito kept his most precious possessions; it was a small, select library, half in English, the rest in Italian.

"So?" Vito hitched his shoulders and got up. Without his clown makeup, he was nothing more than an aging fat man; with it, he was something out of a fairy tale or nightmare. He opened the refrigerator and stared into the depths as if some great secret were contained there. "I wish I hadn't eaten that pizza for lunch."

"I'll go in to town, if you like," offered Michele without enthusiasm.

"No. No, that's okay." He moved away from the place he was standing, letting the refrigerator door close behind him. "I've got coffee and some scones; I guess that will hold me." He patted his extensive girth.

"If that's what you want," said Michele. "I've got the gun ready, and I'll get rid of it as soon as I use it. So far as anyone will know, it came from around here—that was part of the deal and it's all taken care of—and if they think anything else, we'll be long gone, and who could have done it, anyway? Who'd think of the carnival? Not anyone in town, and none of our people. We're safe as ever."

"Gattu?" suggested Vito with half a smile. "What about Gattu?"

"I wouldn't joke about him," warned Michele, suddenly very serious. His light blue eyes were sharp as ice in his olive face. "Something about that guy gives me the creeps, and it isn't that damned leopard of his." He folded his arms and looked at his uncle. "Why'd you take him on?"

"You've seen his act. Who's ever had a snow leopard who could do so many tricks?" He looked down at his hands and spread them wide as if to palm a dinner plate. "It was the leopard that convinced me; but he's hard to take."

"É vero, and no shit," said Michele, and began to assemble a sandwich, wrestling with the lid of the mayonnaise jar. "I wish he weren't here, but I don't know why."

"You know what carnival folk are," said Vito as philosophically as he could. "It takes all kinds."

"Including those of us from *la Famiglia?*" challenged Michele as he spread mustard on wheat bread. "No. Never mind: It isn't sensible to answer that."

"For us or for *la Famiglia?*" asked Vito. He went to the cupboard and took out a large mug, then selected a day-old scone from the bag beside the microwave. "You want one?"

"Sure," said Michele without thought, his mind on other matters. "Where did Gattu work last, do you know?" He frowned with concentration.

"The Circus of Strange Things," said Vito, waiting for the microwave to do its work.

"The Canadians?" Michele asked in surprise. "They're good."

"That they are. Travel all over the world. Command performances for crowned heads. They've done it all. I've seen 'em maybe three times. They're damned wonderful, strange or not. Gattu's gone with them twice. He said he doesn't want to travel so far again. It's hard on his cat. Makes sense to me." He busied himself preparing his mug for tea, putting in two bags and filling it with water, intending to exchange it for the scone in a few seconds.

"The Circus of Strange Things is big-time," said Michele slowly.

"Meaning we're not?" interjected his uncle. "I know."

Michele shook his head. "I didn't say that, but we're not in their league, and you know it. It's an accomplishment to . . . to be part of it." He sighed. "Are we going to open this evening?"

"I don't know," said Vito. "We'll play it by ear. If it keeps raining, no; it lets up, then we can get ready for the fishermen. They like carnivals." He nodded as the microwave dinged. "These things are a lifesaver. How the hell did we cook all those meals for so many years?"

"You didn't," Michele reminded him. "Sophia did."

Vito's face was transformed by a beneficent, fleeting smile as he remembered his wife; now he was not an aging clown trying to look like a rotund bloodhound, he was an old man who had loved long and well. "I don't know how she did it."

"You miss her," said Michele.

"Every time I breathe," Vito agreed.

By ten the last of the fishermen had left and Vito, still in whiteface, was trudging across the small midway toward the main tent when he heard someone call his name. "Yes? *Qui sei?*"

"It is I," said Simon—or Osama—Gattu, stepping out of the shadows. He was a small man, not quite five feet tall. There was nothing childlike about him other than his size; nothing in the way he moved or spoke or behaved made him appear little. His body was unobtrusively muscular and graceful as a dancer's. It was impossible to guess his age, which might have been twenty or forty-five. He had an indefinable accent. "*Don* Vito, I must speak with you."

Vito was so taken aback to hear his old honorific that he almost could not bring himself to speak, and when he did he stammered. "I have . . . I have not . . ." He could not continue.

"You are Vito Cotelli, a man of respect." Simon bowed slightly. "Your nephew is Michele Cotelli, also a man to respect."

The two men faced each other for several seconds before Vito could bring himself to speak. "You are certain of yourself, Gattu."

"Yes," said Gattu without a trace of insolence.

"You have reason, I suppose?" The last was intended to be an afterthought but it gave away Vito's assumptions.

"I always have reason for what I do," said Gattu. "Everyone has a reason."

Vito nodded, wishing he knew what this fellow wanted of him. "Certainly."

Gattu's smile curled, predatory instead of cordial. "I have need of your advice, *Don* Vito."

"On what matter, *Signore* Gattu?" Vito inquired politely. He did not often use this formality, but now it seemed appropriate, and alarming. What was this man doing, reminding him of what was past? "What makes you ask this of me?"

"I have need; that is all you have to know." He cocked his head to the side, watching Vito expressionlessly.

"What is it?" Vito prompted when Gattu said nothing more.

"I must be allowed to move my caravan . . . my motor home."

"I know what a caravan is, Gattu," said Vito, feeling testy.

"Yes; I must move it away from these grounds. These grounds—like the town itself—are disturbed." His eyes swept over the carnival and the field where it was set up. "It is in the earth and in the air. I smell it, like death on the wind. It is bad for my leopard."

"Okay. So you want to move your RV. I'll ask in the morning if our permit allows it. If it does, go ahead." He sighed. He had feared something like this from Gattu, but not so soon.

"Tonight," said Gattu.

Vito shook his head several times. "Can't be done, pal. Even if we had the paperwork square, we'd have to go through the right motions. It's not like the old days, Gattu. We have to play by the rules like everyone else. If we don't have the paperwork, they shut us down." He shoved his hands into his capacious pockets. "We can't afford that, can we?"

Gattu moved back and regarded Vito narrowly. Finally he nodded once. "All right. I will wait if you insist, but I will not be responsible for what happens in this place. Remember I warned you." With that he turned on his toe and sprinted away toward his Winnebago.

Watching Gattu move away from him, Vito was struck with the strength in the small man. He had seen enough acrobats and musclemen to know that Gattu was tough and springy. "Disturbed place," he muttered, shaking his head. He wondered briefly if he ought to speak with Gattu's assistant, Tatiana, but decided against it—one encounter with Gattu was enough for the night. As he ambled back to his Itasca, he started to whistle, one of those spritely tarantellas he had loved in his youth. But the sound was lost and forlorn in the deserted midway, and he soon fell silent.

Friday morning the snow leopard was out of his cage, pacing the area behind Gattu's Winnebago, making a low, coughing growl in his throat.

"Something wrong with him?" Vito demanded of Tatiana when Clara, the bearded lady, had reported it. "How the hell did he get out, anyway? He has to be in his cage or on a leash." It was a chill morning, and a filmy mist lay over the ground, swirling around knees as if to ensnare each step in wraithlike fingers.

"He will not hurt you," she answered shortly.

"It's the rules. The SPCA will cage him if you don't." He kept his eye on the leopard, not trusting the animal. There was something about that steady gaze which troubled Vito, yet he could not explain it. "Be careful with him."

Tatiana gave a single, harsh laugh. "You worry about the wrong things, Mr. Cotelli. You think the leopard can hurt you, but he will not. You think that the place cannot hurt you, but it will." She shook her head, her glossy dark hair shining as if glazed.

"You watch what you're saying to me, lady," said Vito, not wanting to yell at the pretty woman.

"And you as well," she countered, unintimidated. In the next instant she picked up the heavy leather collar and went to secure the snow leopard, crooning to the cat as she fastened the buckles. She rubbed the cat's head, all the while turning her basilisk eyes on Vito. As she straightened up, the leopard began to purr, the sound like a well-tuned engine.

Vito shook his head and started to walk away. "I talked to Mr. Webster at the city planners' this morning, and he said you can move the Winnebago nearer to the fence. There aren't any power and sewage hookups beyond it, so you got to keep to this side." He did not turn to look at her as he gave her the information. "Jenkins will help you, if you need it."

"It will not be necessary," said Tatiana in a strained voice.

"What is it now?" Vito asked, facing her reluctantly.

"The edge of this ground is not far enough. We might as well remain where we are." She patted the leopard as if offering consolation.

"Suit yourself," snapped Vito, suddenly very irritated.

Tatiana led the leopard back toward the Winnebago, a troubled look in her large, slanted eyes.

"There's been a change of plans," Michele announced over a hurried dinner of chili and grated cheese. His face was troubled, his anxiety detracting from his good looks. "I had word half an hour ago."

"What?" asked Vito fatalistically. He refused to think back to the old days, though memory pulled at him as intensely as a burn.

"They want it done here. They're afraid that he might be

guarded where he is. They say the old Buchman place is an armed safe house. There's no point going for him there. If I cannot kill him, the government will provide him yet another identity, and who knows how long it will take to find him next time." He put his hands flat on the table. "I asked them not to insist, I reminded them of the contract, but you know what they are like."

Vito nodded and reached for the cheese, sprinkling it with great care over the half-eaten chili. "What else do they expect of us?" For he was certain that *la Famiglia* wanted something specific.

"They want us to get him here, and then to be rid of him." Michele shook his head. "I asked them not to insist, *Zio,* I did. I told them it was a disservice to you and to our carnival. I said that you had withdrawn from *la Famiglia* in good faith, to keep the war from happening, but they would not be persuaded. They said that was different, another time. You are still part of *la Famiglia.* Blood will tell." He tore a section of French bread from the loaf and stuffed it into his mouth as if to stop the words.

"Who has ordered this?" Vito asked heavily.

"*Don* Domenico. He does not know all you have done; he's too young to know." He said this last a bit desperately, as if he needed to have an explanation for himself as much as for his uncle.

"Domenico. What did he say?" Vito picked up his fork and fussed with the cheese. He did not eat.

"He said that we are obligated to him. He said that we must do this as he orders it or we will be the ones needing protection." His eyes darkened as he reported the last.

"How like his father he is," said Vito distantly. "He said much the same thing before I got this carnival." He sniffed at the chili. "It does not have enough onions." He reached for the bottle of wine he had opened.

Michele would not be turned from his anger. "It isn't right. You gave up *la Famiglia* because of Domenico's father. There is no reason for you to serve the son." He got up suddenly and began to pace in the cramped quarters. "If they wanted someone killed in public, it should be in a city, a big one, where there is room to hide. A town like Greystone Bay, so small, strange,"—he kissed his fingers in mock tribute—"there is no safety for me."

"That does not concern *Don* Domenico," said Vito quietly. "More garlic and cumin, too. It's bland." He took a single bite and set his fork aside. "Sit down, Michele. Have something to eat, a little wine."

It seemed that Michele did not hear him. "He does not care what happens so long as Sardinero is killed, and everyone knows he has died because of *la Famiglia*. Compared to Sardinero, we are nothing, only pawns to be used to execute the traitor." He was abruptly silent as there was a hard knock at the Itasca's door.

Vito shrugged. "Come."

The door opened; Clara Marsden stood in the door, hands on her hips, her dark beard set in rollers above a lace-trimmed blouse. "I have to talk to you, Vito," she said in her incongruous little-girl voice.

"Come in, Clara," said Vito with an air of courtliness. "Michele, see that Clara has a chair."

Michele shot an irate look at his uncle, but brought the pretty Queen Anne chair—the company chair—for Clara, positioning it at the end of the table. "Please. Sit." He was not nearly so gracious as Vito.

"Now, what can I do for you?" asked Vito once Clara was

seated. "Would you care to join us? It's nothing fancy, but we'd—"

"No, thanks. I've had dinner." She looked down at her folded hands as if inspecting for a flaw in her nail polish. "For one thing, there's a guy who's been coming around."

"Wanting what?" asked Vito.

"Not the usual," said Clara with a slight smile. At thirty-eight she was still a very attractive woman, and over the years her beard had created a disturbing excitement for a great many men. "I can handle that. It's easy." She frowned. "No, this one was something else. This one was in a grey suit, very smooth, very sure of himself. He wanted to know about you. He asked me a lot of questions. He talked to Gattu and to Terry; I saw him. He probably talked to everyone."

"A reporter?" suggested Michele, his voice flat with sudden nervousness.

Clara shook her head. "Not like any reporter I've ever seen," she said cautiously. "More like a detective, or a spook; Gattu wouldn't say anything to him. He claimed he had to take care of his cat. Terry was pretty scared. She talked a lot. That's not like Terry." Terry Bannister had been with the carnival for six years—a tall, pencil-thin black woman from East Texas who was their contortionist. For her the carnival was the closest thing to a stable home she had ever known.

"That's not like Terry. Perhaps you will have a little wine with us?" Vito reached to pour himself a glass of Barbera and indicated that Michele should fetch a glass for Clara.

"It's not like Terry not to tell you, either," said Clara. "But Gattu? You figure it. Who knows what Gattu would do." She accepted the glass and held it out for the rich red wine. "But you better tell everyone what you want them to do. I know that guy's going to be back tomorrow. He's got more questions. I feel it in my bones." She took a sip. "Not bad."

"Zio Vito," Michele said softly.

Vito held up his hand in placation. "I cannot order silence, or cooperation, or anything else. No matter what I do, if the man is an investigator, it will appear suspicious to him. If he is not an investigator, then it will not matter what we say, in any case." He stared at the wine in his glass.

"You mean you don't care if we talk to the guy?" Clara demanded, incredulity making her voice even higher.

"Oh, I care, but not that you answer him," said Vito, for the first time appearing angry. "I care that he asks." He drained his wine glass and refilled it, offering more to Clara and Michele. "I am shamed that such a man would come here. It dishonors me."

"How can he do that?" Clara asked, hesitating to drink the wine.

"It is dishonorable to be questioned, and through one's employees." His eyes were fixed on a distant place. "If he thought me a man of respect, he would come to me directly. He behaves as if I am without merit." He looked up at Michele. "I want you to find out who this man is and who has sent him. Then I will decide what is to be done." There was a pause that neither Michele nor Clara dared to end. "Let me speak to the rest," Vito said at last.

"I'll call them into the main tent," said Michele at once.

"No," said Vito at once. "I'll have to speak to all of them separately. Anything else might appear that I have given orders." He looked directly at Clara. "Do you think you might be able to ask a few questions yourself? Can you get this man to tell you what he wants?"

Clara thought carefully. "I don't know," she said at last. "We don't see many like him, so smooth and . . ."

"And what?" prompted Vito.

"Bad. There's something very bad about that one." She

looked from Vito to Michele and back. "Not crazy; worse than crazy."

"You're certain?" Michele drew up his chair again.

"Carny people see enough crazies to know one when they find one," Clara said with weary cynicism. "This one isn't like that. His eyes are stone."

Vito nodded. "Yes." He glanced at Michele. "Tomorrow, *Nipote*, you and I will change places for the day. You will be the clown, in motley and whiteface. Sell balloons for Max. I will tend to your duties."

"But he might know you," Michele warned.

"That is the general idea," said Vito with a furious smile.

Vito saved Simon Gattu's Winnebago for last, knocking on the door at 10:45, and waiting reluctantly in the fog. In the distance the lights of Greystone Bay were like will-o'-the-wisps.

Tatiana opened the door. She was wearing lime green sweats that set off the green of her eyes and she carried a five-pound weight in her hand. "*Signore* Cotelli," she said, not offering to admit him.

"I must talk with you, Tatiana," said Vito, unable to fathom why this woman held herself so aloof from the rest of the carnival. Usually carnival folk banded together, like actors and soldiers. Though Gattu had joined them late, it was odd that he and Tatiana made no effort at all to know the others.

"Gattu is not here." She prepared to close the door.

"Then I will speak with you," Vito said, and braced his arm to keep it open. "It's urgent. You can relay what we discuss to Gattu." He wondered briefly where Gattu might be, but dismissed the question before he could voice it. "Tatiana?"

She stepped back. "Then, of course, you must come in. It's your carnival." Her manner was polite enough but those green eyes mocked him.

The Winnebago was meticulously neat, and there were several unexpected touches that surprised Vito, who had never been inside before: On one wall there were a number of photographs of Gattu in various circuses and carnivals, and others of his phenomenal cat. No photograph showed them together. On the other side of the RV was a small but formidable sound system and a large collection of tapes.

Tatiana put her weight beside its twin on the floor, then straightened up and indicated a place on the small sofa. "What do you have to tell me? Us?"

Perhaps it was because he had repeated himself too often in the last two hours that Vito suddenly felt that his request made no sense. "I have been told there has been a man on the midway, asking questions."

"People always ask questions," Tatiana said, nullifying them all with a wave of her hand.

"Not as this man does," said Vito. "He is looking for someone or something. He is more than curious."

"And so?"

Was it his imagination, or did Vito truly see a flicker of dread in the back of her disturbing eyes? "And so, we must do what we can to find out who this man is and what he seeks."

"Is that the one in grey, who does not look like the rest?" She pressed her hands together, then separated them in an effort to appear calm.

"You saw him?" Vito could not conceal his surprise. "You said nothing."

"There was nothing to say. This is a carnival." She was

composed again, her manner serene. "Gattu saw him. That was all that mattered."

Vito wanted to question her, but would not allow himself to be distracted from his purpose. "If you see this man again, and he speaks to you, I would appreciate it if you could find out more about him."

"Why?" Tatiana asked with—was it feigned?—innocence.

"Because he does not belong here and he is asking questions," said Vito, more directly than he wished. "Surely that is sufficient reason."

"If that is what you require," she said. "I will tell Gattu when he returns." There was a short silence, then she stood up. "If that is all?"

Vito took the hint. "Yes. Unless Gattu has questions; he can speak to me before we set up tomorrow." He was almost at the door when he added, "If there is anything else he might want to discuss . . ."

Tatiana laughed; she was still laughing as she closed the door behind Vito.

Standing in the dark outside the Winnebago Vito thought he heard the leopard cough, but he could not be certain, and as he walked away he was able to convince himself he was mistaken.

His ludicrous makeup disguised Michele quite thoroughly. The lopsided grin painted over his expressive mouth threw his handsome face entirely out of proportion, and the tear—in blue greasepaint outlined in black like the rest of his clown features—which depended from his left eye served to mar the regularity of his face. His fright wig was as white as his face, and stuck out a good eight inches all around his head. He was wearing a baggy version of a waiter's or usher's uniform, and his shoes were large enough to provide shelter for half a dozen kittens without crowding his feet.

"I feel like a fool," Michele told his uncle, as he was about to go out of the Itasca.

"Well, you look like one, which you are supposed to do, so it's fine," said Vito as he struggled to button his red vest over his paunch. He puffed with the task. "It seems to me that I am more a fool than you."

"I'll do the—" Michele began, only to be silenced by a gesture from Vito.

"No. I need you to watch, and you cannot do that if they can see you. A clown on a midway is invisible." He sucked in air and finally eased the treacherous button into place. "I dare not laugh."

"Not at me; you'd better not," said Michele, his smile lost in the painted expression he wore. "I know you are right, *Zio,* but I fear for you. If this is someone who knows you from . . . before, then it could be dangerous for you to appear."

"If he is someone from before, then it will not matter what I do." He shook his head once, slowly. "It will mean that *la Famiglia* has broken the promise made to me, and done a dishonorable thing. If that is the case, they might as well kill me." He reached for the swallowtailed red coat that was hung over the back of his chair.

Michele shifted uneasily, not knowing what to say. In order to do something, he helped Vito ease his coat on properly and smoothed the back and shoulders. "You will do well."

"Especially if they don't start shooting at me." He grinned without a trace of amusement in his eyes. "That would be bad for business, wouldn't it? Well, perhaps if it is *la Famiglia,* they will wait until after the midway closes."

"Do you think it is?" asked Michele.

"I hope not," said Vito, reaching for his shiny top hat. "Have you seen Simon and Tatiana? I went by the Winnebago and they weren't there. The show's got to start on time." He was determined to change the subject now, and added, "Tell Jenkins to have the second row of seats in place. I don't want to have to turn people away."

"It's already done." He looked at his uncle. "It would shame me to have to kill this witness here at the carnival. I am worried, *Zio.*"

"So am I," said Vito. "Why could they not have asked this in another place? It is not only because they are hiding Sardinero here. They have asked you to kill him so that if there is a mistake, it will be the end of us, as a carnival, as men. *Don* Domenico has set out to finish what his father started, but without a war." He picked up the long longe whip that was part of the ringmaster's uniform. "Are you ready to sell balloons?"

"If I must," said Michele with an exaggerated bow.

Vito opened the door for his nephew and stood aside as Michele made his way awkwardly down the three short steps. "Careful with your shoes," warned Vito as Michele all but missed the last step.

"Thanks," said Michele, catching himself at the last. "I'm going over to Max's now." He did his best to smooth the front of his motley. "When do the gates open?"

"Fifteen minutes. First show in forty-five. You know the drill." Vito frowned. "Perhaps I should not admit it: I love this life. When I came to it I thought I would never bear it, and now I know I have had my happiest days here. I do not want to lose it."

"Uncle Vito—"

But Vito did not want to say anything more. "Go sell balloons. And if you see Gattu, tell him he's late." He almost thrust Michele aside as he tromped off toward the central tent.

Michele stared after his uncle, feeling entirely at a loss. He was about to move when someone plucked his sleeve.

"This place is the cause of it all," said Simon Gattu when Michele looked down at him. "This place . . . attracts things."

"You're late," said Michele, pointing toward the tent. "My uncle is waiting for you."

Gattu went on as if there had been no interruption. "There have been difficulties before, haven't there? Blood calls to blood. But it's nothing like what calls you here. Tell your uncle that Greystone Bay is a haunted place." He gave a courtly, old-world bow to Michele. "I must hurry." And with that he sprinted away toward the tent.

At the end of the first show, Vito found two men waiting for him at the entrance to the performers' area. He hesitated, regarding them suspiciously, then decided that they were not the same kind of man as the one Clara had described.

Hale Crittenden, at fifty-four, had been on the Greystone Bay Town Council for more than a decade. He prided himself of being the voice of tradition and conservatism. He wore old-fashioned breeches and glossy riding boots with a turtleneck sweater and tweed hacking jacket—clothing more reminiscent of an English country estate than the six restaurants and four hotels he owned. He was fair, his hair thinning, his eyes a washed-out blue. Before he spoke, he cleared his throat twice. "Mr. Cotelli?"

"I am Vito Cotelli, yes."

With Crittenden was Silas Thomas, an angular man with sharp cheekbones and elbows who seemed always to be sniffing at the wind. He dressed less obviously than his companion, in business flannel of an unfashionable cut, which was all but required of the Director of the Board of Education, a post he had taken on eight years ago. "I am Mr. Thomas and this is Mr. Crittenden. We're from Greystone Bay," Thomas began. "We have . . . certain matters we have been . . . asked to . . . discuss with you."

Vito paused and looked at the two visitors. "What is it, gentlemen? Have you received some complaint?"

The two men exchanged glances, Crittenden clearing his throat once more. "You'd better explain, Silas," he said.

"Well, you see," said Thomas, his sharp face darkening, "we have had a complaint of sorts. Of sorts. Not"—he went on hurriedly—"about the carnival itself. No, not the carnival; that's not an issue." He touched his chin, a fussy, irritated movement.

"We have only favorable comments about the carnival," Crittenden interjected. "Everyone here looks forward to your visit. It's the last amusement in the fall, don't you know."

Vito smiled faintly at Crittenden's affectation. "So. What is it you want to speak with me about, then? This carnival is the only thing I suppose you'd have reason to—"

Silas Thomas cut him off. "You see, having the carnival here . . . Well, I know you've come here for a long time. It's been—what?—twenty years since you took over from old Franklin Zane, as I recall."

"Something like that," said Vito; it had been, in fact, twenty-six years.

"A substantial time." He rubbed his hands together nervously. "But we've had certain . . . developments. They have nothing directly to do with you. That's not significant. They make it necessary to ask . . . Well, I know the permits were issued long ago."

"Last year before we left town, in fact," said Vito. "I have the copies with my other records. Would you rather discuss this in my RV? This might seem a bit public."

"No," said Crittenden at once. "We don't want to make an issue of this, but we . . . Oh, this is so terribly awkward."

"If I knew what it was, I might agree," said Vito, wanting to hurry the two men along. "Please. My time is short. I have to prepare for the next performance. It's still an hour away, but—"

"We understand," said Crittenden. "I know how hard it is to get entertainment on time." He essayed a knowing chuckle that came out a high, irritated cackle.

"Then you will know why I must tend to my duties at—"

"Mr. Cotelli," said Silas Thomas with renewed intensity, "there are compelling reasons for us to request that you either move your carnival tomorrow to the area we designate, over on the bluffs, or be willing to cut your week here short. With full compensation, of course." He made a gesture to hold off any objections. "It has to do with the government." The way he said the last word, it ought to have been cut in brass and bolted to a granite monument. "If it were just Greystone Bay, we would have no objections to you continuing in this location. I know how hard it is to part with a loved tradition. But you see, the government"—again that reverential pronunciation—"has an interest in this land, and they have requested, through us, that you vacate this location and accept the other. They are most adamant. The costs of the move will be covered, naturally, and the revenues for the time it takes you to move will be provided in compensation." He looked away from Vito, out through the flaps of the tent. "My family has lived here for a little over five generations. We came in 1877. We're comparative newcomers." He laughed. "We've always had a carnival in the autumn. In this field. It's unthinkable to—"

Hale Crittenden interrupted this reverie. "Silas, for Harry's sake."

Silas Thomas nodded. "You see, the government did not know that this is where the carnival has played for almost two hundred years. When Jeptha Warring first farmed here before the Revolution, he kept this for a pasture and for the carnival. It's been that way ever since. But because the government needs the Freeman place, they're asking that we move you out of the field, over to South Horn Park, on the bluffs."

Vito was about to protest when the inner tent flap was lifted and Simon Gattu stepped out. "Excuse me, Mr. Cotelli. I overheard some mention of a move. I must tell you it would be very hard on my leopard to take him to the bluffs. The sound of the ocean would disturb him. The place would make him restless. I don't think he would be safe there." He bowed to the two men. "Pardon my interruption; I do not mean to intrude but I am concerned for the safety of my animal."

"Who . . . ?" Silas Thomas started.

"I am Simon Gattu. You may have seen my snow leopard perform with my partner Tatiana." His fey, sinister smile played over his face. "Forgive me; I did not mean to intrude." Again he bowed, and before anything more could be said, stepped back through the flap.

After a short, edgy silence, Hale Crittenden tried his chuckle out again. "A most interesting character. I suppose you meet all sorts in the carnival."

"Yes; all sorts," said Vito, too puzzled to be annoyed by what Gattu had just done. "Well, you have the answer from one of our company."

Silas Thomas cracked his knuckles in his distress. "We must insist. The government needs this land to remain open.

They filed the request with us last winter. We should have notified you, but . . . Well, actually, no one noticed that it would impinge on your visit."

"A misunderstanding. You know how these things happen," Hale Crittenden appended.

"I know how they happen. But as Mr. Gattu already indicated, it is very inconvenient for us to move, perhaps even unsafe." Long ago Vito had developed the knack of speaking in such a way that he was very hard to interrupt; he used that skill now, before either Crittenden or Thomas could object. "Would you permit us to set up our Ferris wheel, for example, near the bluffs, or would you think it unsafe? They don't let us run it in Kinsmans Landing because of the cliffs there, because of the wind and the drop. In such a location, you might not want us to use our other midway rides. What about our animal displays? Where can we keep them protected, so that the public won't be at risk? You want to put us in a park, and that makes security more difficult. You know how kids get fascinated with animals, and we're not in a position to have an all-night patrol." He gave them his easiest smile. "I want to stay here, of course. We're as fond of this field as you are. We don't want to move, though you say we must. All right. But there are good reasons for us to locate away from the bluffs. Perhaps there is a farm nearby. I don't like breaking such a long tradition, just as you don't, though it appears we must; I'd like the opportunity to find a better location than the bluffs, for all our sakes."

The two men from Greystone Bay exchanged glances once again. Finally Crittenden spoke. "I'll do what I can, but I don't know what the government will say. If you find a location they approve, we'll see if they will accept it."

"We'll try to persuade one of the farmers to let you use their land. It's the fair thing to do," Thomas seconded. Both men looked relieved. "We'll be sure there are announcements throughout the town, and we will meet all your expenses. We're sorry to do this. Really." He slipped his hands into his pockets. "Well, I am pleased that we can agree."

"We'll speak with you at the close of your business day," said Crittenden, doing his best to look affable. "Meet us at nine-thirty at the Chancellor Inn, and we'll discuss this further over dinner. We'll see what we can do to accommodate your requests." He had recently acquired the Chancellor Inn and knew he could extend this invitation without any inconvenience to himself; it was good business to conduct meetings at his own properties.

"Yes," said Thomas. "But we must be prepared to have you move by noon tomorrow. That's all the time the government would permit. I regret we've had to inconvenience you in this way. And I am more grateful than I can say that you are being so very . . . reasonable about this."

"I am a professional, gentlemen, just as you are," said Vito with great dignity. He held the longe whip a little tighter.

"Yes, certainly," said Silas Thomas.

"A very capable one," Crittenden concurred. "We'll call out to the farmers in Cross Valley. Most of them grow vegetables and, at this time of year, might be willing to have you there, the harvest being over for most of them. Unless they grow winter crops. They have water hookups for irrigation, some of them." It was nothing more than a minor offering, but Vito accepted it gracefully.

"I will speak to my . . . foreman, Willis Jenkins. He's from this part of the country. He might have a few ideas." He paused. "I'll see you at nine-thirty. I may be a few minutes late, but I will arrive. My nephew will be with me."

Crittenden shook his head and coughed delicately. "We'd like to keep this private. It's less awkward that way."

"Less embarrassing," said Thomas more candidly. "We'd rather deal with you alone."

Vito offered them his smile again. "Gentlemen, my nephew is my partner, and anything I approve he must also approve. You'll see his name on our permits along with my own." He lifted the tent flap. "I have a lot to do before the end of our day, gentlemen." As he turned to go he added, as an afterthought, "Is Fred Borg still on the police force?" Over the years Vito had had some dealing with the pragmatic, pipe-smoking Borg and knew the cop would not escalate their predicament.

"Yes; assistant to Chief Copely. He's a lieutenant now." Thomas did his best not to look bewildered.

"I'll want to talk to him about security, wherever we move," said Vito, knowing that the mere mention of the police would serve to calm the men from Greystone Bay and might gain more cooperation.

"Certainly," said Crittenden, taking the hint at last. "We'll notify him at once."

By the time Vito locked away the day's take—as yet uncounted—it was raining again, heavily. "We'll take number two pickup," he told Michele as the young man toweled himself dry from the shower.

"Anything you say," he responded. "How do you think I ought to dress?" His smile was sarcastic, but since Vito did not see it he gave a serious answer.

"The teal turtleneck and the charcoal slacks and black blazer would be best. Professional but not office types; they'll understand that. Better wear something warm on your feet. This rain's not going to warm up." He had changed into a good but nondescript sport coat over camel-hair slacks and a beige shirt worn with a knitted vest. He looked like a successful furniture salesman.

"Sta bene," said Michele as he knotted his towel around his waist and began to take clothes from the closet.

"Better hurry," added Vito without much pressure. "I'd like to get there on time, and in this weather it'll take us a bit longer to get into town."

Michele was pulling on his turtleneck over his thermal underwear, so his words were muffled. "Why do you care about being on time? They're the ones who want us to move. They can damn well wait for us."

Vito gave his nephew a long, thoughtful stare. "We want them to help us, *Nipote*. We do not want them finding excuses to turn us away without money."

Now Michele was drawing on his slacks. "All right. You got a point. But I don't like accommodating those upright, uptight townies. I just don't." The sound of his zipper served to underline his words.

"I'm not pleased about it myself," said Vito. "But we might as well try to do what we can; they will have to live up to their word if it seems we are living up to ours." He went to the little closet by the door and took out a long, oiled-cotton poncho. "Make sure you wear your raingear."

"Sure," said Michele as he finished dressing. He sat to pull on his boots. "The government men—do you think they have anything to do with Sardinero? It seems like it to me. But why would they want us to move the carnival because of Sardinero?"

"I don't know. Perhaps they've heard something. *Don* Domenico might have made sure they were warned, so that you would kill Sardinero for him and be caught yourself. If they are suspicious of the carnival, then it limits what you can do." He started to snap the poncho closed.

"Do you think *Don* Domenico would do that?" Michele asked, as much of himself as of Vito. "What would be the point? He's the one who wants Sardinero dead. He's the one Sardinero informed on. It doesn't have anything to do with us, so why do this?"

"It's *la Famiglia,*" said Vito slowly. "Come on." He fished in his pocket for keys. "I'll drive."

They were the last occupied table at the Chancellor Inn. By ten the other patrons had left, but Hale Crittenden and Silas Thomas remained with Vito and Michele Cotelli. Spread between the coffee cups and brandy snifters—all that was left of a splendid meal—was a map, and the four men were concentrating on it, not an easy task in the low light of the restaurant.

"That won't do," said Vito as Thomas indicated one field about three miles north of his current location. "It's fallow, and that's convenient, but look at the lay of the land," he went on, pointing out the contour lines. "With this rain, that will be a basin of mud. No wonder the farmer leaves it fallow."

Hale Crittenden frowned as he looked toward the windows. "Well, what other location would be acceptable to you?"

Vito had prepared himself for this moment since they had shaken hands in the bar. He pointed to a spot on the map. "I think this might be best. You see, it's high ground, just about the same elevation as where we are now, there's nothing around it, and it appears we can get a hookup for electricity from the old resort that joins it." He looked to Michele for support.

"Seems fine to me, Uncle," he said dutifully.

Silas Thomas was frowning. "I don't know. Oh, dear, I was

afraid you might want that spot." He took the last of his brandy in a gulp.

"What's wrong with it?" asked Michele, less subtly than Vito would have done. "The government again?"

"No; not the government," said Thomas. "They think it was a graveyard once, back in the earliest days of the town. There was a charter given by Charles II to a Wesleigh Thorne and six families accompanying him. Most of them died in the first two years, and we have reason to believe that's where they were buried. You understand the records weren't very complete, not with most of the colonists dying so suddenly. Three of those first settlers survived and some of their descendants are still in Greystone Bay. They might not like it if you were to have a carnival on top of their ancestors."

A log in the fireplace broke and scattered sparks over the tile hearth.

"What if you ask them?" suggested Michele.

Hale Crittenden glanced at Silas Thomas. "It might work. We could start calling first thing in the morning. I'll do it, if you'd rather not," he offered, seeing unhappy lines in Thomas' face. "You married a Thorne."

"No, I'll help. It's just that Abigail Carton won't like it. She never likes anything." Thomas looked down at the map one last time. "Assuming the descendants agree, this is the place you'd like to relocate the carnival?"

"Yes, it is," said Vito in his most polite manner, to compensate for the way Michele had behaved. "Are you certain that the government will approve?"

Thomas nodded at once. "Oh, yes. I stopped off to talk to them after we spoke with you, and they let me know what areas are not acceptable to them. I don't anticipate any problem there."

"Just with Abigail Carton; she a Thorne," said Crittenden. "In more ways than one. Well, remind her that no one is certain that that was the burial ground, just that local legend says it was. There are no headstones left—not that they would be there after so long a time—and no other indications of graves. No bodies have ever been discovered there, and there have been two attempts to find some, the most recent being in 1959." He smiled, priding himself on his knowledge of regional history.

"Some time ago," remarked Michele.

"The bodies aren't going anywhere," Vito said, adding: "No disrespect."

"Of course not," said Crittenden. "Well, I think we can conclude this discussion. It is late, and the wind has picked up. If it were two weeks later, I'd worry about sleet." He folded his tweedy arms to demonstrate the additional cold of sleet. "Glad we could work this out."

"Rain's bad enough in our business," said Vito. "Very well. We'll close the midway at sundown and pack up. That will lose an evening's revenue, you realize. We'll go to the new site and set up before dawn, and we'll open for business in the new location at noon." He gave both Crittenden and Thomas a careful look. "I assume that preparations will be made, and we'll be able to hook up in the new location as soon as we arrive."

"Yes," said Silas Thomas. "We'll arrange all that. Electricity by midnight tomorrow, if that's satisfactory."

"By nine P.M.," said Vito. "We need to have lights to show our people where to put their RVs and their concessions. Electricity by nine. Michele will be in charge of that end, I'll be taking care of the actual move." He reached for the map as he rose; Michele stood with him. "Do you mind if we keep this until we're established in the new location?"

"Go ahead," Thomas said. "It's a copy of one in my office." He looked in his cup for another sip of coffee and was disappointed to find it was empty.

"And you'll have Fred Borg help us with the traffic?" was the last question Vito posed to the townsmen.

"Fine. Of course; glad you reminded me," said Crittenden. He glanced toward the windows. "I should have brought my foul-weather gear."

"It's not going to make the move any easier," said Vito, truthfully enough, but with the certainty that they would have had few or no people come to the carnival in weather like this.

Silas Thomas got to his feet and held out his hand. "Good of you to be so reasonable, Mr. Cotelli. I must say, we'd anticipated more resistance than you've given."

As Vito took the townsman's hand he said, "We want to be welcome here again next year, Mr. Thomas. And for that reason, we'll want to have signed permits for next year before we leave this year, same as always."

"Same as always," Thomas echoed, looking nervous again. "Well, yes. We can do that, I think." He hesitated. "I'll see if there's any conflict with government interests."

Vito managed to continue smiling though his temper was making it more difficult. "Whatever you wish," he made himself say.

"Excellent, excellent," said Crittenden, on his feet now as well. "A most satisfactory evening." He started toward the door. "I am going to enlarge this place, as soon as I can buy the building on that side. That will double the footage and I'll be able to put in a second restaurant and extend the bar into what is the lobby now, and build a new, larger lobby. The couple I bought it from took my first offer. They'd only had it a few years and didn't have any idea how to run a hotel."

By now they were in the lobby and Crittenden signaled the hat-check boy to bring their coats. "It was a pleasure. We must do it again next year, when you're all in town once more."

"Very kind of you," said Vito with the same lack of sincerity as was in the invitation.

Moments later Michele held the door for his uncle and both stepped out into the storm. They huddled in their coats and hastened along the street to the pickup. As they got in, Vito turned on the ignition and pushed the fan to high.

"The windows'll be fogged over in a second or two. This way it won't last long." He glowered through the glass at the torrents of rain riding a blustery wind. "Moving in this is gonna be a bitch."

"Yes," said Michele, faltering before adding, "but the new location is helpful to me."

Against his better judgment, Vito asked, "How do you mean?"

Michele shrugged. "The safe house is protected, but there are places at the back of the property where the patrols are not as frequent. There's a lot of undergrowth and the slope is pretty steep. I guess they figure that anyone coming down the hill would make themselves known."

"And?" Vito asked, hating himself for wanting to know.

"That abuts the far end of the resort property. I can get there, do the job and get back before anyone knows I'm gone. No one will see me." He made a sound that was not quite a laugh. "Funny. The government moves us, I guess to protect the safe house, and they make my work easier."

Vito shook his head. "Could be a trap, Michele. Anything that easy could be a trap. Did you ever think of that?"

"Oh, sure. It would be a pretty good one if I had to get down that hill, but with the rifle I've got, I can watch at the top, hidden in the brush, and wait for Sardinero come out on the back porch." He hitched his shoulders. "If Sardinero stays indoors, I'll have to think of something else."

"If it keeps raining like this, you'd better," said Vito as he started the pickup. "Hand me the towel in the glove compartment, will you? I want to get this window a little clearer."

Clara Marsden spoke for everyone in the carnival when she said, "Well, fucking shit."

The large tent was chilly, the canvas thrumming with rain and wind. Most of the carnival folk were there, most of them tired and irritable. "So why are we bothering?" asked Terry the contortionist.

"Because this is a good place, when the weather's better. We want to come back again, and this way we can. Greystone Bay usually turns out when we're here. The people like us." Vito paused. "We close at sunset and break down at once. Michele and Jenkins will go to the new location with Augustin and Winkey, and be ready to get us in place when we come. We're supposed to have electricity by nine. We can open at noon the next day. Anyone against it?"

There were mutters and one or two derogatory hoots, but only one man raised his voice.

"*Signore* Cotelli," said Simon Gattu, "I am concerned for my cat."

"Your cat has moved before," said Vito, unwilling to put up with Gattu's temperament. "He can move again. For Ognissanti, he's in a carnival. You've taken him to Europe and Asia, haven't you? What's so difficult about moving a couple of miles?"

"The distance is the least of the trouble. Nevertheless, I would want to go with your nephew, in order to find the . . . the least disturbing place for my cat." He looked older than he usually did; it might have been a trick of the light or the mask of fatigue.

"Ask Michele; so long as you're ready to move with the rest of us, it doesn't matter to me how you do it." Vito looked over the people huddled in the center section of the bleachers. "More questions?"

Winkey de Vere, who was three feet tall and spent his time being shot from cannons and wrestling alligators, got to his feet. "Vito, why not move on, go right to Kinsmans Landing and add a couple days to our run there?"

"Because they're having their pumpkin festival through this weekend and there wouldn't be a place for us. I asked last year if we could come for the festival, but they said no. They want to sell pumpkins, not bring money into the carnival." He showed open hands for helplessness. "I can't blame them," he added. "It's the single largest tourist attraction they can offer, and they want to make the most of it."

"Pumpkins," scoffed Rusty Mueller, who ran all the food concessions.

"Well, it beats that place that had the radish festival," Michele said. "Pumpkins at this time of year makes some sense, but what do you do with radishes, except put them in salad?"

"Go to the festival and find out," said Clara. "Okay, we'll do it. It'll be something to do in the rain." She looked directly at Vito. "What about mud?"

"The place is like this one, on a bit of a hill. If we have mud, Greystone Bay will have more trouble than a relocated carnival." He laughed, and half the carnival folk joined him. "That's it. Sorry it has to be bad news. Remember now: Break down tomorrow at sunset. I want to be moved by midnight, if we can manage it."

There were nods of acquiescence, and a few dissenting

grumbles, but no other protest was lodged. "Might as well get some sleep," said Jenkins, his long New Englander face making him look a good ten years older than his actual forty-one years. "It's gonna be a long day tomorrow."

The gathering began to break up, most of the folk moving quickly, glad for an excuse to be out of the drafty tent. A few paused to light cigarettes or pipes before venturing out into the storm.

"I think I'll get to bed, *Zio,*" Michele said to Vito, rubbing his head. "Motley and whiteface tomorrow?"

"I think so; it's safest," said Vito, waiting until the tent was empty to turn off the lights and secure it. "Max is on perimeter tonight; we won't have any disturbances." The balloon vendor was a genius at spotting intruders of any kind.

"Good for Max," said Michele. "When do you want me at the new site?"

"As soon after we shut down as you can manage. Will six be too hard? Try for six if you can. By ten most of us will be at the new location, and we'll start hooking up. You can work out the positions better than I can. I've sketched a few things on the map, but you'll be there, and you should decide what the arrangements are. I'll need you for that, and for traffic control." He did not ask the obvious question, but he regarded his nephew with concern. "Don't try to fit it in. It won't work."

"Just a thought," said Michele, hurrying with his uncle toward their Itasca. He opened the door and stood aside to permit Vito to enter first. "What can I say? We all have our jobs on our minds."

"This time, that job better be set aside, at least until we're moved." Vito looked around the Itasca. "I promised Sophia a big house, with servants and all the trimmings. She always took it in good humor, and said she liked this better. I wish I knew it was the truth."

"She stayed with you, didn't she?" Michele asked. "Then you have to assume she knew what she wanted."

"Not with women of her generation," said Vito slowly. "They were taught always to put the man first—"

"How fortunate," interjected Michele.

"—and to accommodate husbands and family no matter what the cost to themselves. It's a hard way to live." He looked in the kitchen and frowned. "No more scones."

"I'll pick up some tomorrow morning, when I go to town for food." Michele was already undressing, preparing for bed. "Go on, *Zio.* It's time to sleep."

"Ah, you sleep. I need to do a little reading before I can sleep. You ignore me, I'll ignore you." It was an old routine with them, one that rarely varied. Vito ignored Michele as he finished undressing; he stripped to his underwear and pulled on an enormous robe of muted paisley in greens and browns. Going to his bookshelf he selected *Ten Centuries of English Poetry,* and went to his bed where he propped himself up with half a dozen pillows and dozed off with the broad rhythms of Edmund Spenser.

In place of rain there was fog, thick and clingy. Vito closed the entrance of the midway as the light faded and shouted instructions to Jenkins. "You and Winkey and Gattu and Michele, get to the new site. We've got to *move.* Fred Borg'll be waiting for you."

"We're almost ready," called back Michele. "I just want to get out of this." In the fog his paint and motley made him look hideous, ghostly. The wide red smile seemed now a grimace of pain, the single tear was more like a fatal wound.

He patted Vito on the arm. "Fifteen minutes, *Zio.* That's all I need."

Vito inadvertently crossed himself, then did his best to laugh at his own dread. "Fifteen minutes," he conceded. "Jenkins, Winkey, Gattu, you can get a cup of coffee and something to eat."

Jenkins offered Vito a salute, and from somewhere down the midway, Gattu called back, "I'll tend to my cat."

"Damn, it all looks spooky," said Terry Bannister as she came up to Vito, shivering a little, but not from the cold. "I packed up most of my stuff this morning. Jenkins' boys will take care of the big equipment."

"That it does," said Vito, responding to her first remark. "The Ferris wheel might as well be a dinosaur, the way it looks in the fog. The way the lights catch it, the gondolas might as well be jaws, opening and opening." He shook his head as if to clear away the image. "So you're ready. Good to hear it. Let's hope everyone else does as well." He was going down the midway toward the main tent, feeling the chill seep into his bones. It was going to be a very long night.

Terry tagged after him. "Can I have my RV near Clara's?" she asked.

"Check with Michele. He's doing the space assignments. Tell him what you want and he'll handle it. Or talk to Winkey." His mind was not on Terry, and so he missed the first part of her next question.

". . . a place like that?"

"Who knows?" answered Vito, in order to say something. He raised his hand. "Benson! Kelly! Caudet! Let's get started!" His big voice rang through the shrouded twilight, so powerful that it seemed to part the fog for an instant.

Ho-Ho Kelly—who had been christened Horace Horatio

forty-one years ago—showed up beside Vito, already out of motley and whiteface. "I'm ready, boss," he announced.

"Good. Where's Benson and Caudet? Are they ready to get to work? And what's happened to the musicians?" There was an ensemble of eight who traveled with them, though every year it was a different eight.

"Already packed up," said Kelly, unable to keep the smugness out of his tone. "They're all in their trailers and ready to roll as soon as Michele gives the word."

Vito was surprised, for usually the musicians were the most undependable of the carnival folk, not being truly part of the carnival at all. "Good for them," he approved.

Ted Benson came out of the big tent, his fleece-lined denim jacket making him look more like a cowboy than a roustabout. He wore his cuffs deliberately long to conceal the sixth finger on his left hand. "We're almost ready. I've assigned Hill and Paarfeld to the midway. Caudet's doing the Ferris wheel. We've got Salis and Choza here. Jenkins gave us our assignments last night."

"Good, good," said Vito as he peered at the fog. "Driving's going to be a ball-breaker." He looked around at Benson again. "Everything in hand here, would you say?"

"Unless something goes wrong," said Benson. "It's not like we haven't done it before." He folded his arms. "The last of the performers' stuff'll be out of here in ten minutes, and then we'll get to work. Don't worry, boss; we'll meet your schedule."

"I hope so." He glanced over his shoulder to see if Terry Bannister was still there, but she had vanished into the darkening fog. "I want to check the performers. Carry on."

"Glad to," said Benson, giving himself the luxury of an extra cigarette.

The first RV was Clara's, and she was busily putting the

last of her various sequined dresses into a wardrobe. "Almost done," she called out, stopping her work long enough to say: "Say, Vito, can you spare a driver for me? I can't see a bloody thing in this soup."

"I'll ask Benson if he can lend you someone. Maybe Salis, if that's okay with you? He's dependable, and as soon as the main tent is down, Benson can spare him. Better him than someone on the midway. You and Terry and the Tschenkos will be the first ones out. Then the—"

"I don't care about the order of march, Vito. I just want to be sure I get where we're going in one piece. You get me that driver, and I'll feel a whole lot better about it." She fingered her beard nervously.

"All right," said Vito, and continued on his rounds. By the time he reached Gattu's Winnebago, his voice had turned raspy. As he knocked on the door, he swallowed hard to clear his throat, but it did not work.

Tatiana appeared in the door, looking cool and efficient as always. "I have the cat in his cage. I am prepared to drive as soon as you give the signal. Doubtless we still have the last position in the line?"

"You're the newest here," said Vito.

"Exactly. That is not a problem. Simon will choose the best place for us, if such a place exists." She looked up into the night and fog. "It could be an omen, this terrible weather."

"It's October, Tatiana," said Vito as patiently as he could. "What do you expect in New England in October?"

"I expect rain, but not torrents, and fog, but not this." She gave him her most professional smile. "Thank you for stopping, *Signore* Cotelli."

Vito stepped back to avoid being struck by the closing door.

* * *

It was closer to five than four in the morning when Vito and Michele finally went to their Itasca, exhausted. The new midway was set up and the tent was ready to be raised half an hour before they opened for the day.

"At least the electricity was on," muttered Vito as he clambered into bed, too tired to read.

"Rusty Mueller threw a fit about it," said Michele. "He claimed there wasn't enough juice for the midway, let alone the tent. Fred Borg took care of it." He looked incongruous in his long flannel nightshirt. "We got a third line in, and that should be enough."

"Rusty worries too much," said Vito.

"And you don't?" countered his nephew. "I thought with this fog we'd never be done. It's like working blindfolded, part of the time. I swear I couldn't see three feet in front of me, even with the lights on." Michele stretched. "I used every curse I ever learned tonight."

"It was very bad," said Vito.

"I hope it isn't like this tomorrow. No one will be able to find us if the fog hangs on." He pummeled his pillow. "It's bad business, having to move to a new place after so long. If it weren't a good place for my other job, I would have said no to the whole thing. Getting the trailers and RVs into position! If it weren't for Gattu, we'd still be out there jockeying. Nobody bothered to let us know about the trees. I've got half a mind to tell them we won't bother with Greystone Bay next year." As he drew the blankets up, he said, "Well, *Zio,* do you want to come back here next year?"

"Go to sleep, *Minchione,*" Vito said affectionately.

"Look out who you're calling *minchione,*" warned Michele with a laugh.

Vito yawned. "Go to sleep, whatever you are."

* * *

By noon the fog had turned to a fine, blinding mist which gave the whole carnival the look of a washed-out photograph. The Ferris wheel and merry-go-round were working, as was the snake and the bumper cars, but Rusty Mueller had not got all the food concessions up and running by the time the first townies were admitted, and it irritated him.

"What am I going to do?" he railed at Vito. "We won't have the pizza slices ready for at least half an hour. That means money lost, Vito." He slammed his fist into his open palm, his face puckering with dismay and rage. His forehead was sweaty. "This move is a six-way-from-Sunday fuckup!"

"But you've got the extra electrical line and the ovens are on, aren't they?" said Vito at his most placating. "We aren't getting huge crowds anyway. Let them get by on hot dogs and cotton candy and sno-cones for another hour."

"It's not funny," Mueller insisted. "Damned townies."

"It's not a disaster, either," said Vito. He was once again in motley, his clown's face masking his features with an enormous comic grin and giddy starred eyes. He had not yet donned his wig, and his own greying hair looked out of place with the rest of him. "Go and talk to Jenkins, and find out if he can speed up things for you. Or check the RVs for a couple spare microwaves. Maybe you could do your pizza that way."

"Ha-ha," said Mueller sullenly.

Vito took his wig and carefully put it on. "The thing is," he said in a remote voice, "we're making the best of a bad situation. If you keep bitching about it, some of the others are going to get as miffed as you are, and then we will have a problem. You know that as well as I do. All I'm asking"—the wig was in place now, properly adjusted, a manic creation of bright orange corkscrew curls—"is that you give it an hour. If you aren't up and running by then—"

"I'll be bankrupt."

"If you aren't up and running in an hour," Vito repeated more sternly, the tone of his beautiful voice at odds with his appearance, "then we can discuss what's to be done. In the meantime, I want you to tend to your other concessions and leave the pizza hookups to Jenkins." He stood up and reached for the bouquet of enormous plastic flowers he always carried when in motley. "Is that all, or has something else got a hair up your ass?"

Mueller pouted. "That's all."

"Good. I'll make sure Jenkins is on it." He patted Mueller on the shoulder with his soft, gloved hands. Each finger had an extension filled with two inches of foam rubber, making the gloves unwieldy. "Is Michele ready for the first show?" It was intended as a polite way to end the conversation, not to create another uproar.

"I haven't seen him. He wasn't in the tent. I looked there before I came here. He wasn't on the midway." Mueller slapped his thighs. "What are we supposed to do if Michele isn't on the job?" He rounded on Vito again. "Don't tell me this is nothing."

Although Vito was concerned, he shrugged for Mueller's benefit. "He's probably trying to do something about your electricity. You have talked to him, haven't you?" He was at the door now and prepared to leave. "Come on, Rusty. Show time."

Mueller followed him grudgingly out into the shattering, filmy light. As he fumbled for his dark glasses, he said, "I want to bill the town for the pizzas I can't sell, thanks to them."

"I'll arrange it. You won't have to take a loss," said Vito, clumping off toward the midway, his flowers held out in front of him as if to part the crowd. He stopped at the gate and nodded to Ho-Ho Kelly, who was in full motley as well. "How's it going?"

"Slow," said Kelly. "Not too bad, though. Word's got out. I think business will pick up later in the day. We're doing about seventy percent of normal, and considering the move . . ." The lift of his brow was lost on everyone but Vito.

"It could be worse. You keep at it." He was about to turn away when he asked, "Have you seen Michele?"

"About an hour ago." Kelly took a $1.50 from a wide-eyed boy, and handed him a ticket. "You keep this with you, son. If anyone asks if you paid your admission, you tell them to talk to the clown in blue. I'll vouch for you, I promise."

The boy looked at Kelly, his eyes enormous. "Really?"

"You bet," said Kelly before giving his attention to Vito. "What is it?"

"You think we can up the kids' admission to two bucks?" Vito asked, avoiding the question, and went on without waiting for an answer: "What was Michele doing an hour ago?"

"He was over near that resort. I noticed," Kelly went on, "because he was in whiteface. He was wearing regular clothes, but his face was done. I figured it was some kind of emergency."

"Yeah," said Vito, his face set under his makeup. "Yeah, some kind of emergency, all right."

Kelly frowned at Vito. "What's the matter? You look like someone took away your lollipop."

"Nothing quite that bad," said Vito. "I thought Michele was going to ringmaster the first show, but I guess I was wrong. I better get ready to do it myself."

"In motley?" asked Kelly in surprise. "You aren't really going to do that, are you?" He saw Vito's gesture of dismissal.

"Come on. You can't be serious. You never ringmaster in motley."

"Maybe not as serious as you'd like," said Vito. "How long to the first show? You got a watch on you?"

Kelly pulled back his long, baggy sleeve and consulted the old Timex strapped to his wrist. "Figure twenty minutes at most. What the hell's going on, Vito? Isn't Mike supposed to take care of the ringmaster job?"

"I think something's come up," said Vito, his mind on other things. "I'll have to get the show on the road. Is Gattu ready, do you know?"

"I haven't seen him, but I guess he is. Tatiana was here earlier, and she looked ready to ride bears, kind of wild." Kelly smiled an instant. "Well, she's that kind of woman, isn't she?"

"I suppose so; she works that cat with nothing more than a riding crop," said Vito, his mind already spinning with anticipation. "I'll try to find him, so we can get started." Even as he said it, he was filled with worry that Michele might have tried to bring down Sardinero without any help. How could he find his nephew if he had taken to the wilderness—and in whiteface?

"What's the matter, Vito?" asked Kelly. "You look so strange."

"Oh, nothing," said Vito with a visible effort to dismiss the worry from his mind. "I thought the electricity might be wrong. Rusty's having difficulty getting power for his pizza ovens. I'm borrowing trouble, I know it. Don't pay any attention to me." He started away from the gate, his hands in his capacious pockets, when Kelly called after him.

"Mike had something on his back when he went. A bag maybe, for tools. It was pretty bulky. I don't know what was in it, but I reckon I'd better mention it." He waved good-naturedly to Vito. "If you go looking for him, remember the pack he's got."

"Yes," said Vito, refusing to think of what Michele carried in his pack. "I'll do that." Inwardly he cursed his nephew in a rich mixture of Italian and English. *"Stolto!* What a fucking stupid thing to do!" he exclaimed under his breath. Going on a job like that in whiteface!

Clara waved from her booth, dressed now in an elaborate evening gown of the Gibson Girl era. "Something wrong?"

"The move," answered Vito with a wave of his hand, knowing his explanation would be accepted. "You know what I mean. Are you ready to work yet?"

"I'll start my act in about ten minutes, after we've got a little bigger crowd." She flashed him her warmest smile. "It'll turn out okay, Vito. It always does."

"I hope you're right," said Vito, then added, with an attempt at casualness that did not succeed: "You seen Michele around?"

Clara frowned. "No. Not for an hour or more. He said he was going to get into motley. I thought he was going to be ringmaster." She giggled a bit. "Get your wires crossed, you two?"

"I'm afraid so," said Vito. "Looks like we're both in motley." He shook his head slowly. "Well, if this is the worst we have to contend with, I suppose I should be happy."

"Sure," said Clara, blowing him a kiss before stepping back through the protective flap of her booth.

"Oh, Michele, Michele, what have you done?" Vito whispered as he came to the side of the main tent. The familiar setting provided the illusion of normality, and he welcomed it. He could see the six liberty horses—all saffron-colored Andalusians—and their trainer, Basil; he was checking the cavessons and side-reins one last time. Beyond the horses

Henry and Sandy were getting their three chimps dressed. Where, Vito asked himself, are Tatiana and that snow leopard? Where was Gattu? The leopard's cage was not where it was supposed to be. Frowning, Vito looked around a second time. No sign of Gattu or Tatiana.

"Basil, you seen Gattu?" he called to the horse trainer.

Basil was ready to perform, all rigged out in green-and-gold Elizabethan finery. He could not shake his head because of the ruff he wore. "Not today. He looked pretty done in after the move. Maybe they overslept." As he said this he patted the neck of his lead horse. "We're ready when you are."

"Good," said Vito, though he sounded disoriented. He looked toward the tent entrance and noticed the line was not very long. "I think we'll hold the first show for fifteen minutes, to get more people in."

Basil sighed. "Whatever you say."

Vito was about to repeat this to Henry and Sandy, but Sandy called out, "We heard you," before he could say anything.

Nodding, he left the tent, making his way to the part of the field where Gattu had parked his Winnebago. He was not certain if he was angry or worried as he strode up to the door and rapped on it with his outsized hands. "Gattu? We got a show to do, remember?"

He heard a sound from inside the RV that he could not identify, something between a cough and a cry, and then the door was flung open and Tatiana, looking distraught, stood facing him, mascara streaks marking the path of tears down her face. She almost whimpered as she reached out to Vito.

"Oh, thank God you're here," she said as she took his arm and all but dragged him into the RV. "You've got to help."

Vito was taken aback by her appearance, and more so by

her manner. *"Ch'e fai?"* he demanded, and saw blankness in her eyes. He switched to English. "What's wrong?"

"Gattu," she said comprehensively, shuddering at the name. "In the bedroom. Oh, God. You must see him. In the bedroom."

More puzzled than worried, Vito followed her. "Should I call a doctor? Is he ill? Hurt?"

"No." She turned on him so quickly and said it so emphatically that Vito was stunned. "No doctor. No priest." The last word was spoken with spitting contempt. "You must talk to him." At that, she opened the bedroom door and stepped aside to admit Vito.

In contrast to the rest of the RV, the bedroom was a shambles. Simon Gattu lay on his back on the disheveled bed, his eyes half-closed as if in delirium. Sweat drenched his body and his breathing was quick and shallow. "This place," he muttered. "This place."

After one stunned look, Vito approached the bed. "What about this place?" he asked in a low, reasonable tone; he was shocked by Gattu's appearance, but he had been through enough emergencies that he had learned to set his reaction aside until the crisis was over. "What's the matter, Simon?"

"A slaughterhouse," said Gattu, his speech a bit clearer than before. "Not a graveyard. No rest here. A massacre." He tossed about as if his bones hurt him. "Nothing rests here."

In the doorway, Tatiana put one hand to her mouth to stifle her sobs.

"Simon," said Vito, going a few steps nearer the bed, "what's wrong?" He glanced back at Tatiana, realizing he had yet to see the cage. "Where's the leopard? Tatiana?"

Tatiana turned away, wailing in grief.

"Has something happened to the leopard?" Vito asked, keeping his voice even. Dear God, suppose the animal had been hurt in the move. He wasn't certain his insurance would cover injuries to the snow leopard, or the cat's worth, if he had to replace the leopard. With an effort he put such concerns from his mind. "What's happened here?"

Gattu twitched, spasmed, and Vito was afraid the man was about to have a seizure. Panting with exertion, Gattu strove to answer. "There are dead here. So many dead. Betrayed. Over thirty of them, unavenged. Long dead, long restless." He broke off, shaking violently.

"I'm going to get some help," said Vito, starting from the room.

"NO!" Gattu roared. "No."

Vito shook his head. "You need attention, Simon. You should be in a hospital." This time he ignored the bellow of protest and left the bedroom.

Tatiana was standing by the door, her eyes hollow with fear. "Don't call anyone. It will pass. If we move off this ground, it will pass." She touched Vito's arm. "Please. Move us. Away from this ground. Somewhere clean. If he does not improve, then I will help you get him to a doctor."

"We can't move you now. We're open for business." He took her hands in his, the extra length of his gloves making the gesture awkward. "He's got to have help, Tatiana. Look at him."

"Move us," she pleaded. "Do that first. Now."

"You know that's not possible," Vito said at his most reasonable.

"This place maddens the cat. Don't you understand that? We cannot stay here. It isn't safe." She began to cry again, a steady, hopeless sobbing that tried Vito's patience even as it wrung his heart.

"We'll make sure nothing happens to the cat," he said, hoping he would be able to keep his promise. "But Gattu needs help. Urgently." He broke away from her and reached for the door when there was the sound of splintering glass from the bedroom and the choking scream of the snow leopard.

Tatiana shrieked and stumbled back against the speakers, her face pasty as bread dough.

Vito stared at her. "The leopard?" How in the name of Christ could it have gotten into the trailer? Vito asked himself. "Was that the leopard?"

She nodded but could not speak.

At that Vito rushed toward the bedroom, dreading what he would find.

The bed was empty; the window had been smashed from the inside. Gattu was gone. There was no sign of the leopard.

Michele found his perch and settled down to wait, his rifle at the ready. He had given himself half an hour for this first attempt. He would be able to return to the carnival and get into motley in less than five minutes. With the confusion the shot was sure to cause, he would be safe long before anyone suspected he had been there. He thought of Sardinero, feeling a momentary regret that he had to kill the fellow. He had nothing against Sardinero, but his betrayal of *la Famiglia* could not be allowed. Still, he knew, in similar circumstances he might have well done the same thing himself. The visor he had brought in his backpack along with his disassembled rifle was ready. He lowered his visor over his face, so that if he were spotted the whiteface he wore would not be seen. Once he removed the visor, the whiteface would provide a perfect disguise. It was still warm in the sunshine, but here in the shadows chill lingered, a constant reminder that fall was ending and winter was gearing up for a long run.

At the house down the slope, four men in grey suits walked

their ill-concealed sentry routes. Each was armed, each carried communication equipment and wore a headphone. Their attention was clearly directed to the front and sides of the property, not to the wild tangle behind it.

How much more obvious could they be? Michele wondered, checking his watch for the second time. He had another fifteen minutes before he would have to leave. With any luck, Sardinero would step outside, or open a window. It would take so little to give Michele his chance. He braced the rifle and checked the sights, satisfied he was ready.

Vito held the receiver so tightly he was surprised he did not leave fingerprints embedded in the plastic. "I have to speak to Crittenden at once. I don't give a flying fuck if it's convenient."

The secretary sputtered, but said she would try to find her boss, and returned a few minutes later with Crittenden in tow. "What is the matter now, Mr. Cotelli?" asked the hotelier with practiced smoothness. "I've been told you're distressed about something."

"What happened here? On this place, in this field. What happened?" Vito inquired without preamble. "What kind of place is this?"

For once Crittenden had no easy answer. "How do you mean? It's a field we could all agree upon. You wanted to be located there." He paused an instant. "Is something wrong?"

"In history. You're supposed to know about that," said Vito. "What happened here, a long time ago? Why do you call this place a graveyard?"

This time Hale Crittenden's pause was noticeable. "Well, it's only a story, and we don't put much stock in it," he said reluctantly.

"Tell me," Vito ordered.

"It's not confirmed fact." Crittenden cleared his throat. "It's said that some privateers or pirates were using Greystone Bay as a . . . a hiding place, the Horns making it protected and all. Anyway, after the first settlers came, the ones with Wesleigh Thorne ended up facing the pirates. According to the tales, the pirates waited for them and killed most of them. That field is supposed to be one of the places it happened." He coughed. "The pirates might have thrown the bodies into the sea. They did that sometimes." There was a longer pause. "Why? Have you found something?"

"Not exactly," said Vito. He looked across from the office booth down the midway, idly wondering who could be dragooned into doing the ringmaster duties while he went looking for his nephew and a *were*leopard.

"What is it, then?" Crittenden demanded testily.

"I'll try to explain later," said Vito. "When it's settled." He added a hasty word of thanks and hung up. "Jenkins," he shouted as he left the office booth. "Here."

"What is it, boss?" Willis Jenkins asked as he came to Vito's side.

"I . . . There's a problem. I need your help."

"Okay," said Jenkins in his usual phlegmatic way. "When?"

"Right away. Put someone in charge while we're gone." He had pulled off his clown's gloves and stuffed them inside his motley. "I'm getting out of the rig. Meet me in five minutes at the Itasca. Put Max or someone in charge while we're gone and tell . . . Oh, tell Basil to get the show going without the . . . leopard." It was more difficult to say the word than he would have thought possible. "And bring your pistol."

"It's not supposed to leave the grounds of the carnival," Jenkins reminded Vito, who was already striding away through the booths, attracting the attention of a few of the incoming patrons.

"Bring it!" Vito told him, adding as he continued toward his RV. "And Tatiana."

There was a flurry of calls from one headset and hand-held unit among the men in grey suits. Michele watched with interest, and leaned forward a little to have a better view of the house. One of the men at the house pulled an automatic from his underarm holster and started toward the front of the property, a second coming behind him.

"Damn!" whispered Michele as he realized that his quarry was going out the front of the house and not the back. He watched helplessly as a car was brought to the front of the house. The angle of the roof kept Michele from seeing Sardinero leave the house, but he knew by the way the car was driven from the property that he had been spirited away.

The remaining two men in grey suits turned their attention to the hillside at the back of the property.

Michele sank back into the brush, and began to disassemble his rifle. There would have to be another time. He slipped the barrel and stock back into his pack, putting the sights into a protective bag. At last he removed his visor and added that to what was in the pack. He slid back through the brush into deeper shadows; certain that he was concealed, he listened to the movements and orders of the men at the foot of the slope. He would have to hide his pack and come back for it later. He could not afford to be caught with the rifle in his possession.

One of the men in grey barked several sharp orders; two more men emerged from the house, both in dark clothes made for hunting, both carrying assault rifles.

Hurriedly Michele found a good-sized tree and began to

dig out a hollow at the roots. He breathed with his mouth open, taking care to make as little noise as possible. When he had enough of an indentation, he shoved his pack into it and began to pull leaves and earth back over it, trusting it would be sufficient concealment until he could return at night and get it.

"I swore on blood I would not—" Tatiana protested as Vito and Jenkins all but dragged her toward the old resort.

"It's too late for that," said Vito, who knew something of blood oaths. "He's in danger, don't you get that? Michele is out there. If . . . Gattu gets close, he could kill him."

Tatiana attempted to break free of the two men. "I can't. I can't."

"We can't do it ourselves," said Jenkins. "You know him; he trusts you. Maybe we can keep him alive."

"No," she cried. "No, no, no." Her eyes were wild.

"Do you want him dead?" Vito asked bluntly.

"No. Please. Please, no." She set her jaw. "All right. I'll try. But I don't know if I can do anything. I've never seen him like this. It's the place. It . . . does something to him." Her voice dropped. "He's feral now. He isn't most of the time, not really. You've seen him in the ring. You know."

They had passed the boarded-up buildings and had come to the edge of the wilderness at the back of the resort.

"He's got to be in there somewhere. So does Michele," said Vito, preparing to enter the undergrowth.

Michele was alert to all the sounds in the woods now, trying to locate the men coming up the slope. He was about a quarter of a mile away from where he had left his rifle. Another quarter mile and he would be back at the resort. He could tell his face was smeared; he would have to do it over, or dress for ringmastering. The whiteface might be better—he knew there were cuts and scratches on his face that would be more easily concealed by makeup.

A sound in the underbrush caught his attention. He turned. The pale, baleful face of the snow leopard emerged from the darkness.

Animals did not often frighten Michele, but now he felt terror go through him, turning his bones to ice and sinking talons into his guts. He tried to shout, but only a high, strangled bleat came from his lips.

Vito halted the other two as they stumbled through the undergrowth. "I heard something," he said, holding up his hand for silence.

"I don't—" Tatiana began.

Then came the scream, long and ragged.

Michele was borne backward by the snow leopard's rush. As the fangs ripped into his shoulder and the claws fixed themselves in his back and thighs, he recalled with idiotic composure that snow leopards were not supposed to attack men. He wanted to laugh but what came out was a second, more guttural scream. There was something in his body, something more alive than the cat that crouched on his chest. It raged and burned through him, and then there was a tearing so immense that Michele thought his body had exploded. Then there was no more thought, or feeling, or life.

Just as Vito and Tatiana blundered into the little hollow where Michele lay, the two black-clad men burst upon the sight. Both moved swiftly, lethally.

Their assault rifles spat and the snow leopard collapsed on top of his still-bleeding victim.

"No!" yelled Vito as the snow leopard died.

"Osama!" wailed Tatiana as she broke away from Vito and ran toward the two dead figures.

"Hold it!" ordered one of the men in black.

Vito responded first. "They're from my carnival," he said, knowing that his whiteface identified him as it identified his nephew.

The man in black motioned with the barrel of his gun and Vito remained still, signaling to Jenkins to do the same as he ran into the little clearing.

Tatiana was trying to pull the snow leopard away from Michele. She shrieked as she dragged at the cat, and all her body shivered with fright.

"What the—" the first man in black said.

For the snow leopard was now not so much a cat as a small, athletic man. Tatiana's sobs were mixed now with horrible laughter.

"May I . . . He's my nephew," said Vito, indicating Michele. "I . . . ought to close his eyes."

The two men in black nodded.

As Vito approached Michele, Gattu gave a sudden, impossible shudder. "It is . . . murderous here," he whispered, and then fell forever silent.

Kneeling beside the ruin of Michele, Vito nodded.

Jenkins lingered at the edge of the tragedy. "Boss?"

Vito looked up. His clown's face was smeared and streaked. "Enough. No more." He looked from Jenkins to Gattu, to the hysterical Tatiana, to the two men in black. "We don't belong here. No one belongs here."

Only Jenkins nodded.

O Love, Thy Kiss

by Nancy Holder

IT WAS 1938, THE HOTTEST SUMMER ON RECORD, and the gee-gawkers gathered at the top of North Hill to watch the Covingtons—who were, as Miriam's mother termed them, *nouveau riche*—receive into their home the first electric refrigerator in Greystone Bay.

The machine was a massive white box with a circle of porcelain on top and the name Coldspot emblazoned on the door. The muscles of the colored men who carried it up the first set of stairs of the Covington's white Queen Anne quivered; their brows beneath their caps dripped clear sweat. Then the men disappeared around the side of the house, their destination the kitchen, and the crowd murmured among themselves.

"Of course the Covingtons got one first," Miriam sniffed. She twisted her scented handkerchief between her long, white fingers and dabbed her face. "Mama says it'll fall apart in a week and they'll be back to buying ice."

Cody Greystone Montague smiled faintly at Miriam's show of loyalty. She'd been his girl for the past year, and though her parents were pleased that she'd found favor with the youngest son of the distinguished family, the direct descendants of Greystone Bay's founder, Winston Andrews Greystone, still they knew of his determination to leave the Bay and didn't want to see her hurt. They encouraged her to date other boys, those not as "radical-minded" as Cody, but she remained steadfast in her devotion.

Miriam and he had talked of his plans for Yale; he promised to be faithful and to send for her eventually. But he would not promise to return to the Bay. That frightened her: People stayed in Greystone Bay, where they belonged. The only person she knew who had left came back in a coffin.

Oh, Cody, my Cody, she thought, her heart pounding; and she said again, "It'll break," not sure if she were still speaking of the refrigerator.

He clasped her hand and she felt heat rise to her cheeks, if that were possible in the blast furnace the town had become that record-breaking summer. Beneath the brim of her brand-new Coral Rose acetate sun hat, she struggled with herself for a moment, gazing down at their fingers. How she prayed an engagement ring would appear there before he went off! She contrasted their two hands; hers was as white as the paint on the boards of the Covington mansion. As was the rest of her, though she wore cotton floral sundresses and no hose all summer. Most of the onlookers were as pale as she: Greystone Bay folk didn't tan well. Cody was an oddity, fair and blond and brown as a nut; and for all that, voted Most Handsome Boy of Greystone Bay High for the Class of 1938.

"They've plugged it in!" someone proclaimed from the other side of the Covingtons' house.

"A week, if that," Miriam muttered.

Cody shrugged as if he didn't care one way or the other, crossing his arms to prove it as he leaned nonchalantly against the banister. The others glanced at him; some averted their gazes and Miriam figured they'd ordered refrigerators, too.

"My pop's not worried," he said, although her father had said Mr. Montague was very worried. He and Cody's three brothers—his much, much older brothers—had been spending hours behind the closed office doors of the Greystone Ice House, which they owned, ever since news of the Convingtons' refrigerator had spread through town.

"Ice is good enough for the Peixe brothers," Mr. Montague had told Miriam's father, referring to the Portuguese who ran the fish market, "and for all the other merchants too. My ice men are honest—they give three hundred pounds for three hundred pounds, not slicing off an extra chunk like they do up in New York. And the ice is cut square so it fits in the box. So what do they want with refrigerators?"

"It's change, Andrew," her father had replied, and was startled by Mr. Montague's look of anger.

"We don't like change much in Greystone Bay," Mr. Montague had snapped. "Especially not a change like this."

"God, I can't wait to get out of here," Cody told Miriam.

She pretended not to understand. Arranging her handkerchief across the top of her pocket, she smiled brightly at him. "Then let's go."

"It's working!" the same voice cried. A cheer of excitement erupted from the crowd.

Miriam and Cody didn't hold hands as they walked farther up the hill. Below them limp, nickel-colored sheets of fog hung over the equally nickel-colored waters of the Bay, grey on grey, an impenetrable wall of steamy heat that drove Miriam deep into unhappiness. Pangs of guilt welled inside her: If the ice business began to slack off because of the refrigerators, maybe Cody wouldn't be able to go to Yale after all. And they'd get married and—

"Jesus Christ, I'm going to die here, grey-white like everyone else, dead in their souls and hearts!" Cody cried, and Miriam took his hand and gave it a squeeze.

"No, you won't," she soothed. Then, to make up for her disloyal thoughts, she added, "You'll be off to Yale in two months, Cody. Studying philosophy and living in a fraternity house and doing all the things you've dreamed about."

Cody stopped walking and put his arms on her shoulders. His bright blue eyes blazed at her and a thrill shot up her spine. When Cody Montague looked at you like that, you wanted to do whatever he asked of you.

Indeed, she had done everything he'd asked. Everything.

"Don't you want to leave here?" he asked passionately. "Don't you despise it?"

"Oh, yes," she murmured. He released her.

"Miriam." He sounded disappointed.

"I do. Only—" she began, but stopped herself, because she was about to say, "only if we were married first."

"Damn summer," Cody said, as they reached the edge of Colony Avenue, where both the Montagues' Victorian mansion and the Greystone Ice House perched at the very top of the hill.

The ice house was a squat, ugly building of aging, many-times-painted wood and no windows except one beneath the Office sign; it had been built in the early 1800s—quite revolutionary for its time—when Greystones still ruled the Bay with complete authority and could put their businesses where it suited them. And it had suited old Thaddeus Greystone to put his ice house next to his home. The ice was collected from the freshwater lake just preceding the marshland, guided down the slope of the hill to the ice house, and from there the delivery men slid it down the streets of Greystone Bay in an ingenious system of troughs, since fallen into disuse. Indeed, the location of the old ice house made little sense now that the real estate of North Hill was so valuable; now and then a banker would suggest to the Greystone family that they relocate it to the west of town, where the other factories and warehouses took advantage of cheaper land. But the ice house, eyesore that it was, remained beside the Greystone mansion, which was remodeled and refurbished with as much care by successive generations as the ice house had received neglect.

Miriam herself had developed a fondness for the building because Cody took her there. He would show her a few of the underground rooms—most of the ice house was underground, to keep the ice from melting—but some of the doors were chained or padlocked and the stairways didn't look safe, and it had become boring to survey floor after floor of nothing but chunks of ice. Now, as they walked in, Miriam smelled the familiar blue odor of frozen water and shivered with the first blast of freezing temperatures, so welcome after the summer heat.

Cody peeled the front of his shirt away from his chest and fanned it back and forth several times while Miriam raised her face to help the perspiration evaporate. They threaded their way around the huge cubes, which were wrapped in burlap and salt, to a small cubbyhole in the back. Cody pulled off his shirt and sat in the sawdust, pressing his forehead against the edge of a block. Miriam seated herself beside him, arranging her flowered skirt around herself like a garden, hoping Cody would notice how nice it was. His bare skin excited her; she couldn't imagine how he could stand being shirtless for more than a couple minutes, for it really was cold in the ice house. But she loved to look at his chest; there were hairs on it and it looked so manly. She thought of the muscles of the colored men and blushed again.

Cody rummaged in his secret hole in the wall and produced two bottles of beer. He opened them and handed one to Miriam, saluting her.

"To Yale," he toasted, then hesitated while Miriam took a little sip. She didn't much care for beer, but she drank it with him to cement the bond between them.

"Oh, Jesus. I hope I can still go." Cody rolled the bottle between his palms.

"Cody, don't worry. There's only been one refrigerator sold."

"There'll be more." He hefted his beer to his lips and savagely swallowed.

"We'll never buy one," Miriam promised. "I'll move out if they buy one."

"You're a peach." Cody put his arm around her and kissed her cheek. She smelled his beery breath. His lips traveled down the side of her face to her neck, and she gave a little gasp. She began to feel hot, despite the fact that she was shivering from the cold; hot especially between her thighs, where she had allowed Cody because she knew he loved her.

Awkwardly, she shifted. "Cody, not here. Not now," she begged.

"But I love you, Miriam. I really do."

Outside, cicadas buzzed in the heat; the air was frigid in the ice house, the cold seeping through Miriam's dress, soon to make its way into her skin, her bones. She let him push her onto her back, let his hands steal inside her dress. Oh, cripes, what was going to happen when he moved to wherever Yale was? What if someone found out that she'd ruined herself for him?

What if he didn't come back for her?

"Cody, hold me," she whispered, putting her arms around him. "I'm so cold."

"God, I'm on fire," he replied, opening his shorts. "Feel me, Miriam. I'm burning up."

He thrust inside her; she made the proper motions, though she was consumed, as she always was, by guilt and fear. Only wops and micks got pregnant without being married; and colored girls, too—that's what her father said. "A girl's purity is the best gift she can give her husband on their wedding night," her mother had lectured when Miriam began to date Cody exclusively. Miriam had agreed; and now here she was, writhing on the floor of the ice house like a colored girl, her purity long ago bestowed on Cody Montague.

"Oh, Miriam, Miriam," he moaned. For a moment she imagined he was saying, "Yale, Yale," as if he were thinking of another girl while making love to Miriam. It occurred to her—not for the first time—that if he got her pregnant, he would have to stay, and she moved her hips to encourage him to go deeper. Then, frightened by the lurking thought that he might not stay even then, she pulled back—not for the first time—and hid her tears against his sweaty chest.

Then he was finished, and he fell against her. Tenderness washed over her and she played with his hair, one ear cocked for the sound of intruders. It was after five, and the ice house was closed.

"The last summer," Cody said, sighing. "The last summer I'll ever spend in the rotting hellhole that is my childhood home."

"Oh." Miriam swallowed hard.

"Master Cody!" It was Brigid, the Irish maid.

"Oh, damn. Supper." Cody pulled out of her and picked up his beer. The back of Miriam's dress was caked with sawdust. She sat up and pulled down her skirt, brushing the lovely floral print as she rose unsteadily to her feet. Something warm trickled down her thigh and a yeasty odor like beer filled the air.

"Oh, cripes, Miriam, better clean up," Cody said. "You smell like . . . me."

She hesitated. There was nothing to wipe herself off with except Cody's shirt, and he would have to wear that.

They looked at each other. He took another pull on his beer and said, "Sit on some ice."

She gaped at him. He chuckled.

"Just kind of, you know, rub back and forth."

Miriam drew herself up. "Cody, I can't do a thing like that. I'm not a—a—girl like that."

But he looked at her with his bright blue eyes, and she did it while he watched. Then she finished dressing and let him brush the sawdust and straw off her, did the same for him, and left to go to home, filled with misery and love, hopelessness and hope.

She stood in the doorway of the ice house and watched him walk the short distance to his family's immense Victorian house. A pleasant daydream wafted through her mind of arranging flowers in all the lovely china vases throughout the house, as Cody's elderly mother did. Of having the Literary Society over for tea, of being among the premiere ladies of Greystone Bay, as Greystone wives always were.

Like Miriam, Mrs. Montague adored Cody. He was her youngest, and she'd had him when most other women were dandling their grandchildren on their knees. She, too, had wept when Cody announced his plans to go to Yale, and consented only when Mr. Montague said, in his low, gruff voice, "Let the boy go. At least one of us will get to do what he wants. Three's enough for the ice house."

"Damn you, Mr. Montague," Miriam said fiercely; and then, because she felt more miserable and guiltier than before, she took her time walking down the hill and across Port Boulevard to the small, cramped house that was her home. And thus it was that she was one of the last to hear that Cody's father and brothers had gone into the ice house almost as soon as she had left it, and there they had all died.

At the funeral, Miriam sat behind Cody and his mother, mumbling words she dimly knew were prayers. Her throat ached so bad she couldn't swallow. She was boiling in her black dress; it was so hot she thought she might faint. Perspiration dripped down the tip of her nose, mingled with her tears.

His three strapping brothers. His father. Some kind of accident no one could explain; the doctor vague, not able to tell poor Cody how it had happened. His father and Albert scalded by steam, Kenneth and Gerald bruised and broken as if they had fallen.

Or been thrown, the gossips were saying, and Miriam gave a choked cry of shame, because mixed with her unhappiness for Cody was the thought that she had damned Mr. Montague and now he was dead.

And now there was no one but Cody to run the family business.

Miriam went with her parents to the reception. It was awful to see the black wreath on the door, the big brass bell hanging in the middle. The beautiful, red flocked wallpaper was swathed in black crepe; the mirrors were covered.

Cody was dressed in black with a black armband around his biceps; his mother hunched small and grey in a black dress and veil. It was stifling in the parlor, where food and punch sagged on a cherrywood table. Miriam didn't know how everyone could move through the heat, it was so thick and steamy.

She knew she couldn't stay long; she drew Cody aside and said, "I'll come back at midnight. I'll throw rocks at your window." And then she stood on tiptoe and kissed his brown cheek, not caring who saw her.

"I'm still going," he said, as if she'd asked. "This damn town isn't going to stop me."

"Miriam," her mother said behind her. "I think we should leave now. Mrs. Montague needs to rest."

Miriam returned exactly as she had promised, creeping up the walkway. The house blazed with lights, and when she began to tiptoe across the vast expanse of lawn toward Cody's window, Mrs. Montague opened the door and appeared on the threshold.

"Miriam," she whispered. "Miriam, come here."

"Oh." Miriam put her hand to her mouth. "Mrs. Montague. I—I—"

"Miriam, he must do his duty." Mrs. Montague held a small leather book in her hands, which she held out to Miriam. Miriam thought it was a Bible, and took it.

"He says he doesn't believe me. But I know he does, deep down. He's afraid, and rightly so. But Miriam, we have to do it."

"Mrs. Montague?" Miriam asked, looking down at the book.

"Mother!" Cody bellowed from inside the house.

"He's drunk," Mrs. Montague said. "There's a puddle of whiskey on my Aubusson. . . ." She stopped speaking and began to cry. "He was my darling. He was so much younger. I had such hopes."

Crying harder, she gripped Miriam's wrist in a surprisingly strong grip and pulled her into the house.

"Help me, Miriam. Everything depends on us. We both love him."

"Cody?" Miriam called.

Mrs. Montague urged her to sit on the oyster-colored satin couch Miriam loved so much and pointed to the book.

"Read that. And then help me get him to the ice house."

Bewildered, Miriam frowned. Then she opened the book:

THE CONFESSION OF WINSTON ANDREWS GREYSTONE,
AS WRIT ON HIS DEATHBED

Greystone Bay, in the Year of Our Lord, 1723

Oh, my sons, those of you who yet remain upon this earth, this is the last writing of a father who loved you more than you can ever credit. Breath never stirred within a breast more adoring, more careful of your good fortunes. And yet, it is my bitter task to vouchsafe to you the secrets of our house and the charge I must lay at your feet, which I do with the agony of the condemned, as I know myself to be. Forgive me, you who sprang from my loins, as I pray your own sons may one day forgive you.

It is summer now, hotter than ever I can recall, as I take pen to hand, though it be the winter of my life; a winter, I confess, that covers my very heart and mind with frozen dread. A winter that appalls me with its terrible consequence. It be an end I deserve, though now as I look o'er the bay that bears my name and that I love more than even I once loved her, *as I look upon the sparkling beauty of the waves cresting with gold and the rocks, so often grey but now glittering with silver—oh, my sons, I cannot credit what I did. What acts I committed, in the name of love—and what a love I owned, what a hideous mask I put on and took off, and watched another bear my sins—*

watched. *I cannot believe; yet mine unbelief, like all else about me, is false.*

My fear has altered my mind, which I am aware ye have noted in the long months since your return from your wanderings abroad. How loath I was to call you back, but my time grows short and I have such terror that you will not believe my spoken words, that I have resolved to set down my story for you to read this very night. I shall call you in and bid you read while I watch you silently, praying that you shall credit this tale as more than the ravings of a dying old man.

Gods, it is so hot. I feel the very heat of hell seeping into this chamber. Alack, to die in summer, that most dangerous of seasons! Fate's hand has a helper, I assure you. Do not help further with the destruction of not only my own soul, but your own and that of every member of our village. . . .

Ah, my sons. I grow so weary. My mind travels back to simpler days. When we landed here, not twoscore years ago. I hold in my mind the face of our captain, Brian Fletcher, who did not fathom our secret until the very day we cleared the fog. (A pun, my boys, which you may take as such.) How amazed he was by us, and how frightened. He thought we meant to kill him if he did not join us. And yet, he has been happy. He took Jacob Plummer's sister to wife and yes, those are his children ye have played with. But this you knew. My command of myself weakens; I muse like the old man I be.

Repent! Find a way to free the House of Greystone! Ay, me, what a misery I have brought upon ye!

You cannot know what it was like then, to be free, and unknown, to live among ourselves with no fear that men like James and William would scourge and murder us. James, and his Bible, so badly writ into English by priests slavish to his power, who knew how he hated our kind and so lied in their Holy Book about us. James. I pray he is burning in hell as I write this.

But for me, for me, the hope of not burning. The hope of salvation. Oh, my sons, you must believe. I shall make you believe. When you are finished with your father's last words, you must look in the cellar of this house, and then you will have no choice but to believe.

But I tire. I must not die before you read this. I must tarry yet a while, or all is lost.

She came to us in summer, in the Year of Our Lord 1692. I was on watch that night; I stood on the roof of this very house. The small room where now you watch was not built then.

I surveyed with pleasure my domain; summers were pleasant then, and we had but lately celebrated Midsummer's Eve. Our Maypole still stood in the center of town, festooned with flowers and ribbons and garlands. Houses were freshly painted, roofs mended, fresh straw lay in the barns. It were a lovely place then, my Greystone Bay, my own, and I was well satisfied with it.

By the moon, I saw Harris Croome on the beach below. He paced; his child was due that night and he was filled with anxiety. I had offered to put someone in his place; but the man, who was most pompous, drew himself up like a courtier and said, "Zounds, Greystone, I'm not an old woman! I shall do my duty like a man."

So there he paced, pretending he did not—I could scarce keep my laughter from the air. I settled upon the roof with a pasty and a pint, crossing my legs as ye have oft seen me do, and watched the water.

How I loved that task, guarding the waters of our little inlet. I observed with unflagging delight the crashing waves upon the beach, black and white like the clothes we wore then, our Godly garb, our disguises. I recall my observation that the water was likewise a disguise upon which enemies might creep, or swim to harm us; but those depths were our friends—had I not made them so? Had I not allies that skittered and danced with fishes and sea dragons? So sure of all was I! So filled with the pride that has now destroyed my house!

Gods, how cold a shudder runs through me now. My hand shakes. I must hold or ye shall never read this, never know. Of what was I writing? My mind. My heart. My sons. Oh, my beloved sons.

She came to us in summer.

Croome saw her before I did; it was the wave of his hand and not the moon-flushed bark that caught my attention. My tankard halfway to my lips, I stared out to sea, and saw the three-masted vessel. Her sails were filled with mist, cat's-paw-soft and grey like a kitten, but fatal as a wild beast. Shrouds of fog rolled over our hills, as if the bark had shot a cannonade of grey at us.

The moon moved behind clouds, and the ship was obscured for a moment by trailing ether. Behind and below my watchtower, my people stirred. The first to appear was my own wife, my beautiful Gabriella; altered by the fog, other women emerged from their houses, skirting round my darling with naught but unhappy looks for her. Soon they were joined by their men. They stood in the wet night, wiping perspiration from their foreheads as they squinted into the gathering mists.

Then Gabriella, whose jet hair and belladonna eyes bespoke her Venetian heritage, peered up at me and shook her head.

" 'Tis a pity, caro mio,*" she said.*

In reply, I nodded. I felt the sorrow of it myself, but there was nothing else to be done. I could not permit strangers to land; the safety of my folk was my charge. That of those on the ship was not. With a heavy heart, I pointed to my lieutenants, who had already passed torches among themselves in preparation for signalling the ship not to shore, but to the treacherous rocks on the western end of the bay.

Gabriella sat on the stoop of our house. Her back bowed with the weight of the sin, but the sight of her dejection served to strengthen my resolve. She had suffered much: that gentle back crossed with thick white scars, the brand on her forehead forever red and ugly. To my disappointment, my colonists still had not accepted her. I grew angry as I thought back to the day I had brought her to our safe house in Cornwall. How she trembled in her mud-caked traveling clothes, exhausted, while the women barred the door.

"Gypsy!" spat Old Woman Lorcaster.

"Foreigner!" Mistress Adams flung at Gabriella, who raised her chin and walked toward the door.

"Wait," I ordered her, and Gabriella obeyed. I strode past her, furious.

"I am ashamed! I cannot credit the depths of my astonishment! You act like the very people you despise! Shall we drag her to the hanging tree, then, or burn her as they do on the continent? Do you know she was half-dead when I rescued her from her village? Do you think she would ever betray you?"

And so I bullied and harried them into allowing her into our company, but they never warmed to her. They did not see the sense of a foreign woman, they told me, when any of the maids among us would be honored to be my wife. Indeed, I saw grave heartsickness on some of the comeliest faces in our band, but I was steadfast. I had taken Gabriella to wife, and I would bring her to our colony in the New World to bear my children and brighten my soul.

This they permitted me, grudgingly. But on that summer night a score of years and odd months ago, they set to work with an eagerness that hurt my spirit, confounding the fog-laden ship with misplaced beacons, knowing the fate of those aboard to be sure death. It were a pity, as my lady asserted, but it could not be helped. As for myself, I would swim to the side of that unfortunate ship and toss each of her occupants overboard before I would risk harm to me and mine. No man, no woman, no dog could know of the existence of Greystone Bay.

The ship approached; the fog thickened. Gabriella dropped her hands to her lap and gazed at me. I fought against looking into her huge, dark eyes; for, once lost inside them, there was nothing I would not do for her. I looked instead to the foundering of the ship, saw the perplexity in the sails. My heart sank as the ship surely would; then, as if Gabriella had touched my chin and pulled my head around to face her, I swam into the gaze of my wife, and drowned there. For as the fog swirled about me, I found himself doing that which I planned not to do, something I knew to be wrong; but there was to it a contrary feeling of rightness, and relief. I began life as a gentle man; my care perpetually was for my flock. But Gabriella, my exquisite love, was the supplicant for wider care. For mercy.

I cleared my throat and said, "Put the torches right. Make haste, so they have time to take a proper tack."

All looked surprised, and even angry. While the men obeyed, the women murmured among themselves. The ship took shape behind the veils that lifted from the moon, and from Greystone Bay. I knew the village grew clear to those aboard the ship, as the ship did to those who watched along the shoreline. A great weight descended upon me, not lightened by the look of joy on Gabriella's face. She was *an outsider, I thought uncharitably. She didn't know how it was.*

But she did, poor darling. I knew that she did.

The ship drew nearer. White faces grew visible; a voice cried, "Ahoy!" and I answered back.

"Welcome! Follow our torches. We'll guide you in."

For a moment I had the thought to extinguish the lights and call for muskets, but Gabriella's gaze held me. Within an hour, the ship dropped anchor. Rowboats were lowered from her side and figures climbed down into them.

I went down to the water's edge, I alone. The rest of my folk hung back, even Gabriella, chary and shy.

The waves brought three boats to us. The first touched the beach; two rough men, sailors by the looks of them, jumped out and dragged the prow into the sand. A gentleman then stood and doffed his hat.

"I'm Captain van Haarlem," he said in thickly accented English. "Prithee, may we come ashore?"

It seemed an odd request, for obviously the boat was ashore already. But before he could answer, a figure wrapped in a grey cloak rose from the stern and stood poised as if waiting for consent to move.

"Indeed," I said, and the cloak fell to the floor of the boat, revealing the fairest young girl ever I had seen. It was as if she were fashioned of marble, of crystal; she was as white as the crests of the waves. Her

hair captured the merest tint of gold from the moonbeams. Her maidenly gown was alabaster. She glowed with whiteness, and when she smiled diffidently at the assembled company, my heart leaped within my breast.

I fell to one knee. "Mistress," I said, "welcome."

She made as if to curtsy, then held her hands out as if she desired me to help her out.

"Please, sir, has another boat been by?" she asked. Her voice was musical; her sentence was a melody, each word a note.

"Another ship?" I echoed dumbly.

She cast an anxious glance at the captain. "Aye, me." She covered her mouth with her hands; above her fingers, her eyes glistened.

"Perhaps he shall come after," the captain said; and at his words, the girl cried out and collapsed.

One of the sailors caught her as she fell. The captain shook his head and said, "He's been missing these five months now."

"Who, her husband?" Gabriella asked.

The captain opened his mouth, but it was the girl who spoke. "Yes," she murmured, fast in the arms of the sailor. "My poor husband!" Then she fainted again.

"Take her into our house," Gabriella directed the sailors. "And come ye, also, captain."

Our soft summer waxed into a raging, feverish season. Overnight, the temperatures rose to unbearable levels and we were eager for the strangers to be gone, so that we might reduce our clothing to that more accustomed by us. The girl lay in a stupor for five days, which grew hotter in succession, she thrashing and calling for water, complaining of the heat, the awful heat; then calling for someone whose name no one could decipher. Captain van Haarlem told us all he knew of her. She was Goodwife Elizabeth Hever, and she was sixteen. She was from a small village in Massachusetts; she had hired his ship in Boston, explaining that she was to meet a man named John Proctor in a hamlet down the coast. Then, once there, she received intelligence that he had gone on to Greystone Bay and that he was in grave danger there. That unless she came posthaste, he would be hanged.

"Told me exactly how to find ye," the captain told Winston. "Longitude and latitude. I knew ye were there in that fog. I was never afeared."

This information troubled me greatly, and I meant to call a meeting to disclose it to my men. But something stayed me, some sense that I must not alarm them, and I uneasily kept silent. I told no one, not even Gabriella, from whom I had hidden nothing since the day I had rescued her in Venice. What man knew of Greystone Bay? And why had he planned to come here?

"I was given to think the man we sought was her brother, not her husband," he said, which confused me more. And what, I pondered, had she been doing on such a tender night wrapped in a woolen cloak?

After three days, the captain left with his ship, and we were left with the girl. The doctor came and bled her, and spoke his concern over the temperature of her skin.

"Most hot," he grumbled. "She is burning with fever. You must apply cold cloths upon her forehead and extremities. Day and night, she must be kept as cool as possible."

"What? In this heat?" Gabriella demanded, but the doctor, who did not like my wife, ignored her and looked to our two servant girls.

"Day and night," he repeated, and took his leave.

And so they toiled, the three females, over the young girl. As was fitting, I remained aloof, inquiring at intervals about her condition. At the first, all three expressed their concern and their interest over the comely patient, but I noticed after an interval of days that my wife became most reticent on the subject, responding to my queries with hesitant, vague replies and cast down gazes.

When we were alone in our own room, I quizzed Gabriella on the meaning of such behavior and she paused before answering me.

"When I tend her, I have such a feeling about her. I am uneasy in

the room alone with her. Yesterday I turned my back to her and I felt such a chill, bello mio. *And I thought I heard her laugh. But when I turned around, she was asleep."*

I was moved to share my secret, but unaccountably held back. "And what do Birgit and Hester feel?"

She shrugged her shoulders. "They are pleased to sit with her. They pity her and care for her as if she were a sister. But caro, *I have such misgivings—"*

" 'Tis nothing. You are cautious for the sake of all of us, which is good. We cannot have strangers among us. You know that."

"As I am a stranger?" she blurted with unaccustomed bitterness. "Am I forever to be friendless and suspected?"

"Why, wife," I asked, "has something happened? Was someone unkind to you?"

"Is anyone ever kind to me?" She rose from our bed and walked to the window. The black night parted and the moon glowed upon her hair; my black beauty, I called her. She was too lovely for this world. The portrait that hangs in the main hall— Ah, but I lose myself. The portrait was taken down many years ago. I could not stand to look at it.

No, faith, that's not so. It was she who . . .

"Cara mia," *I urged, "tell me who it is has been cruel with thee."*

"Oh, Winston, if I told you all of the times . . ." She sighed and sat upon the windowsill. "I wonder, often, if I was wise to come with you. If I should have made a life elsewhere." Her eyes glistened with tears.

"How can you say that? You are my life. Without you, I should never have governed this colony. You are my heart, my compassion."

"I wish I had let you dash that ship upon the rocks!" she cried wretchedly.

"Is it the maid? Has she been in some wise unfair?" I could scarce credit such an idea, for Goodwife Hever had done naught but languish in bed, twisting and turning. Gabriella shut her mouth and looked again to sea.

"Can you make the pixies come for me, and take me to a place where I have friends?" she asked in a soft, mournful voice.

I rose from the bed and took her in my arms. She smelled of almonds and roses, my lovely, dark wife, and I pressed her tightly and held her for many minutes.

"Gabriella, I am your friend, and shall always be."

She said nothing for a long time. We stood together, watching the great waves blacken the beach. "Ah, Winston, hold me." And I did.

After, when she slept, I got out of bed and crept into the room where our odd guest lay as one dying, her poor, white face a mask of death above the coverings. I surveyed her skin, the pale golden color of her hair, jumbled over her shoulders like the sea kelp. I confess I watched the soft rise and fall of her breasts, and found myself breathing in her rhythm. In the hot, darkened room, it seemed she looked upon me with powerful eyes, as if she spoke. And I spoke in reply, with words, asking, "Who art thou, wondrous, sleeping lady? Hast come to harm us?" As I stood there, worries pressed me down; and those of Gabriella likewise, for I felt with a deep surety that something, indeed, was wrong with the young lady. For the space of a few seconds—a few seconds only—I had the violent urge to lift her from her sickbed and fling her into the sea. Yet I said nothing.

Did nothing.

The summer heat grew.

And with that heat, mine own uneasiness. For a fortnight I continued my clandestine visitations to her bower; I watched over her as a lover might. I guarded her in much the same way I guarded Greystone Bay, with a jealousy and a single-mindedness that perplexed me. I began to realize I was protecting her. That confounded me even more.

My wife detected much alteration in me. She chided me for watching the sleeping girl, saying it was not a decent thing. I sensed the increase of her uneasiness; I saw her shadow beneath the door as I sat with Goody Hever.

And one night, near midnight, the girl opened her eyes and whispered my name. I was so startled I rose from my chair.

"Winston," she said softly, "my throat is hot."

I reached for the ladle and trickled water carefully into her mouth. Most of it slid down her cheek. She smiled and said, "You must lift my head."

I was shy to touch her, I knew not why. I thought to call for a servant, but she licked her lips with thirst. With care, I slid my hand beneath her neck and cradled her head in my open palm.

And I smelled fire, the scent of burning branches. I felt fire; she was burning as if from within. The flesh of my hand stung. When I gasped aloud, she raised a shaking hand and touched my wrist. It pained me so, I spilled the water.

"Yes," she whispered, and her word was like a hiss. "You must be brave. I know how it is with you and your folk, Winston Greystone. Believe me."

"Do you?" I asked carefully, my heart pounding with fear. For if she did, then others must, and we were in peril.

"I shall protect you. I shall save you. You see, I have . . ." She closed her mouth. "I am weary. I speak too much."

"I shall fetch the doctor," I said.

She touched me again with her hot fingers. "No." The fingers trailed down my arm; I stared at their path. Surely she was not . . . caressing me? "He can do nothing about it." She pressed a finger against my mouth. "No one can." Her lips pulled back in a strange little smile.

How does a maid make a man fall in love with her? How does her scent intoxicate him? How does she bestir him without a glance, a word? In other nations, and other villages they say that she has bewitched him. I, of course, deemed this nonsense. Who better than I to know what was witchcraft, and what wasn't? My pride, my grievous pride. But that was not the greatest of my sins.

I should confess it in every detail, I know. I should tell of each lecherous glance, each caress, each lie. But my time grows short; suffice to say we became lovers. She would open her gown and await me, and I would come and kiss her neck, her shoulders, those full, high breasts. . . .

Even now, I rise with desire. I think to go down to her. I think to stop it. I think of madness. I think of evil.

At first I was careful of Gabriella's feelings. I stole in the dark into the room where my sweet girl lay, dreading the few muffled noises I made, covering her mouth when she moaned with pleasure. But slowly my care translated into purest contempt. How could I have ever loved Gabriella? No one else did. Not one woman had befriended her. Not a single young boy left herbs and flowers at her door, as others did for other wives and girls in Greystone Bay. I had thought her beautiful, but it was a voluptuousness of the commonest kind. Whereas my young lady, my love, was a goddess. Oh, and a fiery one, too. No man has ever had such a flame in his bed.

Flames . . .

It were vile enough, if this were my only sin. But as my desire for the girl grew, so did my desire to cast Gabriella aside and instate Elizabeth as my wife. Yet how could I do so honorably? I had forbidden the sundering of marriage in Greystone Bay, so that we might bear many children and flourish without rancor. How could I, the ruler of the town, break my own code?

Besides, I believed that Elizabeth had a husband, one who was searching for her. "I mispoke myself," she assured me. "It is my brother seeks me." But I guessed that it was not, and told her so.

"He is only my lover, and he would not mind." She laughed at my expression and touched me with her burning fingers. "I promise you, he would be pleased to know I had found true love."

And then she rose from bed and begged sweetly to be let out, and I walked through the town with her on my arm while my Gabriella sat in the window of our room, watching the water that separated us from England and the Continent. My wife neither stitched, nor knitted, nor read, as had been her pleasure. And I cared not.

For the villagers loved Elizabeth! To a man, to a boy, to a lass, they came out of their houses to comment on her health, and how glad they were that she was rescued. And I thought this very pretty, but dissembling. For I had resumed the ceaseless vigil on our shores, and all had aided me in that effort, thus affirming our mutual conviction that we must protect ourself from strangers. And yet, as I walked her daily through the streets of our place, venturing up the hills and, briefly, to the marshes, I came to see that my folk felt genuine love for her, and I was amazed.

"Do you see how it is, Winston?" she said as we walked. Her arm through mine near scalded me; I smelled smoke in the air. I started and stared at her, and she laughed. "I mean to make you a king."

"To them, I am a king," I replied with no false modesty.

"But Greystone Bay is such a small place. The kingdom I speak of is far larger." She laughed again, throwing back her head, and she gave such a look, a smoldering glance, that it was all I could do, in the middle of the street, before the eyes of my people, to refrain from kissing her. Nay, from taking her, then and there, from flinging her down and joining my flesh with hers. Somehow, I know not how, I restrained myself, and she seemed to know it, for she laughed again.

I was much shaken by the time we returned to my house. She stopped walking and turned to face me, saying, "You know what you must do, Winston. Your kingdom awaits and I mean to give it to you."

"You cannot speak to me of these things," I said, but my heart ached as she took her leave and wandered to the back of the house.

I followed her and saw not Elizabeth, but Gabriella, weeping on her knees in our garden. She had been picking summer daisies; they were strewn around her and her basket overturned. She searched blindly for them, moaning, and as I watched her, a seeping cold pervaded my bones. My heart shuddered in my chest—I thought I would die from its convulsing. I shivered; my flesh raised on my arms. In the worst heat of summer, I suffered as a man in a blizzard as I watched my wife in her agonies.

When my fit was over, it was as if I had awakened from a nightmare. What had I been doing? I beheld my dear wife, whom I loved more dearly than anything in the world, awash in the misery I had caused her. With great shame and contrition, I lifted her up.

"Cara mia, bellissima," *I said, striving to cheer her. "My darling, why do you weep so?"*

"I want to go home." She pulled away from me and buried her face in her hands. "I want to go home."

"This is your home."

"Nay, nay! Send me home."

"In that other place, death awaits you," I rejoined.

"Death awaits us wherever we go," she said. "And ofttimes, it is preferable to life."

You cannot know then the shame that consumed me, as all-powerful as the lust that had blinded me to the virtues of my beloved life companion. I took her hand and said, "She shall leave, Gabriella. I swear to you that by the next full moon, she shall be gone."

The joy reappeared on her face. She fell on me, kissing me. Her black hair entwined in my fingers and I kissed each black strand, each curl. My Gabriella! My dark love. My own.

"I swear to you," I said again, and I meant it. And I would have done, would have sent Elizabeth away, but Fate conspired against me.

For, two days later, the most evil man I know—second only to myself—arrived unbidden on our shores in the late, clear breeze of a summer's morn. His name was James Strand, from Massachusetts, and he was the First Lieutenant of the Witchfinder General.

Strand was a pale man of extraordinary height, gaunt as William Everson, and possessed of the darkest, coldest eyes ever I have seen. You can imagine how afrighted we were that a second ship had discovered us, but when I learned his reason in approaching us, my horror became too great to hide. For he sought to capture an accused woman, one Abigail Williams, escaped from Salem, and take her back "to justice."

"Be she a fair maid?" asked Master Lorcaster. And I stared at him with terror.

"Ay, passing fair," the Witchfinder said. "Not of great stature, with golden hair." He continued for some time in his description, and of course we all knew who it was he sought.

My spirit plummeted to my boots. I thought of Elizabeth—or was her true name Abigail?—in her room in my house, yet ignorant that I had resolved to send her away. She was dreaming her dreams, mayhap, of a life with me; and I realized with a rush of pain that I loved her still. I adored her. I wondered if, after all, I could have made her go.

But not with this man, surely. I raised my chin and said, "There be none among us we do not know, sir," and with a glance dared my people to proclaim otherwise. No one played me false, not even Gabriella, who looked at me with love and sorrow. Again shame replaced passion within me and I thought, How good she is, that she protects the girl. Though she has cause to be rid of her, yet she will not deliver her to this witch-hunter.

The man looked puzzled. He took from his pocket a piece of paper and read it to himself, then looked at me. "I have the sworn statement of a sea captain that he delivered a maid to your village not a month ago. She fits the description of my lost wanton perfectly."

My folk looked to me.

"Ah, that one. It be ill to speak of the dead," I said. "She died soon after he left her here." Some of my folk nodded, to assert the truth of this.

"I should like to see her grave, then," the man said, "as I have brought my Bible and must exorcise the ground where she lies."

I hesitated, caught in my lie. I thought desperately of the state of our little kirkyard. It was most carefully tended, with stones upon each mound, and none unnamed. Then it occurred to me that of course the outer world would not bury a witch in hallowed ground, and so I said, "We did not provide a grave for her, sir. We threw her in the marsh, just beyond that hill."

The man nodded. "A wise action. Otherwise, she should have polluted those in your company who rest in the bosom of the Lord. Well then, I will speak my words over your marsh. But first, Mistress," he said, looking at Gabriella, "may I refresh myself at your home? My voyage has been long, and I am tired and hungry."

Gabriella sank into a low curtsy. Like the others, she was shaking and fought to hide it. "Of course, milord," she murmured, and I did not like his look as she did so. His eyes narrowed and he made a thin line of his lips, and cocked his head as men do when reflecting.

Gabriella led him to our house while I hastily conferred with my people.

"What if he discovers her?" Mistress Adams demanded.

"What if he discovers us*?" Mistress Lorcaster said. "He is a finder of—"*

"Do not be alarmed. This man's work is based on superstition. He will be unable to see the truth. We are safe."

"I know men like this. They are not appeased until they uncover evil," Harris Croome said unhappily. "What they perceive as evil."

"He shall be satisfied with his little rituals at the marsh. And then he shall leave us alone."

"How haps it that so many come to our shore? It were a bad thing. A grievous, bad thing," said old Dame Alice Tanner.

"He shall soon leave," I promised.

But he did not. He supped with Gabriella and me, then sat back in his chair while I smoked my pipe and said, "Your village is uneasy, Mr. Greystone. Do you have trouble I might help with?"

Gabriella licked her lips and summoned the serving girl. "Pour our guest more cider," she said, and the poor girl was so overset by the man's presence she spilled the majority on the table.

The man regarded the spreading stain. "Most uneasy."

"We are unaccustomed to strangers," I explained. "Our place here is isolated, by intention. To have visitors twice in one summer alarms us, though—"

"Are you saying, sir, that I am unwelcome?"

"Not at all," I said quickly. "A man like you is, of course, most welcome. I am only sorry we did not detect the . . . presence of evil . . . while this Abigail still lived. Then perhaps we could have helped her to cast out the Devil and find everlasting peace in heaven."

Gabriella swallowed hard. I bade her, with my eyes, to keep silent, though I knew how offensive my words were to her.

The man nodded, all the while watching Gabriella. "Aye. It were a pity." He dabbed his mouth with the edge of the cloth and made as if to rise.

"Might I stay the night? I am weary, and my work requires much strength."

"Oh!" Gabriella cried, then recovered herself. "You have robbed me of the opportunity to prove myself a good hostess, Mr. Strand, by asking before I could offer. Please let me show you to a room."

"Allow me to assist you," I said, rising from my chair, but Gabriella stayed me with her hand.

"It is my duty." She looked at me long and hard. Oh, no, I thought. She means to betray Elizabeth.

But she did not. I heard her mount the stair and say, "The room at the end of this hall is our best." That was not the room where Elizabeth lived.

But the sound of his boots stopped just above my head, in front of the door where she did live!

"Merciful heavens, this room's on fire!" he shouted.

I ran up the stairs in time to see him open the door. A blast of hot air burst forth, and we all three stepped back. Then I rushed past Mr. Strand and ran inside the room.

It was as hot as if it were aflame; and Gabriella gave a cry when she touched the jamb as she swept in. The wood burned her; she held her palm out and said, "What can it be, Winston?" Then, not thinking, she pressed her sore hand to her forehead, thereby rearranging her hair so that her brand was visible.

And the Witch finder saw it. Sucking in his breath, he drew back and whispered, "Witch! Witch! You are discovered. Abigail, hast changed thy shape?"

"I am not Abigail!" Gabriella said, pulling her hair over the mark. "I was falsely accused, in Venice. I am no evil creature such as you seek!"

The Witch finder looked at me. " 'Tis truth," I said. "She were falsely accused. I was there. I witnessed her trial, in Venice."

The man shook his head. "If the charges proved false, then why the brand? You do me a grave misservice, sir, hiding this concubine of hell. You know what must be done."

"Nothing by you here, sir. I am ruler of these lands," I said.

"You are amiss in your command, then. And I have sworn to stamp out evil wherever I find it."

He grabbed Gabriella's wrist and began dragging her down the hall toward the stairs. "I shall expose her to the townspeople, as you have seen fit to hide the truth from them!"

I took Gabriella's other wrist and pulled her from him. Then I shielded her with my body. "You shall not harm her, sir! You have no jurisdiction here. If you do not desist, I shall be bound to stop you in any way I can."

The man's outrage burned in his eyes. "An' you touch me, sir; a committee of inquiry would appear on your shores. I have left instructions as to where exactly I am, and the reason for my mission. And furthermore, that if I am obstructed, others are to follow and investigate."

More intruders! I despaired. "Very well," I said, "I shall accompany you to the town square, where my people will explain all to you. That they know there is no evil in my wife, and that she is a good and a patient—"

"Winston, no!" Gabriella screamed. "They hate me!"

"And why is that?" Mr. Sounder asked with icy calm. "Because they know the foul corruption that you are?"

Oh, my sons, can you not guess the rest? Must I bare my entire sin? I let him take her. I did not rush ahead and command the people to be silent, to aid her. I did not command the men to arms. And why not? Why not?

Because I was detained. Because as I ran after them, the passageway filled with heat; I gasped and fell against the wall, which scalded my shoulder. And when my servants found me, they dragged me to my room and laid me on the bed.

"Can you not feel it? The heat! The fire!" I cried; and they said no. "The heat in her room?" No again. No one felt anything save the wretched heat of summer, and that they expected.

"Go to my wife," I begged. "He will take her to our jail and hurt her. You must speak in my name. You must protect her."

Why did I not rise from the bed? I felt as though I writhed in hell; the bed was a bed of coals. I was in agony. I suffered unimaginably. They felt nothing, and were free to go, but moved slowly, out of fear. Anyone in our town could be accused, and most bore brands or marks.

"Go, or I shall curse you forever!" I shouted, and at last they went.

And while they were gone, Elizabeth came to me. She appeared in a shimmering haze; her hair was on fire, and she laughed merrily.

"Blessed be," she said. "You shall soon enter your kingdom. It is being prepared for you, below."

"Save her and I shall go with you." I held out hands that felt charred to the bone. "I shall do whatever you wish."

"Aye, you shall." She sat down on the bed and stroked my face with fiery fingers. "You shall."

And then she took me, fiercely, and I cannot tell you of the pain that engulfed me. I thought I should die of it.

But then I entered a fearsome place, a cave whose walls were fire, whose floor was burning coals, and I heard the most beauteous music ever I have heard. When I heard these sounds, such happiness roared over me that I threw back my head and laughed. The space around me grew cool, and pleasant. I cannot describe the joy that flowered inside me.

"Relief from the worry," murmured a voice inside my head, and I knew it to be Elizabeth's. "Your people forever safe. Forever."

The great weight that had descended upon her arrival lifted. I was more carefree than when I was a child, innocent of suffering and persecution. A full measure of delight was mine, such as I had never tasted, in that cave of fire, with Elizabeth inside my soul.

And then I heard screaming, of the most agonized and pitiful kind, and I realized I was in the basement of mine own house. I ran through it, seeking the source of the cries, thinking it to be my love, my Elizabeth.

But she cried, "No! Winston, stop!" I faltered and the screams grew louder. And so I ran up the stairs, and through my house, ran to the edge of the hill—

—And looked down at the square, where the Maypole still stood, Gabriella tied to it, and faggots loaded about her feet. And my people, my own people, with blood in their eyes, shrieking, "Witch! Witch!" at her.

"No! Stop!" I screamed, and ran as fast as I could down the hill, but I moved as one in a dream; and I was too late.

Have you seen someone die like that, my sons? Worse, to see a woman you have loved die like that? Words fail—ah, my heart. My heart. Gabriella, my soul.

My own people. Those who yet survive and whom ye know. No one moved to save her. You must know that. All betrayed her. Every member of Greystone Bay Colony sinned against her.

I, most of all, for as I fell to my knees in horror, Elizabeth caught me up; and in that moment, she recaptured me. I found myself back inside the fiery chamber beneath my house.

And the first of you were born within the normal passage of time.

How did I move through those years? I know not. Truly bewitched, by a fiend I cannot explain. But I know that she took from me more of my soul every year; that she meant to make me a lieutenant of hell: When she came to us she sought the Devil, who had beckoned her to Greystone Bay. And not finding him—or did she?—she fashioned me in his image.

And when I die? What then?

I know only this: that I lived with her as one in heaven. No one loved more greatly than I. She was my passion, my life, my darling. I cannot describe the delirium I moved in, for all the years of your births, my sons. I was not my own man. No thoughts of the horror that occurred entered my mind. Indeed, I can now recall staring at a portrait of my Gabriella and wondering who she was; Elizabeth spirited the picture away and burned it in our basement chamber, where fires raged all day and all night.

For three years, I loved more greatly, I think, than any man has ever loved.

And then I was saved. I know not how—perhaps there is a divine Providence after all and not the world I had once believed in, I and my folk. But it was winter, and she always hated the winter, and wrapped herself in blankets and sat by the fire, enduring the season fearfully. She would not move from the house until all the snow was gone, and then with much trepidation. She came to us in summer; she lived for summer; she was summer.

And she loved you boys as I loved her, with the ferocity and devotion of maternal feelings. She told me how you would grow to inherit our kingdom; she never tired of holding you and singing to you and calling you her little demons. And everyone in our town loved you as well, as they loved her.

No one spoke of Gabriella.

And one day you, Bromley, grew tired of staying indoors all winter and contrived to steal away. You climbed down the tree that guarded your room and ran as fast as you could, onto the frozen lake.

And she saw you, as she saw all the things that happened in Greystone Bay, and ran after you, and the ice was too thin—

You were too little to understand; you sat down and began to cry, and that is how I found you when I came looking for you both.

Steam rose from the surface of the lake, which fast was melting. I grabbed you and looked into the gaping hole, and saw her.

She was encapsulated in a perfect square of ice, in all her beauty. Her eyes were open, but their life appeared extinguished. And when I looked on her, I was freed. I felt nothing but revulsion, and memories of Gabriella flooded into my brain. I was overcome with horror and desolation, and I plunged myself into the ice as well.

Steam rose around me; I burned as though set aflame, and then I shook horribly. I put my arms around her icy coffin, determined to put an end to myself, but I heard you crying.

"These are her babes, and must be killed, too," I thought. But fatherly love overcame me. I stared at Elizabeth and she stared back, and now I saw hatred in her eyes. She was alive—if ever she was alive—but powerless to affect me. And she hated me for being free of her.

I let go of her and swam to the surface, where I plucked you up and ran to our house. On the way, Mistress Lorcaster saw me and fell to wailing.

"What have we done? The evil we have done!" she cried.

I saw others, coming out of their houses, shaking their heads as though waking from a deep sleep. And they looked with horror at the charred Maypole in the center of the square, and a wild lamentation ascended the heavens, such as you have never heard.

"I have captured Elizabeth!" I told them. "Help me!"

Someone took you, Bromley, and threw a blanket over my shoulders. Then my men assembled with ropes and axes and we went to the lake and pulled her out.

"She must stay frozen," Davy O'Connel said.

"Ay, and we must guard her. We must take care she doesn't get out," said another.

After much deliberating, what we proposed was this: that we should build a tomb for her and fill it with ice, and put her into it. And that we must replenish it. And that each of you must be baptized in ice water, as you were, and no fault found with ye.

Then, because the most grievous fault lay with me, we determined that those of my line must guard her forever, until such time as we are clever enough to dispose of her in a more final way. For believe me, my sons, she lives within the ice. She lives! And now it falls to the eldest of ye, and then to the next, and the next, to prevent her escape.

Ah, my heart! I cannot die yet! I must speak to ye. My sons! My sons! I am so hot!

"My whole goddamned family's crazy," Cody said.

Miriam jumped. He was standing behind her with a glass of whiskey in his hand, and he threw it back in a single gulp while Miriam shut the book and laid it beside her.

"Cody, she's down there, and she's *melting,*" Mrs. Montague said, picking up the book and cradling it against her chest. "The summer's been so hot."

He laughed. "No problem, then. We'll stick her in one of those new refrigerators."

"Don't trifle with this!" she shouted, then hesitated. "Do you think we could?"

Miriam stood. She didn't know what to do. She was shocked that Mrs. Montague could believe such a thing. Then she reminded herself that the lady had just lost three sons and a husband—hysteria made sense.

"Oh, brother," Cody slurred, lurching across the room toward the whiskey decanter.

Miriam cleared her throat and said, "Why don't we go into the ice house and look, Cody? Then we can settle this."

He shook his head. "I'm not wandering around that place in the middle of the night."

Mrs. Montague began to cry.

"Cody, for your mother's sake. So you can prove to her there's nothing to worry about." Miriam held out her hands. "Please, Cody."

"Oh, all right." He pursed his lips and set down his glass. "I'm sorry, Mom. I know you're upset."

—And so we went into the ice house, and the first thing I noticed was the smell. It was an awful stench, of decay, and Miriam looked at me and said, "It's hot in here."

It was stifling. My mother screamed, "She's loose!" I was so drunk I could hardly stand up, but I motioned them to follow me down the stairs.

We seemed to descend forever, past walls of melting ice. The stairs were slick; there were puddles in the sawdust and our shoes got covered with mulch. The smell was unbelievable.

As you may have guessed, the locked doors hid the secret. Mom had the key; the padlock opened easily, and I was the first to step into the room.

How can I describe what I saw? The first thing I did was fall down. Just keeled over, I was so overwhelmed. Miriam screamed. Mom cried harder. I think I went into shock. That's how I rationalize what I did, anyway.

There must have been two hundred, no, three hundred separate blocks of ice in there. And each one held the corpse of some ancestor of ours. The Greystones, arranged like the bodies in an Italian catacomb—effigies frozen in repose. Men in Quaker-style outfits, ladies in bustles. The captured dead of centuries of Greystones, buried all those years beneath our obsolete ice house. The smell. They were melting.

The smell. The way they looked.

They moved.

And surrounded by a large steel cage in the back of the room, standing upright, there she *was.*

She was just as Winston Greystone described her, blonde and lovely, imprisoned in ice as the others were. Fire raged behind her, casting shadows of red and orange over her whiteness, sparking her eyes. She stared at us with her eyes blue, then red, then blue, then red.

I knew she was alive. She stared.

Miriam shouted, "The walls are burning!" and I saw that what I'd assumed was steam was smoke; the whole place had ignited. Steam and smoke—that's what the fog of Greystone Bay is, you know. That's why there's so much of it.

Flames shot above our heads and around us, the icy coffins dripped.

"They mustn't get out!" Mom yelled, grabbing me, and I tore my gaze away from the woman.

"Why not?"

With a sob, she flung herself away from me and ran to the opposite end of the room. She fell, got up, fell again. I thought she was dying.

"Darling! Darling!" she pleaded, bending over a block of ice. "Tell me what to do!"

"Oh, my God, Cody!" Miriam shouted. "It's your father!"

I heard them, but I didn't. Once more, I was staring at the woman in the ice. I couldn't help it. She smiled at me, and I heard her voice inside my head: Let me out, and I'll make everything all right. Images of Yale rushed through me like warm water. Of leaving Greystone Bay forever.

Leaving it to her.

I don't know why, or how. You've read Winston's confession and now you're reading mine.

But I knew I never wanted to leave her. The world was nothing compared to her. Yale a child's dream. She smiled as if she understood—but of course she did; my God, she understood everything. I'm sure she knows I'm dying. I'm sure she's planning something.

I kissed her. I pressed my lips against that block of ice and looked into her eyes. And when I did, I thought I'd been electrocuted. There was nothing in life like kissing Elizabeth.

The block of ice shattered. Shards cut into my hands and face, and I didn't care. I didn't feel them, though I was far from numb. I kissed her again, and again. Water rushed up to my knees, and the room filled with steam, and my heart exploded when she put her sopping arms around me and said, "You look so like John Proctor."

—and I fully understood when she looked at Miriam and said, "The others will take care of her. Lie with me now. Now."

—and Miriam's screams were nothing to me, nothing, as the townspeople went for her, yelling the old word over and over, which was both a word of murder and a chant of homage.

God help me, I loved Miriam in my young, callow way. And what they did to her—what I *did to her. What I did.*

What I have done.

But when you have Elizabeth, you don't care. You don't. Greystone Bay is paradise when she's with you.

And she's with us. I can't believe you don't remember her. But I'm grateful. Then, perhaps you won't be tempted, as I have been, to go down there again. To go down and—

O love, thy kiss would wake the dead.

She was summer. She came to us in summer.

And this is why you must never, my poor children, never ever, *close down the Greystone Bay ice rink.*

I hope she knows I'm dying. The hope of not burning. The hope of salvation.

She sought the devil in Greystone Bay. In summer.

—Greystone Bay, August 29, 1990

Ice House Pond

by Steve Rasnic Tem

I

"THAT POND IS MUCH BIGGER THAN IT IS," Rudy had said to the realtor the last time, the first time, he'd seen Ice House Pond. He would never be sure exactly where the perception came from: something about the way the great stretch of level ice—pewter-colored that late in the afternoon, highlighted with occasional painful stabs of silver—disappeared into blinding snow that rose in clouds he would have thought more typical of high altitudes, snow that expanded and exploded as if with an angry energy. It had been a silly thing to say, really, and he had felt a little embarrassed around this proper New Englander. But it had also been the perfect thing to say, and now, on his return trip to take over ownership of the pond and everything attached to it, Rudy was pleased to see that his original perception still held true. The pond *was* much bigger than it was.

And Rudy was in desperate need of just such a place. In the real world, in his old world, things surprised you: They seemed so pitifully small after you'd lived with them for a while.

"I can't honestly say that this is the perfect deal, you

understand," the realtor had said that first time. His name was Lorcaster, which, the fellow at the gas station where Rudy'd asked for directions was quick to point out, was one of the oldest names in the Bay. "Unless, of course, it's *exactly* what you're looking for." He didn't look like the scion of a great family. He had the belly, certainly, but none of the air. His clothes were a mismatch of pale greens and dark blues. And here he was, actively discouraging the sale and they hadn't even gotten to the place yet.

A small, wooded hill, more like a bump really, still obscured the property. The dirt road to the pond was so iced over they'd had to park on the narrow secondary that had brought them out of town, then walk a "short" jog cross-country. Lorcaster had supplied an extra coat and snowshoes. Although there was very little wind, it seemed much colder out here than in town. "It'll require some fixing up, no doubt about that. But if you're handy with tools—"

"I'm not," Rudy interrupted. "But I have a little money set aside." More than a little. The deaths of two families in ten years and the resulting insurance payoffs had seen to that. His father had believed in insurance, had insisted on it for himself and for Rudy's families, but Rudy would always wonder if he hadn't, literally, bought himself trouble. And now he was about to buy himself a new life with the death money, the pain money.

Lorcaster said nothing more about money for the rest of their walk. In fact, he seemed a bit uncomfortable that Rudy had brought up the subject in the first place.

"Just a few feet more," Lorcaster had puffed, trudging up the wooded rise, grabbing on to occasional nude trunks for support. "Watch your step, real slippery through here. You know, I'd hoped to be selling this place in the summertime. Beautiful out here in the summer." He paused at the top of the small hill, holding fast to a thick branch, and looked back down at Rudy, who still struggled. "You'll need to be getting a snowmobile, or a Cat."

Rudy stopped and looked around. The snow here was wet and heavy, not the fluff he was used to. And for the most part the snow surfaces were rough and icy. It was like a hardened white sludge that stuck to everything. The trees, instead of looking decorated with lace, seemed assaulted by the snow, encased in it as it froze. Not exactly pretty, but he would hardly call it ugly, either. Perhaps *uncompromising* was the word he wanted. "I don't know." Rudy grimaced from the cold. The temperature appeared to drop noticably each foot closer to the place. Rudy had never experienced such cold, but he was reluctant to tell Lorcaster that. "Maybe I'll want to stay put all winter."

Lorcaster stared at him appraisingly, as if at some questionable piece of property. "Maybe you will at that," he said after a while. "Anyplace you go, there's always some that stay to themselves, and don't mingle in town. Old Finney, the one that built the house and the ice house as well, they say he was like that. Well . . . speaking of . . . looks like we're there."

Rudy forced himself up the few remaining feet, chagrined that this fat old man was actually in better shape than he was.

He couldn't believe the increase in cold.

"Heating system's in good shape, or so they tell me. You'll *need* it."

The property was in an enormous saucer of land, edged by the small rise, with its trees, around two-thirds the circumference, and a short arc of hand-fitted stones along the remaining third. Beyond that wall were the far edges of the forest, and beyond that, farmland, although Lorcaster had made it clear that the closest farm was still some miles away. He could see the bright white, two-story house with the odd angles that so often characterized owner-built homes—unassuming but interesting—and connected to that was another large white building with a walkway around it, but with no windows, which Rudy assumed to be the ice house itself. The truly dramatic feature of the landscape was the pond, which extended in all directions beyond the buildings: Ice House Pond. From this angle, it seemed more like a lake than a pond, and it seemed to have its own movements, its own weather.

The air moving above the pond was whiter than the air surrounding it, and more active, with eddies and sudden swirls, transient movements of white and silver which disappeared as soon as Rudy thought he had found some pattern. Now he knew where the intense cold lay: The pond obviously trapped cold, but he had no idea how. It appeared to be snowing just over the pond, but nowhere else.

"The old-timers, the ones who knew about it before Old Finney bought the property, called it Bear Paw Pond," Lorcaster said. "I suppose because of those four little projections along the north shore. They kept calling it that even after Finney had renamed it and posted that sign—Ice House Pond." Lorcaster paused. "Well, there *was* a sign. Looks like somebody's torn the blamed thing down. Anyway, even before that some of the old maps have it named as 'The Hand,' but it doesn't look like any hand to me." Rudy could detect five long shadows growing out of that north end, four of them being extensions of the four small projections; during high water periods, or maybe times of flooding, they might indeed make the pond look like a hand. But he didn't argue. "Don't know where the water comes from. No sign of a spring, or any kind of exit. There may be some sort of tunnel under the surface, I suppose, that would lead up into an underground body of water. Folks around here will give you more explanations of exactly how the pond came to be than you'll ever need. Or maybe you'll just want to make up your own."

Every now and then the snowy air above the pond would clear a space, and Rudy could then see all the way to the surface of the ice. It was gray and silver, like frozen fog. Rudy thought he could detect streaks, dark branching cracks—shadowed areas like smudges, mounds, or many small things, or one large thing, floating or swimming just beneath the surface of the ice.

That was when he said the thing that would later embarrass him: "That pond is much bigger than it is." He hadn't meant to say something so provocative, or poetic as that. His mouth had just acted on its own, giving voice to a silly thought he'd been unable to shake from his consciousness.

He had been uncomfortably aware of Lorcaster staring at him. But he couldn't bring himself to turn and look at the man. "Do tell," Lorcaster finally said. "Then I suppose you'd be getting more for your money that way."

The deal had gone swiftly after that. After a cursory examination of the property (although that first glimpse had told him everything he needed to know), Rudy told Lorcaster he wanted the place and flew home to settle his affairs, which mostly consisted of calling up the relatives of his two dead wives and letting them know that they could have whatever they wanted from the house. The remainder of the dealings with Lorcaster were handled by mail and over the phone with his secretary, a Miss Pater. Rudy eventually came to believe that Lorcaster found discussions of contracts and money ill suited to his old-money background. The man probably believed that such dealings left the founders of the first families of Greystone Bay rolling in their graves. Except he did pass on one note directly, and in his own hand rather than Miss Pater's errorless typing, suggesting perhaps that Rudy might prefer moving in during the spring. Lorcaster even offered to supply a short-term caretaker "with my compliments." But Rudy wouldn't hear of it. Although he couldn't have put his reasons into words, more than anything he wanted to reside at Ice House Pond before winter was out, when there was still plenty of rough snow and hard ice on those grounds.

But even when he got back to Greystone Bay he had to live a few days at the SeaHarp Hotel—the locals seemed oddly reluctant to rent him a truck capable of negotiating the road, and the small moving van bearing the few household furnishings he hadn't given away to in-laws refused to take them out there in those conditions. Fortunately, a cooperative manager at the hotel agreed to store the items for a small fee until Rudy was able to get to a neighboring town, buy his own pickup truck, and return. By the time he got out to the pond with his belongings, it was near dark on the fifth day.

And the pond *was* much bigger than it was, even bigger than in the dreams he'd had of it every night since that first visit.

Rudy had a little trouble with slippage getting the new truck up over the shallow rim of hills, but the snow-packed road leading down into the saucer itself was in much better shape than what had preceded it, as if getting around on the property itself had long been a higher priority than getting back into town. The surrounding trees had already blended into one large, irregular shadow, but the difference in the air suspended over the pond was even more pronounced than before. Floating ice crystals caught the light and magnified it, like dancing, low-hanging stars. Rudy pulled his topcoat more tightly around him, hoping he had brought enough warm clothes. An extensive shopping trip before he left the city had readied him at least for an arctic expedition, but already he was having his doubts. The reality of such hard, inexplicable cold as that generated by the pond was a bit difficult to accept.

An intense storm again was blowing the width of the pond, lifting the snow off the ice into towering clouds of mist, white as powdered sugar. Then the mist began to tear apart into arms and fingers, and, like any schoolchild watching clouds some late summer, Rudy imagined dancers and boxers, fleeing men and drowning women in the separating mist. Just as the truck was leaving the rise for the flat drive to the house, the mist was blown away completely and Rudy got a clear view of the entire pond. And there was the broad palm scarred with life and death and fortune lines, the slight knobs to the north elongated, by drifting ice and snow and moon-silvered shadow, into long white fingers, as ready to stroke a sad cheek as tear out a heart with their razor-sharp nails.

The truck bumped its way into the front drive and slid sideways to a halt. Rudy leaned over the wheel, trying to cough out the slivers of ice that he'd suddenly sucked into his lungs.

Rudy brought in only what he knew he'd need that first night, along with anything that might be damaged by freezing. The rest of the truck could wait until tomorrow. He'd need more furniture from town, but he had plenty of time—years—to get it.

The house was even emptier than he remembered it, but then that wasn't what had concerned him most during his first visit. Of the few furnishings which remained, a good number were in such bad repair they were unusable. Rudy collected such debris from three of the front rooms into one large room, to give him a little bit of living space for now.

The empty rooms reminded him of life back before he was married, when he either couldn't afford the furniture or didn't think he needed it, or because his life hadn't yet been full enough to leave him with bits and pieces to haul around from one place to the next.

After Eva, his first wife, and their daughter Julie had died in the car accident, he'd held on to every furnishing from that life he possibly could, including most of Julie's toys. He thought it protected him from the empty rooms. Not until a few days prior to his marriage to Marsha had he thrown those items away. With Marsha had come still more things to fill his life. A fire at a downtown theater took her from him, and the unnamed baby she'd been carrying, and again he discovered he could not let go of her things. He had surrounded himself with them, even put them out on display.

His father used to tell him that in the concentration camps the "veterans" encouraged the newcomers to let go of their personal possessions as soon as possible. Sooner or later, they had to learn that their past, their lives, their status meant nothing now—they had only their naked bodies to depend on. The major reason his father had changed the name from Greensburg to Green when he came to America wasn't because of anticipated anti-Semitism, but because he didn't want to rely on his old name for comfort. If he had had a choice, he claimed, he would have preferred to go by no name at all. Names meant nothing in such a world.

So his first night at Ice House Pond, Rudy Green would sleep naked, in an empty room. At least he had heat. Within a few hours of turning on the furnace the place was like an oven. If anything, the heating plant worked too well. He would have to bring someone out to check the thermostat.

He took a flashlight and made a quick tour of the remaining rooms. The house certainly wasn't in as bad a shape as

Lorcaster had suggested; the walls in what he supposed had been the living room would require a complete replastering, and the wooden baseboards had been removed in a parlor-sized room. Two of the upstairs bedrooms were in fine shape, complete with essentially usable beds, bookcases, and dressers (although he'd certainly want to replace the rotted mattresses). The other two bedrooms—one upstairs, one down—needed some new furniture and a few patches on the walls, but that was about it. The kitchen was old-fashioned, needed new linoleum, but was workable. The only true disaster area in the house was an ancient nursery at the back of the second floor, which for some reason Rudy hadn't seen during his first visit here. He couldn't have forgotten it.

He suspected that the nursery had been out of use much longer than other parts of the house—the crib and bassinet were rotting antiques, and the walls so severely water-damaged that great areas of plaster had melted away, revealing the wooden lathe which itself was rotting and falling. Much of the ceiling had come down, exposing beams just below the roofline and blackened, crumbling electrical cable. Here and there charred areas of the exposed wood revealed intermittent fire damage. At first Rudy was angry, but then decided that that kind of deception didn't fit the realtor's character; Lorcaster must not have known about the damage.

He and Marsha had been about to build a nursery when he'd lost them both. And now, with a sick feeling, he realized he was liking the idea of having a nursery here in this house, whatever its shape. Solitary people didn't have nurseries in their houses, nor did lonely young bachelors, nor did people with no more hope left for the future. Whatever changes he would make to this house, he knew that in some form this nursery would stay. There was something not quite right about that, he knew, but he didn't care. After his first family had died, the thought of having children had terrified him, although he'd still had the desire. He'd never told Marsha about any of these feelings; he'd acted as excited and happy as she was.

More life meant more death—that's what it finally came down to. The awful fecundity of the world, the terrifyingly long reach of life and its death accompaniment seemed to him a perversion. Every birth seemed to take place within a flowering of rot. What had nearly driven his father insane in the camps was having to live in ultimate exposure to so many people, their naked bodies, their bad habits, their stares, their breakdowns, their piss and shit violating his own flesh. And yet with such an overwhelming sense of massed living, breathing, sweating humanity, they still lived in a *cemetery.* There was no escaping it. More life meant more death, and what did it matter that your child died as long as you yourself survived? Rudy's father used to say that his own papa would have pushed him into the ovens before him if he'd had the chance and if it would have helped him save himself. But Rudy's father had lived and his grandfather perished. Who could figure it? Friends, families meant nothing. So much death in life, so much terror of both—the mathematics were unacceptable, yet inescapable.

What little wallpaper remained in the ancient nursery had yellowed to the point of brownness, so murky that its pattern was indecipherable. Rudy came as close to the wall as he dared, for the very walls stank of ancient damp and sewer smell. After a while he determined that the figures painted beneath the brown were cartoonish images of cute tiger cubs and lamb babies playing together, but the browning and other damage had so distorted their features they looked almost depraved, soiled and chewed upon. *Just the thing for a nursery in a mausoleum,* he mused, and felt disgust with himself for this errant thought.

He went to the side of the bassinet and rested his hand there. A miniature baby's pillow of pink silk lay on a greying, dusty blanket. The pillow was creased in such a way that Rudy could almost see the wrinkles where new eyes squeezed shut, where a new nose had just shown itself, where thin lips pursed into an upside-down W. The surface of the face began to crinkle and collapse, rotted cloth giving way, dark insect heads flooding out of pores and blisters and cavities to swarm across the blanket, eating and laying and multiplying even as they filled the bottom of the bassinet with a thick, writhing soup. Rudy stepped back as the tide lapped over the edge of the bassinet, long chains of the insects hanging out like the waving, reaching fingers of a dark hand.

But then he knew that wasn't what he was seeing at all. A *few* insects, no more, stains and shadows imitating the rest. With the little self-control Rudy had remaining, he left the room slowly, pulling the door tightly shut behind him.

Downstairs by the stairwell was the one door in the house he hadn't yet tried. It was cold to the touch, despite the severe heat in the other rooms—so cold his fingertips adhered painfully to the metal knob. He hadn't gone through this door his first visit—Lorcaster had said it led to the ice house. He'd planned to leave any examination of the ice house until he actually moved in. He hadn't been sure if it was usable, if he even wanted to use it, or if he'd have it torn down.

He found himself wrapping his fingers around the cold metal of the knob again and again as if trying to warm it. But the knob would not warm, and each time, he came dangerously close to losing some skin. And yet still his hand seemed to need to caress the painfully cold knob. Finally he brought his hand away bleeding, the fingers extended and spread, unable to touch each other. Rudy waved the hand around in the air to help ease the pain. It fluttered like a wounded, bleeding bird. It fluttered as if seeking something to hold, another hand, or maybe something sharp that would take the skin off.

An exploration of the ice house itself would wait until tomorrow. Rudy went back into the empty living room, skinned out of his clothes, and put his bare body down on the clean white sheet he'd used to cover the floor. A slight trickle of blood from his hand painted the sheet as he tossed and turned, searching for sleep in the worn patterns of the floorboards.

This was all he had left, but it didn't matter. He had plenty of money—death money, pain money, blood money—to buy himself an entire new world of possessions.

II

Rudy woke up cold again. Sometime during the night the furnace had shut off.

His belly, arms, thighs were smeared with cold dried blood. The cold gobbets of blood around the wounds on his hand looked like cherry Jell-O. *Jesus, what have I done to myself?* He thought about the previous night and knew he had had some trouble with a door, but couldn't remember anything more than that. *Jesus* . . . He wadded up the bloodied sheet and tossed it into the corner. *The shock of changing heat and cold must have gotten to me . . . hallucinations* . . . He staggered into the kitchen and pushed hard on the tap with his good hand. He was pleased to see that the pipes weren't frozen, but he would always wonder why not. He shoved his bloody hand under the tap and grimaced. The water wasn't exactly freezing, but cold enough. After a few minutes it began to warm; thin threads of blood and bits of torn skin swirled dizzily down the drain. *Jesus* . . .

He looked out the kitchen window. The sun was high and bright, probably close to ten o'clock. Ice-melt flowing over the window distorted the view, but the bright snow and sun against yellow-and-orange trees actually made the outside world look halfway inviting. He tied his hand up in a towel and padded off to his pile of gear in one corner of the living room to find some warm clothes.

In the morning glare the house appeared even less friendly than it had the afternoon before. The rooms seemed concentrated with dust—transfusing the air, dusting the walls, powdering the rough wooden floorboards—as if the intense cold had sealed the atmosphere inside, permitting nothing to escape. The house needed a good airing out, but Rudy was more than reluctant to open up the windows. As a compromise he cracked one window in the living room and one upstairs. After a few minutes a ribbon of icy cold wound its way past him and up the stairs, dust motes crystallized and shining as they rode along its back.

The walls looked even worse than they had the day before. He began to wonder if any of them were salvageable. He imagined stripping the house down to its skeleton and rebuilding its walls with blocks of ice—thin, hard sheets of it for windows, curtained with lacy frost. His fantasies made him colder; he pulled on long underwear, two pairs of socks, the warmest pants and shirt he could find, shiny virgin boots thick as elephant hide. He felt swollen and uneasy in his new down-filled jacket, but he knew activity would lessen that discomfort.

The front door stuck when he tried to open it. A few hard pushes and it broke free with a snap. Tiny bits of ice stung his scalp, forehead, cheekbones.

Outside, the sun was like a huge white eye with a burning stare. If he looked into it long enough, Rudy knew he'd be able to see the deadly dark pupil hiding within. He pulled on his hood to protect himself—not from moisture, but from that fearsome sun.

During the night, light snow had pushed up on both sides of the door and was frozen in place. Now small holes were melting through the delicate membranes of ice—a woman's dazzling white lingerie dripping on the line. He almost expected her to come walking out of the snowbank that filled half of the yard, naked, pale, and cold. Rudy walked around the side of the house and could see the pond and the distant trees beyond. Snow still capped the branches, but enough had melted so he could now see the distant darkness inside the trees.

From here he could see how badly the exterior of his house had weathered the years. Below one of the upstairs windows the wood had cracked and a brown stain spread from there down to a window on the first floor. Always a bad sign—there was a good possibility of structural damage underneath. But the rest of the structure was promising: A lot of scraping, a little puttying, replacement of a few shingles, and a good paint job would probably take care of it all.

As he continued down the slope to the ice-house portion of the structure, he couldn't help watching the pond, looking for some of the shadows he'd seen the day before. An oval near the center had melted—he could see rough waters rise here and there above the ice as if attempting escape. *That water's too rough for a landlocked pond,* he thought. He could sense the sun's heat battling the cold trapped over the pond.

He found this perceived invisible activity unsettling, and looked away, gazing at his feet as they stalled and slipped their way down the slope by the ice house.

The ice house looked to be as sturdy a wooden building as Rudy had ever seen. It had two whitewashed levels: the ice house itself—level with the main house and with its own wraparound porch—and directly below it, a stone-walled cellar of some sort, or maybe it was an old-fashioned cooling chamber. Dead vines clung to the outside of the stone—he wondered if he would see it green up come spring. A rotting top hat had been nailed directly to the stone, a hole cut into the top. He stepped closer; an ancient bird's nest rested inside. The outside door to this lower level was only a few yards from the pond. Several shade trees planted close together made a protective shield for the southern exposure. A little canal three feet across led from the pond to a small hatch to the right of the door—for transporting the cut ice blocks, apparently. The roof of the ice house had a sharper pitch than that of the house, and its eaves were unusually wide, wide enough to shade the walls of the ice house even when the sun was low in the sky. The wraparound porch was similarly wide, so that thick posts had had to be used to support it. This would leave the outer stone walls of that lower level in shadow virtually all the time.

Of course there were no windows in the ice house, and Rudy could detect no doors off that upstairs porch, just a connecting walkway to the side of the main house and an outside staircase leading down to the pond. Other than the untouchable door inside the house he'd tried the night before, the only other entrance into the structure appeared to be the outside door to the lower level. If he was to find any more he'd have to go through that door.

This wasn't to be easily accomplished. Although the door

had no lock, Rudy couldn't budge it. It was a thick door, heavy wood, and swollen from all the moisture. Rudy didn't think the damage had been caused by snow—the overhanging porch kept the area in front of the door relatively clear, and a small stone wall served as a windbreak for snow blowing off the frozen pond. Rather, it looked to have been underwater for a long period, as if at some time the pond had overflowed its banks. Something else Lorcaster had failed to mention, or perhaps hadn't known about. In any case, if Rudy used the ice house the door would have to be replaced.

Rudy retrieved the heavy-duty crossbar and a large flashlight from the new truck. He rammed the sharp end of the bar into the doorjamb and started prying. Dark wood splintered with a dull, damp sound. He had to pry away chunks all up and down the edge of the door before it finally creaked partway open; the edge looked gnawed by giant teeth. He wedged his heavy boot into the opening and used hands and knees to open it the rest of the way.

Bright, ice-reflected light flooded the stone chamber. The stark shadows of the support posts and Rudy's own upright form alternated with the bright gleamings of ice and metal. He fumbled for the light switch, and was pleased to see that the bulb was still good. The room became evenly brown. He breathed a heavy earth smell. The thick stone walls had troughs on each side, probably for keeping milk, meat, cheeses, vegetables cool during the summer. And, he suddenly recalled from some forgotten novel, for keeping the dead until the undertaker could get there. Tar had been used to seal the joints where walls met ceiling and floor. Antique ice pikes, picks, knives, and saws hung from pegs in the support beams overhead. The floor was sloped for drainage, as was the ceiling overhead, giving it a dangerous, caved-in look. From the lowest point of the ceiling a small pipe protruded above the drain in the floor, several foot-long icicles hanging from its open end. Above him were the press and cold of several tons of ice.

As he walked toward the back, his boot crunched through something brittle. He glanced down. The toe of his boot was wrapped in a tiny rib cage of graying bone threaded with dried flesh. He shook his leg and the bones separated and fell. The skull of the thing peered out at him from the side of one of the support beams.

A staircase rose in the center of the back wall. Rudy began climbing the dark well of it, intent on viewing the ice. With much effort, he was able to push aside the cellar-style doors in the ceiling. Old, dark sawdust rained heavily onto his head and shoulders. He was suddenly afraid of insects in his hair and down his collar, but he didn't really think any could live in such cold. Finally the air overhead was still. With no breeze to distribute it, the cold had the presence and intensity of stone. He turned on the flashlight and directed it overhead.

Tall columns of sawdust-caked ice rose up into the darkness of the roofline where Rudy's flashlight beam could not reach. An ice cathedral. An ice tomb. Rudy moved the beam around. He could see little detail under the grimy sawdust: a collage of shadows, light-absorbing grit, and isolated, jeweled ice reflections.

His back was damp with sweat inside the multiple layers of clothing. He could feel it turning to sleet as the chamber air drifted over him, as he thought about this dark, cold interior, this temporary storage place for the dead.

As a child he'd seen an old black-and-white movie late one night on television, a night like so many others in which he'd tried fruitlessly to sleep. He couldn't remember the name, but it was a science-fiction thing in which a scientist had frozen the bodies of Nazis in order to bring them back later, into a world less cautious, perhaps less aware of the evil. The interior of Rudy's ice house reminded him somewhat of the stark blacks and whites of the mad scientist's freezing chamber.

At the time he'd become obsessed with the image of that freezing place, where sleeping Nazis waited. Strangely enough, he found himself thinking of that freezing place as a kind of analogue for the gas chambers and ovens his father had survived. He felt compelled to reimagine his father's time in the camps as if they had been places of freezing, where the naked bodies had been stacked into great freezers instead of gas chambers, ovens, and mass graves, their postures of agony preserved for all time, until some future scientist devised a way of safely thawing them, and they were able to wander naked among their descendants, minds perhaps damaged by the intense cold so that they shuffled and stared, but still able to bear witness to their terrible ordeal.

Rudy's father had signed himself into a nursing home before the cancer finally took him.

"This is the *worst* place you could have chosen!" Rudy had screamed at him.

His father had smiled sadly. "I know."

"I don't *understand.* You have the money for a good place." The halls bore the constant stench of shit and piss. Half-naked residents shambled through the halls.

His father had looked around dreamily, calling to the residents he had never met before, using the old Jewish names from the distant past. Then Rudy had known: This was his father's own way of reimagining the camps.

Rudy closed the doors to the ice chamber and backed down the steps. He sat on the edge of a stone trough waiting for his eyes to adjust, then he went back out into blinding light and ice, closing the broken door behind him as best he could.

"So, you plannin' to sell some of that ice?"

Rudy spun around so fast his feet slid out from under him. He recovered by throwing his knees together, but not without considerable embarrassment. He felt ridiculous; he was sure he looked even worse. The man staring at him from the other side of an ancient green snowmobile was tall but sickly-looking—lids and eyes so dark it was like looking into two holes. He wore a dirty green-checkered jacket and flop-eared cap—standard New England farmer issue. "Can I help you?" Rudy managed, trying not to betray the aching pain in his ankles.

"Didn't mean . . . to startle you," the man said. Rudy took the comment more as an assertion of position than as an apology.

"No problem," Rudy said. "And you wanted . . . ?" These New Englanders could beat around the bush all they wanted to, but Rudy wasn't about to play that game.

"I asked if you were puttin' the place back into business again. Sellin' the ice. Talk has it you're gonna harvest this year. First time in twenty, I reckon."

"Well, sir . . . I guess I didn't catch your name. Mine's Rudy. Rudy Green."

"Netherwood." He stuck out his hand and Rudy latched onto it with an odd sense of desperation. For such a sickly-looking fellow, Netherwood's hand was enormous, and strong. "B.B. is what folks call me."

"Well, Mr. Netherwood, I don't know where that talk came from, but I've made no such plans. I haven't made any decisions in that area at all, as a matter of fact."

"Folks 'round Greystone love to talk, Mr. Green. That's about all there is to do around here—don't matter if it's true or not. But I take it you haven't decided *not* to open her up then, have you?"

"No, I can't say that I've ruled it out completely. But I don't think it's likely either. I don't know a thing about the ice business. That's not the reason I bought this place. So you're in the market for ice, are you?"

Netherwood shook his head. "Got all I need. Just figured you might be needing some help around here. I work cheap."

"Well, I'll keep that in mind . . ."

"*Real* cheap. I *love* this old place." Netherwood looked almost ridiculous in his sudden enthusiasm. "And I love the ice business. You won't do better than calling on me."

Rudy stared at this man who seemed to have grown healthier even as they talked. He tried to gauge his age, but between the years in his face and the strength in his hands Rudy found he could not. "I'll seriously consider that, Mr. Netherwood," he said. "I certainly will."

That night Rudy spent a few hours hauling debris out of the rooms and piling it onto a snowbank on the north side of the front yard. He figured he could live with the mess in his yard until spring, when he could hire a truck to take it away. He knew he'd be sleeping in the living room temporarily and so swept its floor clean and attacked the windows with ammonia, then caulk and heavy curtains to keep out the cold. This would be the last night he could stand it without a real bed, however. One of the next day's projects was going to consist of moving a bed down from upstairs and fixing it up with some sort of mattress substitute. He couldn't imagine lying down on any of the mattresses that had been left behind.

Rudy was putting the broom back into a narrow closet by the stairwell when one of his stocking feet slipped into a pool of cold water. He looked down. He didn't know why he'd thought it water—it was viscous, like syrup or oil, and when he lifted his foot thin strands of it tugged at his sock.

He jerked his foot and the strands let go. They curled back into the clear pool and then the center of the pool turned milky, then appeared to solidify, looking something like a clump of torn whitefish meat or waterlogged tissue.

Rudy turned on the light hanging by the stairwell. A yellow glow seeped from the bulb. In slow motion, he thought, as if the air were impossibly thick here, or full of dust, but he could neither see nor feel anything unusual in the air.

At least the yellow light allowed him to see the extent of the leak—he was already thinking of it as a leak even though he had no idea what it might be leaking from. It had gathered into a spot approximately two feet across in the center of this section of gray flooring, with a narrow tail that wriggled its way underneath the door to the ice house.

Rudy had a sudden terror of the entire ice house turning to slush and pushing its way through the walls of his home, mashing the place into soggy kindling. He suddenly felt in touch with the terrible *potential* of all that ice.

A thawing was impossible. It was just too damn *cold.*

He grabbed a mop out of the closet and pushed it gingerly into the area of the leak. The mop rapidly filled with the damp and became so heavy Rudy could barely lift it from the floor. After a few seconds the mop head appeared to bleach. Rudy bent closer and discovered the bleached effect was in fact ice. The leak had frozen again, and the mop had frozen to the floor.

Rudy went back into the living room for his boots, picked up his tire bar off the floor, and worked it back and forth between the door and the metal jamb where thin layers of melting and refreezing ice had glued the two pieces together.

His breath made tortured clouds of white mist in the air. Now and then he shoved so hard against the bar he wasn't sure if the resulting cracking noise was the ice or his own bones giving way.

Finally he felt the door beginning to ease open. Tiny fragments of ice showered the floor. A sudden explosion of cold air tightened the skin of his face and forced his eyes closed. As he heard more ice cracking the weight of the door took it out of his hands. His eyes still closed, he heard the door bang against the wall as if from a great distance. He imagined a delicate balance of atmospheres between the space of his house and the space of the ice house. He imagined the ice house melting all at once: boards and timbers melting down to the foundation stones. And as an alternative vision he imagined his house frosting through from the inside, all the walls and floors rimed to a slick, glasslike finish.

But nothing so dramatic occurred when he opened his eyes. The passage into the ice house was dark, and smelled of old, cold air, but the switch just inside the door still made a bank of bulbs recessed into frosted cages overhead burn orange-under-white. Overhead the light disappeared into the dark recesses of the quarter-pitch roof. He could hear the faint whirring of the ventilator up there removing any collected vapor. Ahead of him a series of boards had been slid behind two upright timbers to hide the passage to the ice beyond. Bundles of long straw had been packed tightly around these as insulation. Intense cold had blackened the boards and straw and, as in his fantasy, had turned portions of these to black ice that bled darkly from the heat pushing in from the warm house. Here on the other side of these black boards was the oldest ice, the ice he hadn't been able to see from the cooling chamber below.

Rudy went back for his tire bar and used it to loosen the

ice that cemented the boards together. Then, by wiggling each board back and forth, he was able to free them from the hidden ice blocks. It took him two hours to remove the top five boards, exposing a window of antique ice three feet square.

The array of ice blocks was gray, like frozen fog, with occasional shiny specks buried deep inside which vaguely reflected the light from the caged overheads.

Rudy stepped closer, shielding his eyes for the best view, careful not to actually touch the ice for fear his skin would adhere to it.

Faint shadows melted across the ice. He twisted around, feeling as if someone had stepped behind his shoulder and momentarily blocked the light. But nothing was there.

He came back around, and stared into shadowed sockets, and beneath those a dark gaping mouth frozen in the act of swallowing ice.

Rudy shouted, and the face in the ice before him fogged over. And all his wiping and scraping on the dim ice would not bring it back.

When he finally shut the door behind him he discovered that the mop had become unstuck, fallen over, and the leak was drying. Only a small, pulpy, white residue was left, and that turned to frost, then pale fog even as he watched.

III

The second visitor to Rudy's new home was Mrs. Lorcaster, the realtor's wife.

He'd awakened late. The furnace definitely seemed to have a mind of its own, and his sleep had been disturbed several times during the night because of alternating intense heat and intense cold. He was bound to come down with something serious if he didn't get it taken care of quickly. He'd been dressed only a short time when he heard the knocking at his door.

From what he could see, the woman standing on the other side of the icy door-panes seemed to be warmly but elegantly dressed: a dark suit and white blouse draped with a tailored, muted red cape of brushed wool. She tapped lightly, directly on the ice-covered frame. Ice broke and fell beneath the steady rap of her dark-gloved knuckles.

She was obviously nonplussed to be suddenly viewing his early-morning face distorted on the other side of the icy glass. But she recovered with a practiced smile. Rudy made a feeble attempt to smile back. He pulled as hard as he could on the door. It stuck, then let go all at once, showering her with a blizzard in miniature. Embarrassed, Rudy reached out to dust off her cape, but reconsidered when she reacted with a step backwards into the snow. "I'm sorry," he said quickly. "Can I help you?"

"Quite all right." She stepped past his arm and into the house. "I'm Emily Lorcaster. I believe you know my husband?"

Apparently not as well as I thought. He couldn't match up this elegant creature with Lorcaster. He stared at a silver lock of her hair trapped within a fold in her hood. A snowflake hung within the curl like a jewel, refusing to melt. "Yes. He sold me . . ." Rudy made a nervous, sweeping gesture. "All this." He stopped, not knowing what else to say. "I feel very lucky," he added awkwardly.

"Yes. Of course." She tried to look past him into the rooms beyond. He found himself shifting his stance, purposely blocking her view. He didn't know why—having just moved in he obviously wasn't responsible—but he was embarrassed by the condition of the place. She gave up and looked at him directly. "I used to live here. In fact, I grew up in this house." She looked at him in anticipation, but he had no idea what she expected from him.

"That's very interesting," he said, feeling increasingly inferior to this creature. He wondered if Lorcaster felt the same way. Perhaps that was why the man dressed the way he did.

"I've heard you may start up the ice operation again. My grandfather designed and built the ice house, as well as the living quarters here. My maiden name was Finney, you see."

Rudy quickly tried to remember what Lorcaster had said about "Old Finney." He couldn't remember the specifics, just that it had had a negative tone to it. The previous owner hadn't been a Finney, though—some investor in New York by the name of Carter. So it had passed out of the family. Now Rudy could make some rough guesses concerning Lorcaster's reluctant style of salesmanship. "Just a rumor, I'm afraid," Rudy said. "I don't know how it started. Actually, I hadn't really decided. You know, just yesterday a man named Netherwood came by—"

"Netherwood," she interrupted. "I see. Still about, is he?"

Rudy didn't think she really wanted the question answered. "I have to admit this interest in the ice has me curious," he said. "I might have to look into it."

"Oh, by all *means!* My grandfather, and my father after him had quite a lucrative business. And you'll still find those very interested in the ice from this particular pond."

"Magic ice, eh? Something special?" Rudy tried to chuckle, but it caught in his throat.

She eyed him coldly. "Perhaps. I wouldn't know. But I know there is a market."

"I'm surprised. Surely with modern refrigerators and freezers . . ."

"Tradition, Mr. Green. The people of Greystone value it most seriously. And some would cherish just the novelty of that sort of ice, I'm sure. And then there's the ice palace. We had wonderful ice palaces! Many here still remember them."

"Ice palaces?"

"Winters, for years, the whole town would come out to the pond and help Grandfather cut and haul the ice. Blocks two feet wide and almost three in length. They'd lay the blocks out on a pattern staked out in the snow on the other side of the stone wall; the forest wall made a beautiful backdrop. There they'd build up ice walls, and ramparts, and Grandfather would chisel turrets into the huge towers. People would come from towns many miles away to see the palace and spend their money. It was a great boon to the town."

"I take it the custom eventually stopped?"

"They *used* my grandfather." She looked almost, but not quite angry. "Or at least he thought so. He said they only cared about money, or whatever they had in hand. He said they had changed, all of them. He said they sat around in their houses doing nothing, breathing in the fog off the Bay, letting it fill up their lungs. He said there were just too many of them for comfort. Too many eyes to stare at him in their pain. Too many mouths to feed. Too many bodies old and dying. Finally, too many to bury. He said they didn't even behave like human beings anymore."

"That's pretty strong, isn't it?"

She smiled faintly. "I suppose my grandfather wasn't very well at the time. He worked very hard, you see. Other than the construction of the palace each winter, he would permit no one to help him, except for occasional odd jobs he would offer my father when he was young. He would hire no one, and my grandmother was not allowed near the ice. He discouraged visitors; he no longer had any friends in the town.

He suffered the customers for his ice simply as a necessary evil. 'My own personal poison,' he would say, and laugh—the only time I ever heard him laugh. He'd cut the ice himself and guide it down the trough from the pond to the cooling room. He wore the pike handles down until they snapped from his using them, his hands moving constantly around and around their shafts in that nervous way he had when he worked the ice.

"Back when there were ice palaces he used to let me play inside. I was the *princess,* you see. He said the ice palace was my castle, and I could do what I wanted. Once he stopped building the palaces he had very little to say to me. He'd simply haul the ice that would have gone into the palace up into the ice house, and once the ice house was full he'd still cut the blocks and lay them out on the bank, leaving them there for spring melt. Fewer and fewer customers came, so there was always a large surplus left on the bank."

"So why did he bother cutting up the ice? Just to have something to do?"

"My grandfather never did *anything* 'just to have something to do.' Everything was done with a purpose. I used to think that at his age he believed he needed to repeat the habitual gestures of his job again and again or else his muscles would lose their edge and forget what was required of them. Eventually it became clear that he viewed it as he would view the milking of a cow: It was necessary."

"If you don't milk them they become swollen and in pain. Eventually they go dry," he said. She looked at him quizzically. He smiled. "My father kept a cow in his garage in the city, until enough of his neighbors complained. He had liked that cow more than people, and trusted it far more. He had said that the cow was infinitely more reliable. Forgive me for saying so . . . but I imagine the town found that to be very strange behavior."

"Certainly. They did. But things happened when he failed to harvest the ice. I know. I saw them." She paused, as if waiting for him to guess. *Get on with it,* he thought, but said nothing. And still she waited.

"What happened?" he finally asked, angered by this petty use of power.

"At first the ice turned very gray. Grayer than any fog. If you put your tongue on it it would taste sour. Some got very sick doing that—a few even died. And you could see all kinds of shadows trapped inside, or worse still, vaguely moving if you had the right angle on it. Sometimes you thought you saw faces there, as if someone were looking up at you through a foggy window, but you could never be sure. If you put your hand on the ice too long the ice hurt the skin. It burned, or ached for days. And a few times the ice went completely black, coal black, surely unlike any ice that ever was. Grandfather said harvesting the ice was the only way to keep the pond pure, to put things right again. He said that it was dangerous if left too long."

"You saw this?" he asked.

"I did. And tasted it. And felt it."

Rudy turned and looked out a side window. He could see one corner of the pond where the ice had melted and dead leaves floated, swirling in a small circle. White chunks of ice bobbed to the surface like drowned hunks of flesh. In the yard, snow and ice encrusted the old furniture he'd tossed there, making it resemble brilliant white formations of coral. "How long has it been since the ice was last harvested here?" he asked.

"Too long, Mr. Green." She almost smiled. "Better a dazzling clean ice palace, don't you think, than that great stretch of frozen gray fog?"

The wind picked up after lunch, keeping Rudy inside. He spent several hours staring out of an upstairs window at the pond and the distant trees. By late afternoon white snow-mist was blowing off the frozen water—a solid expanse of it, no breaks now—turning to gray fog once it got a few yards over the land. The brilliant white eye in the sky had shut its lid. Ice trees bent and broke into glistening shards as the wind picked up. The skin of the pond grew grayer still. It seemed to turn to night in the pond before it turned to night in the sky.

The visitors had soured Rudy. He'd come here for escape, and now they wanted him to revive a business—to build ice palaces, no less. Despite his fascination with the ice house and its history, the thought of all the other visitors that that might bring, all the customers, appalled him. He just wanted to be alone. With his thoughts, his memories, his imagined relationships with dead families. He could live with the invisible presence of Old Finney, even his father—that seemed to fit, that seemed inevitable. But no one else.

That night Rudy set up one of the old beds in his living room, tightening all the rusted wood-screws and hammering in a few large nails for additional support, and constructing a mattress out of sewn-together sheets with rags and odd bits of clothing stuffed inside. He shut the furnace off completely, thinking that he'd sleep better in his clothes, with several heavy blankets laid on top.

But after only a short time he was awake again, the sweat pouring off him, the distant sound of the furnace a hot static in his ears. He stared up at the ceiling. He thought he could see the waves of heat flowing there, gesturing to him with their long curves and heated mouths. Sweat popped up out of his flesh and immediately went cold, so that he could track the progress of every drip across his painfully warm skin.

The furnace was working overtime to protect him from the deadly cold. As if it had its own intelligence. The cold was tricky: It hid in the corners, under the bed, around the windows. It could seep through an unprotected electrical outlet or along a pipe coming through the wall. It prowled the floorboards in search of ill-protected feet.

But more than that, a mass of it hid just on the other side of the badly insulated wall. The oldest cold Rudy had ever known, heavy and full of memory.

He'd always insisted that couples who had separate beds—or, worse still, separate bedrooms—could not really call themselves married at all. It was the body heat that was important, that they needed to share, the heat that signified their living, their working and doing. And of course at no time was that plainer than on a cold night, when the skin sent out the messages of *I live, I need,* and *I love.* He wouldn't even allow himself to buy an electric blanket. Now his memories of his wives and children were cool ones—they lacked the heat of life, the heat of love. In memory there was only numbing, deadly cold.

He did not know how long he'd been hearing the dripping before he recognized it for what it was. He slipped his boots on and went out to the stairwell, but there was no leak or stain on the floorboards. And yet he could smell the damp; he could smell the cold. He looked at the door to the ice house, and there the stain of head-shaped damp, the torso, a slow ooze of water through the pores of the cracked and peeling wood making the bare beginnings of the legs.

Rudy walked slowly to the door to examine it. As his warm breath—*life breath, love breath*—hit the stain, it vanished.

He opened the door without much difficulty; he'd pretty much destroyed the jamb the night before. Only a small amount of the light from the stairwell lamp slipped into the chamber, but tonight he was reluctant to switch on the overhead bulbs inside the ice house. The square of ice ahead of him seemed to glow with its own inner, gray light. From this distance fog appeared to swirl just beneath the hard surface.

In the camps, his father had told him, you eventually had nothing but your naked body to protect you from the cold. Any clothing you might have meant very little. As did wealth or status. Then his father had told him the cancer felt like an invasion of ice into his body. Cold, numbing memory that froze his cells one at a time, not at all like the consuming fire he'd always imagined cancer to be.

Rudy approached the square window of gray ice. Staring into it was like staring into a cross section of the frozen pond itself. Shadows flickered across the gray surface. He twisted his head, looking for moths against the light, but there were none. He stared again at the ice, and knew then that the shadows were just beneath the surface, and not on its top. He stretched his hands out, fingers spread, and set them gingerly against the ice, careful to keep the contact on the subtle side, afraid his fingertips might adhere and then he'd lose them, substituting wounds for them. The ice grew dark where he touched it; the shadows of his hands in the ice appeared to grasp the hands themselves. Then the shadows of his hands in the ice floated away from his hands and grasped the sides of his shadow head, his skull head with gaping eye holes and absent mouth screaming and screaming as it stared at him.

Rudy backed away but his shadow self in the ice did not move. Rudy backed away and saw the naked form floating in the ice, emaciated and cold, consumed by hatred, accusing him with its stare. And Rudy thought of Auschwitz, and Treblinka, and that last picture of his father's cancer-ridden body, and some poor soul drowned so long ago in Ice House Pond, harvested and preserved in Old Finney's secret ice palace.

The body disappeared, and the ice was a murky gray again.

IV

The last thing Rudy wanted to do that next morning was negotiate the road into Greystone Bay, but he had little choice now.

Lately, mornings had been warm enough to cause considerable snowmelt each day, but that actually made the roads even more treacherous. The pickup veered dangerously as it topped the slight hill that marked the edge of his property. Rudy fought the wheel and then let the car slide down most of the remainder of the decline.

Greystone Bay's biggest bookstore was the Harbor Bookshop, which had a large selection of local histories, most of them of the privately-printed kind. There were also several volumes of facsimile newspapers, compilations of historically significant police reports, and other document collections of historical interest. A small selection of contemporary paperback novels were displayed on wire racks at the front of the store; they appeared to be largely ignored. During the two hours Rudy spent in the store he saw only one customer examine them: a fat man in a fuzzy red coat who eventually bought one of the dark-covered horror novels whose cover displayed a man's decaying head, worms encircling the fixed iris of the left eye. The man asked for directions to the nearest hotel and the elderly clerk told him how to get to the SeaHarp.

The rest of the stock was about a twenty/eighty percent mix of new and used hardcovers, university and scientific presses, local and small presses, handmade volumes, fine editions, charts and prints, and occasional unclassifiable dusty paperbacks. All in no particular order. In the few instances where shelves had actually been labeled, the labels were nonsensical (Books We Wished We Had Read, Imaginary Countries, Working Titles, Character Assassinations), or useless (the three shelves carefully labeled Classics were empty). But the good gray clerk appeared to know where every book contained within the shop's shadowed walls was located, however obscure. Each of Rudy's inquiries brought a flood of title names and locations. Eventually, he had gathered all the sources he thought he might need. The clerk guided him to an overstuffed chair, almost showing its springs, and left him.

Rudy found what he wanted in *The Greystone Papers: A Century of Headlines, Major Stories, and Oddities,* in the chapters concerning a twenty-year stretch of the Bay's history. Old Finney's stretch.

BAKER CHILD STILL MISSING

Constable Biggs still reports no leads in the case of John Baker, age six, still missing after twelve days. The boy was last seen in a field near The Hand where his father, Philip Baker, was gathering firewood. . . .

PRESUMED ELOPEMENT

Mary Buchanan, mother of Ellen Buchanan, wishes to announce the elopement of her daughter with William Colbert of Hinkley. Earlier reports of foul play, Mrs. Buchanan informs us, are certainly the products of perverse and overactive imaginations. . . .

HUNTERS LOST

County deputies and rescue workers are still searching the North Forest for Joseph Netherwood and his son Paul, who were separated from their hunting party Friday afternoon at approximately three P.M. when their dog Willy . . .

Dozens of other stories described similar events. Rudy gladly paid the exorbitant ransom the clerk wanted for the book.

The Harbor Bookshop sported an old-fashioned pay phone-booth. There were six Netherwoods in the phone book, but only one B.B.

Before leaving the store, Rudy made two more purchases: yellowed handbooks concerning the construction, maintenance, and day-to-day use of ice houses.

He ran into Mrs. Lorcaster coming out of the bookstore. She was bowed from the weight of packages, heading for an old station wagon. He grasped her elbow gently as she walked past, not recognizing him. "You didn't tell me about all the missing people," he said quietly.

She staggered slightly, and part of her load began to tilt. Rudy reached out to steady it. He caught a small bag in mid-fall and nestled it inside one of the larger ones. One of her lovely eyes peeked out at him from between the two largest bags. She didn't seem so self-assured, so powerful now. She seemed more like what he'd have expected Lorcaster's wife to be. "I . . . don't understand," she said.

"Emily." He shook his head. "All those people a number of years back who ended up missing? *Rural* people, for the most part? People your grandfather would have known?"

"You've been talking to Mr. Netherwood. He's a bitter, *disturbed* man," she said.

"I've been talking to him, yes. But not about his missing relatives. I figure he'll tell me all about them in his own good time. But I've seen some things at the ice house, em . . . Mrs. Lorcaster. In ice that must date back to your grandfather's time."

She put her bags down on the hood of the station wagon, letting them tumble. She was a sad lady, suddenly looking old. Now Rudy was feeling insensitive. "He was my grandfather and I loved him very much," she said. "And he . . . he *hated* people around here. He'd come to that, all right. But I cannot believe he would actually *do* anything to anyone. I never knew that to be a part of his nature."

"That house. That pond." Rudy hesitated, searching for the right word. "They aren't *right.*"

"Then *do* something, Mr. Green. At one time my grandfather built palaces."

"And then?"

"And then my aunt died. She was three years old when she lost herself in the fog, and drowned in the pond. My grandmother, who'd always been so quiet, stewing in her silence, became quite mad. And something happened to my grandfather. He grew frightened of people, the way the mass of them intruded, the way life created death. He said that the Bay had its own will and its own way of populating itself out of the fog. He came to see the townspeople as not simply other, but *other.* They were no longer human, as far as he was concerned. But I cannot believe he would have killed. My grandfather built *palaces,* Mr. Green. Those hints of murder . . . that is simply Mr. Netherwood's brand of gossip."

"I'll be hiring Mr. Netherwood, Emily. I think you should know that."

"Whatever for?"

"For the ice business. And maybe I'll be building palaces as well."

V

Two days later, B. B. Netherwood met Rudy by Ice House Pond at six in the morning, as arranged. Netherwood was already there by the time Rudy had gotten out of bed and dressed and made his way through the thick snow around the side of the building. Snow had fallen again all evening, as it had several evenings in a row. And although the sun was out and there were no clouds in the sky, this was the coldest morning Rudy had yet experienced at the pond. It seemed as if his newfound determination to take charge of things had brought out a renewed stubbornness in the weather. The cold seemed to have leeched much of the color out of the trees and sky, even his own clothes. The landscape he saw was like a faded picture in some grandparent's photo album.

The distant trees looked stiff and dead. There was no breeze. The thick snow swallowed his footprints.

He found B. B. Netherland standing by a large pile of gear, apparently unloaded from the battered green snowmobile and its attached sled. Netherwood gazed out over the frozen pond, fixed and motionless, as if frozen himself.

Rudy purposely made as much noise as he could thrashing through the snow. Netherwood turned and went over to the bottom of the slope to wait for him.

"You have a personal interest in the pond, I believe," Rudy said.

Netherwood scratched at his chin. "You must have figured that out from something you read in town, am I correct? An old newspaper or something?"

"According to the papers two Netherwoods were missing. I assumed, of course, they were relatives."

"My daddy and my older brother Paul. Helluva kid, and a helluva dad, if truth be told. Although I was pretty mad at them for going hunting without me that day. But then I was only eight; I could hardly hold up the rifle." Netherwood shuffled his feet, his hands buried in his baggy pants pockets as if that would keep him warmer.

Anxiety makes you cold, especially out here, Rudy thought. And then: *This is crazy.* "And you've thought about it all this time. Considered where, and how."

"You don't stop thinking about it, Mr. Green. The folks around here talk about things—I hear you have a lot on your mind, too. The fact that I was just a kid at the time doesn't make much difference in the thinking about it, the dreaming about it, except maybe I've had a longer time for doing it."

Rudy took a deep breath. The cold air seized his lungs, squeezing until they began to burn. "But why this place? What makes you think you'll find out something about them *here?*"

"The same reason you called me, Rudy. I really didn't see you for somebody who'd go into the ice business, despite my coming to visit you the other day. Same thing that told me I'd find out something about what happened to Daddy and Brother right here on the pond, I suspect." He looked directly into Rudy's eyes. "Seen anything since you been here? Anything you're afraid to tell 'cause folks might think you're crazy?"

Rudy told him about the alternating freezing and melting leak, and the shadowy form in the ice trying to grasp his hand.

B.B. just nodded. "I've seen the worst storms you can imagine, bad as any tornado or hurricane, right over this pond and nowhere else. When they move away from the ice they don't go anywhere—they just disappear. I've seen shadows big as a house floating under the ice. I've seen smaller ones, too, man-size and smaller. And sometimes they do a little dance, a little ballet. And there are days in summer, I swear the water gets all rusty and stinks like a slaughterhouse."

"Something strange here, B.B., something very odd," Rudy said.

"Something cold," B. B. Netherwood replied.

Netherwood had brought his own tools: a carpenter's toolbox and some good door stock, a push broom, some weatherproof paint, and various tools for cutting and handling the ice, although the tools hanging up in the cooling room were still in remarkable shape, greased, with the metal parts wrapped in oilcloth. Rudy told B.B. that frankly he knew nothing himself, except for what he'd read quickly in the two old handbooks he'd purchased, and so B.B. shouldn't hesitate to give the orders. B.B. told Rudy to "get to sweeping, then," while B.B. worked on the splintered door and jamb. "Looks like something *et* it," B.B. said. Rudy told him what he'd had to do to get in and B.B. just shook his head.

The dust, seemingly harder to push in such cold, created a stench when it was disturbed, so bad that Rudy had to tie a handkerchief over his mouth and nose while he worked. He didn't even want to think about what caused that smell. He used a shovel to remove the animal skeleton he'd found the other day.

He was impatient to get to what needed to be done, and find some answers. But he also wanted to do things right, and he knew this man Netherwood knew how to do things right. But still the practical and ultimately meaningless chore of putting the ice house back into working order reminded Rudy of nursing homes and concentration camps.

"You think you'll do the ice palace?" B.B. asked.

"If that's what it takes," Rudy replied.

"Hmmmm . . ." was all B.B. said, working his plane up and down the edge of the door.

Rudy swept until he could see clean stone flooring to all four corners. B.B. was still working on the door, trying to make it fit the opening, muttering about old houses, how there "wasn't a single parallelogram in the whole damn lot of 'em," so Rudy got ammonia and brushes and started scrubbing down the stone troughs. Even under the sharp bite of the ammonia he thought he could smell spoiled milk and vegetables, meat left too long in the season, even its blood starting to gray.

After another hour Rudy's patience was wearing thin. The weight of the ice overhead oppressed him, and he imagined he could feel the pressure of the tons of frozen ice in the pond behind him, pressing its weight against the embankments, pressing against the world, freezing its way slowly to the muddy bottom, pushing its argument toward China, if it could. And turning grayer by the hour. Rudy expected an explosion at any moment would rip off the back of his skull.

"Done," B.B. called from the doorway, his form a silhouette against the brilliant light that filled the doorway. "Give me a few minutes to shovel out the raceway and chip the ice off the gate, then we can start. I brought along a few sandwiches we can munch on while we're working, providing you got a clean jacket pocket."

The raceway and gate took more than a little shoveling and chipping, but B.B. eventually got it done. The ice was like concrete; B.B. was scarlet-cheeked and drenched by the time he finally broke through. The dark, cold water rushed down the raceway to the front of the ice house. "It's full of silt . . . or pollution . . . something . . ." Staring down at the water filling the raceway, Rudy could not see the bottom, even though it was only a couple of feet deep. The water was black, and dangerous-looking. Steam escaped where the water made contact with the warmer metal of the raceway.

"Yeah . . . something . . ." B.B. said, going for two sets of tools. "I just wouldn't put my hand in it if I were you. I wouldn't even *look* at it too long. Come on . . . we got ice to cut."

B.B. brought out two each of two different styles of saw, as well as two "choppers"—something like thin-bladed hatchets. The chopper felt especially good in Rudy's hand—as well-balanced and perfectly formed as a surgeon's instrument.

"Don't waste the ice," B.B. said. He chopped off a little from the edge where he'd begun removing the ice, making a remarkably clean horizontal line by the open, dark water. Then he used the chopper to make his lines. "Two by three feet is a good size," he said. "The size Old Finney designed this setup for anyway. Ice should be about a foot, foot and a half thick here. If we're lucky it won't get much thicker or thinner than that anyplace else in the pond. But I don't suppose we can hope for luck in these particular waters." He chopped deeper through the lines, then used his saws to cut the rest of the way. The block looked remarkably perfect, like a giant ice cube, crisp corners, and gray as woodsmoke.

"I've never been good at estimating measurements," Rudy told him, trying to keep his mind off the gray of the ice, or the even darker shadows that seemed to change position as B.B. used the pike to move the block down through the raceway. Or the vague unpleasant smell when a minuscule portion of the ice block melted, condensing on its upper surfaces.

"Don't worry. The more of these you cut, the closer you'll be getting to a perfect two-by-three. You won't be able to help yourself. Once we cut a certain number of blocks, we move them down the raceway like this, then we'll use a block and tackle to drag them up the ramp into the ice house upstairs. Usually another team works on that end of it, but the two of us'll just have to work it double."

B.B. proceeded to cut out enough of the ice to provide Rudy with a horizontal edge to start his own row. Or, rather, double row: Both men started using five cuts to carve out two huge blocks at a time.

Rudy thought about Old Finney performing the same task so many years ago. He thought he even had Old Finney's saw and chopper—they were far more worn than B.B.'s set. After a time he was able to lose himself in the work, chopping and sawing, aware only of the proscribed movements of his muscles, and the endless gray.

At times the rhythmic chopping made Rudy think of hundreds of pairs of hard boots marching across polished wood floors, across fitted stones, across ice. The wind picked up and blew snow across his knuckles, freezing and burning them, finally numbing them. Now and then he would look up at the sky—he could see no approaching storms, but he could feel them. His joints ached. He looked over at B.B., who stared at the gray ice as he worked, who stared into the dark cold water, into nothing.

"Do you always think about them?" Rudy asked, as he began to saw.

B.B. said nothing for a few moments, letting his saw make the only noise, scratching and tearing through the ice, the sound rising when it reached the really hard sections, sounding like a cat caught on a hook. "Not always," he finally said. "But every day, sometime. Paul was already a pretty good man, the way I remember it. Just like Daddy. I'll never know if I'm as good a man. I was too young when it happened—not much judgment yet. What about you? You thinking about them now?" B.B. asked without looking up, his gaze drawn along with the maddening saw.

Rudy slowed down his own saw so he could hear himself think. "They're there, somewhere, even when I don't have their precise image in front of me. My second wife—this sounds terrible—I think I married her when I did partly so I could start putting an end to the grieving for my first wife."

"But you loved her, too, right?"

"Very much."

"I figured. But you still knew what you did, why you did it, and you felt guilty as hell about it. I know about guilt."

They widened a highway of dark water toward the center of the pond. By lunchtime the dark water was looking grayer and beginning to freeze again. They had to go back down the expanse, breaking up any new connections frozen in between the floating blocks. The tiny specks of snow in the bright air were growing slightly larger.

Walking down either side of the carved-out waterway, they used their pikes to herd the blocks to the raceway. A huge hook at the end of the block and tackle allowed them to pull several blocks up the ramp at a time, although sometimes they had to use B.B.'s ancient snowmobile for additional pulling power. Once up in the ice house, they used portable ramps and levers to stack the blocks.

Rudy kept looking for angular, naked shadows in the stacks of older ice, but he really hadn't the time to do a thorough search. The new ice blocks, even grayer than the old ones, seemed to trap and absorb the light. The overhead caged bulbs in the ice house made little headway.

Once surrounded by the towers of ice, Rudy found it difficult to breathe.

During a rest break, Rudy lay on the frozen pond, a strip of ragged canvas underneath to protect him from the cold, and to keep his skin from adhering to that sticky gray exterior.

He used the edge of the chopper to scrape away a little of the silver rime. His lips looked blue in the reflection, his eyes dark coals, his snowy skin shifting loosely on the bones.

In late afternoon the fog rolled in, thicker than before. Although nothing was said, they both increased the pace of their work, despite their weariness. Rudy's arms grew steadily colder, despite the energy he tried to will into them, the pace at which he pushed them. They looked translucent in the fog-filtered light. Translucent ice skin.

The fog was turning to cold, to ice and snow. Rudy looked up: He seemed to be standing on the bottom of an ice white sea. He waited for the slow drift of generations of small animal skeletons to reach the bottom of his sea and cover him over. If he opened his mouth he could taste their deaths on his tongue.

"I think the pressure's lifting," he heard B.B. say, although he couldn't see him for all the fog and snow.

Rudy looked down at the pond. The gray ice had turned whiter, cleaner. The open expanse of water was clearing.

The huge white eye in the sky was obscured by eddies and winding sheets of hard-driven snow. Whatever remained of the late-afternoon sunlight had diffused, spread itself out so that each of these tiny ice crystals might grab a piece and carry it to the ground. So the world became a darker and colder place as the snow continued to fall.

Rudy had lost track of B.B. some time ago, although every now and then he thought he could hear the sound of metal hitting ice, the steady pace of the chopper, followed a few minutes later by the sound of the cat being torn apart, its screams muffled from the heavy snow filling its mouth. Rudy had lost his ice saws somewhere on the frozen pond—he had no idea where. He hoped he hadn't dropped them into the water.

He wondered how Old Finney had stood it out there. And what kind of wife he must have had, to live with a man who could stand such a thing. He could not imagine a more desolate place to live.

He stopped himself, not quite believing what he had been thinking. He, too, had chosen to live in this place, and despite all that had happened, perhaps *because* of all that had happened, he was still convinced that this was the right place for him. Maybe he was as crazy as Old Finney.

The light was fading rapidly. He could see nothing beyond the few feet of snowy air surrounding him. His feet had gone numb, despite his heavy boots; they felt as if the ice were rising through them, penetrating the skin and infecting the bone. B.B. must have gone back to the shore, he thought. Surely no one could work under such conditions. Rudy turned round and round until he was dizzy, trying to determine in which direction lay his ice house and his home—but the foreground of blowing snow was uniform, and the distant backgrounds of trees or buildings were invisible. He could not find where he had last cut into the ice. He could find nothing.

Sin otra luz y guía, sino la que en el corazón ardía. It was a spanish poem he had read many times. St. John of the Cross, about the Dark Night: *No other light to mark the way but fire pounding my heart.* He would just have to choose a direction and go with it. There was a slight movement in the snow falling ahead of him, a slight turning. He started in that direction.

A pale skirt, twirling. A vague drift of white-blonde hair. *That flaming guided me more firmly than the noonday sun.* A tiny child's face, leeched of color by the cold, her iced hair floating up around her cheeks and blue crystal eyes.

Rudy saw the little girl burning up in the snow, the snow becoming flames. She twirled and twirled, dancing, dressed in the flames. His sweet sweet baby, Julie. His daughter Julie burning up in the car with his wife. Was this reimagining of her death any better? Was ice any easier to take than fire?

That flaming guided me more firmly than the noonday sun. He watched the child stumbling, first snow and then fire attacking her pale form, and he cried out, but did not run to her. He seldom thought of Julie; he couldn't let himself think of Julie. The images of her death were poisonous; he shut them out of his thoughts. He could think of Eva and he could think of Marsha, even of the unborn child Marsha had carried. But he had not been able to think of Julie for a very long time. He wondered if she would hate him for that betrayal.

The girl stumbled and fell to the ice and lay there. Unable to stay away, Rudy stepped slowly through the snow that continued to accumulate on the surface of the pond. He looked down at the small form.

The child was too thin. Her arms too white, too short. This was not his daughter. Then he remembered that Emily Lorcaster had lost an aunt, a little girl, Old Finney's daughter. Who had drowned in the pond.

The blonde head turned and looked up at him. The lips had swollen to fifty times or more their normal size. The child's head was all mouth. It opened, showing its huge hungry tongue. The small white arms lifted to give him a hug.

Rudy screamed and stepped back, slipping on the ice, then crawled away from the monstrous child who wanted to hold him, who wanted to hug him, who more than anything else wanted him to remember her. Children were hungry mouths—that's mostly what they were, "hungry mouths to feed." They would eat you if they could—not out of malice—that's just what they were. Healthy, maturing, growing mouths. People fed off each other; it was the only way they could live. *O tender night that tied lover and the loved one, loved one and the lover fused as one!* But Rudy had gotten far enough away. The child's body diminished, hair disappearing, skin receding to the bone, until finally it was a corpse on a hard slab. It slowly sank into the ice and disappeared. *In darkness I escaped, my house at last was calm and safe.*

Rudy got to his feet. Of the surrounding curtain of snow, one portion appeared lighter than the rest. He went in that direction.

"You cannot know what life is until you have been forced to live with those events which cannot, with any justice, be survived." His father hadn't said it like that, not all in one breath like that. He'd coughed and spat and started over again and again and failed in his search for the right words. Finally he'd demanded a piece of paper and a pencil and Rudy had had to help him get the words down with numerous erasures, strikeouts, substitutions. He'd been drunk when he finally delivered to Rudy this final message of his life, two weeks before he'd signed himself into the nursing home. The cancer had left him bald and ravaged his body. He had broken all the mirrors in the house, unable to look at himself anymore. It was because the concentration camp had finally caught up with him; he now looked too much like those who had failed to survive.

There was much that could not be lived with. His father had been sickened and appalled that he still breathed and walked around, consuming, evacuating his bowels, dribbling his piss like any animal.

"Rudy . . ." his father whispered. Rudy came to him and his father clutched his shoulder with a skeletal hand, pulling him up close to his face. "God made a poor choice in me." The sentence stank of his father's failing organs. "So many died. So *many.*"

Rudy could not bear to think of Julie. Thoughts of Julie were razor-sharp and tore down his throat and through the layers of his belly so that he could not eat, could not sleep. She was too much to survive. God had made a terrible choice.

After his daughter's death Rudy had had fantasies of murdering other children in the neighborhood. He'd imagined that he would sneak up to their bedrooms at night and smother them in their sleep. At least he would not let them suffer as Julie had suffered—their deaths would be quick and relatively painless. They probably would have no idea what was happening to them.

He often wondered how their parents would grieve, what

form it would take. He wondered if any would grieve the way he did and whether it would show in their faces. He was not sure he would ever know the full extent of what he felt until he saw its terrible landmarks in the landscape of another's face.

But these were fantasies, and they passed. Now when he heard of the death of another's child he locked himself in his house and railed. And yet even in his screaming he would not let himself think of Julie.

During those flights of fantasy he had been no better than Old Finney, if indeed Old Finney was guilty of the crimes Rudy and B.B. were accusing him of. Rudy would have brought the world to death if he could, guided by the dark light of his heart.

He imagined he could see the distant white eye up in the sky again, behind the snow, drawn to the cold ice of the pond. As it began to sink, the eye turned red, the falling snow like frozen flakes of blood.

Rudy heard a murmur from the pond as the ice around his feet began to break.

Once the hard ice began to crack, it went rapidly. Rudy opened his mouth to shout as the cold arms of the pond reached up over his body to pull him under, but only cold air came out, the ice of the pond already in him and working its way up to his brain. He pushed frantically with his arms against loose pieces of floating ice, trying to force himself out of the water, but they slipped from his grasp and crashed back into him, forcing him under once again.

His vision went to gray. Cold infected his thoughts. Cold pushed him farther and farther down into the depths of the pond, the ice skin on the pond growing thicker, expanding downward, chasing him and forcing him into the pond's dark heart. Where all he'd ever known or imagined dead swam out to greet him, their narrow arms poised for an embrace, their eyes staring wide in their attempts to see all that he was, their mouths gaping in their hunger for their lost lives, their bellies empty and rotted away, the cold of Ice House Pond filling them through every opening. By the hundreds they crowded and jostled him, begging him, forcing him, pressing the issue of the intolerableness of their deaths.

Rudy twisted away from them, thrashing toward the surface. Old Finney had put them here, not he. These weren't people he had known, but death made all people the same.

Julie's voice was calling him, asking him to come to her room and tell her a story, give her a good-night kiss. But he ignored her, as he had so many times before.

Rudy gasped as he broke the surface, his eyes wide to the darkness. Even before he caught his first breath, it occurred to him that it had stopped snowing—the storm was gone, the night clear and full of stars.

He choked on his first icy gulps. The sudden exposure to cold air numbed him. He could barely see an edge of ice a few yards in front of him. He tried to swim, but his frozen clothes made him stiff.

Suddenly he felt a sharp point at his back. He tried to turn around, but whatever had snagged him was dragging him rapidly with it. He braced himself to be dragged back beneath the surface.

"Don't fight it!" B.B. shouted behind him. "It's just the pike! Have you out in just a second!"

Rudy could barely feel it when his back bumped up against the edge of the ice. Now that he had been exposed to the dark air, the cold in his limbs had gone to work rapidly, spreading and numbing him clean through to the bone. He barely heard B.B. grunt as he grabbed Rudy under the arms and began dragging him backwards up onto the ice. The big man's strong embrace barely registered.

"It's my fault!" B.B. said breathlessly. "I should've been watching you, you being new at this. But I got too busy harvesting the ice, watching the ice, looking at all the shadows under it and trying to figure out what all might be down there."

"It's . . . not . . ."

"Save it. I almost let you drown down there. And one thing this pond sure don't need is another ghost."

Two hours of blankets, hot coffee, and his overactive furnace, and Rudy was beginning to feel a little like a human being again. B.B. hovered over him like a nervous aunt, running back and forth, second-guessing his every need. Rudy felt a little guilty about it, but didn't make an effort to stop him.

B.B. collapsed on the floor beside him. "You could use a little more furniture, you know," B.B. said.

"I've had other things on my mind of late," Rudy replied. "You could have my chair. I'm feeling much better, you know. . . . Thanks."

B.B. made a gesture of dismissal. "I cut a lot of ice. Most of it's still floating out there, so I'll need to break it up a little in the morning—some of the blocks will bond together overnight. But that isn't a big job. If you're feeling up to it we can finish filling the ice house, and stack the rest out on the shore. Then you can do with it what you like."

"You sound disappointed."

B.B. studied his hands. Rudy could see how raw they were, from repeated frostbite and ice abrasion. B.B. finally looked up at him. "I'm no closer now to figuring out exactly what happened here than I was before. It's true we got some of that old gray ice out of there, and things have calmed down a bit—the pressure is off. But what about my father and brother? So you saw things deep down in the pond; I don't even know what they mean."

"It means, B.B., that we'll have to do considerably more to lure out some of the pond's secrets; it means that this year Greystone Bay is going to get its ice palace," Rudy said.

VI

B.B. informed Rudy that once they had all the pieces cut, with generous help from the townspeople the castle would require about a day to assemble. A cold day, of course, would be best. Rudy left it up to B.B. to predict the coldest day for the event.

On the chosen day, the townspeople started gathering by the pond in late afternoon. Some had seen the flyers posted around town; others claimed to have heard the news from friends. Rudy was distressed to see that most of the volunteers were elderly, those who had first-hand memories of the pond. Most of the young people appeared to be relatives they'd dragged along with them, no doubt with promises of great fun. The ones who didn't stand around with looks of interminable boredom immediately occupied themselves with snowball fights or sledding on the ice. Groups of old men and women followed Rudy around wherever he went, telling him stories about Ice House Pond, The Hand, Old Finney, and how the ice was handled back in the old days.

"Oncet me and a few pals helped a fellow over to Maryville—put away five hundred blocks in his ice house in one day!" one old-timer said, his tobacco-stained teeth a mere inch or so away from Rudy's face. The old fellow waved his hands in excitement. "I worked for four of the five ice companies here in Greystone, even worked on one of these here castles. But not for Old Finney. Hell, he didn't want no help, but I'd be damned if I'd a gone to work for him anyway. Cantankerous sonuvabitch!"

Rudy nodded and smiled, looking over the old man's head for B.B. He finally spotted him supervising a motley crew of old men and women and young kids as they attempted to erect a corner of the palace. "So you gonna hire me, Mr. Boss-man?" Rudy looked down at the man. The man winked up at him. Behind the old man a couple of his elderly friends nodded and smiled. Everywhere he looked Rudy saw eager old faces, their bright red lips and cheeks blowing out great clouds of steam.

"I'm afraid there's no pay," Rudy said. "You could just call this a historical ice harvest and castle construction, I guess."

"Oh, I *know* there's no pay," the old man said eagerly. "Couldn't make much of a go at an ice house these days, anyway, what with all the Frigidaires and Whirlpools. I just like working with the ice! Hell, I'd pay *you!*"

"Then Mr. B.B. can show you where you can help out the best."

"B.B.? Oh, B.B. knows me. B.B. knows I'm experienced!"

"I know, sir—you'll be a great help. Mr. B.B. will put you where you'll be the most useful." Rudy glanced over the man's head at his silent, smiling friends. "*All* of you should report to Mr. B.B. for your assignments."

The old man trotted off happily, his elderly contingent struggling to follow with the same energy. It occurred to Rudy then that the one thing he and B.B. had never discussed was liability insurance. Rudy watched as B.B. and his helpers finished erecting the first of four corners for the castle. Then the helpers went on to the next corner while B.B. walked back to Rudy. Rudy was amused to see that the old man he had just talked to now seemed to be in charge of the "corners crew."

"Are you sure these old people can handle all this construction?" Rudy asked. "Those blocks are heavy."

"Two hundred pounds, easy," B.B. replied. "And you got some learning to do about just how much an old person can do." B.B. chuckled. "Don't worry. This is just about the age group I wanted—they'd be the ones that would have the skills and any understanding about what we're trying to do here." His voice went soft. "They won't say anything to you, but most of them have somebody they know that's been lost. They know something's been wrong here a long time." He crouched down in the snow and scratched lightly at its surface. Rudy watched with an odd sort of anxiety. "I laid out a bottom row for a foundation, and once all the corners are up they shouldn't have any trouble filling in the walls. I'll plumb the walls ever' now and then to check the angles, but we got old-time carpenters out there—they know what they're doing. And a few of the young 'uns'll help out where they need a little more strength on the job."

"And the openings?"

"I've got a couple of fellows picked out to help me on those. It should look pretty much the way Old Finney had it, I guess. I'll do a little sculpting on the towers, and once the sun's down it should be cold enough to use a sprayer for freezing up some interesting effects. So that should do it, right?"

Rudy watched the second corner go up. B.B. was right: The old man seemed to know exactly what he was doing. "B.B., you said these old people have an understanding about what we're trying to do here."

"Yeah."

"What *is* it that we're trying to do here?"

B.B. continued to scratch at the snow. Rudy was beginning to find it irritating. "Hell . . . I don't know, Rudy. We're harvesting the ice out of the pond, getting out way more than we need—I've got a fellow and some kids out there now cutting even more—because that's the way Old Finney did it. We're building that castle, too, because that's what Old Finney did. We're doing everything he did, and we'll see what happens. Maybe nothing—I don't know. But what else do we do?"

Rudy looked out over the pond, which today, with so much of its ice removed, looked very much like any other pond. The water was perfectly calm, reflecting the deep blue of the sky. The morning's clouds had blown away so that the afternoon grew steadily colder, but no colder than might be expected in this climate. He tried to trace the steps that had led him to this ice-harvesting party he was throwing, this ice-castle-raising by his pond, but he could not—it was as if he had been on automatic pilot since his arrival here. It had started with some shadows he had seen in the ice, and which had both surprised and appalled him—he knew that much—and it also had something to do with what he had been thinking about survival, and guilt, and terrible grief and what other people meant to you. When they surrounded you so tightly you could not breathe, what did they mean? Were they the essence of life, or the threat of your imminent death? "I don't know," he said out loud.

"Then let's just continue this and see what happens," B.B. said.

After B.B. went back to the construction site, Rudy watched for several hours as the blocks of ice rose rapidly out of the cold, forming walls and entranceways, gates and towers. Every now and then he would go over and lend a hand, raise a block or use a chisel, but most of the time he was obviously just in the way. The blazing white eye overhead gradually went away.

Twilight came and soon God could no longer see what humankind was up to. *That pond is much bigger than it is,* he thought, as the castle expanded, using up more and more ice, far more ice than Rudy thought the pond could possibly contain. He watched as B.B. climbed on top of the towers and created ice domes with tall spires growing from their centers. He watched as B.B. used a hose attachment to throw misted curtains of water over parts of the structure, where they froze into lacy contours and intricate ornamentations. He watched as minarets and turrets were added, ceilings with long icy stalactites, stalagmite pillars, ramparts and slides and secret pockets in the ice.

The castle followed a plan B.B. had drawn up based on a few old photographs and the recollections of a few of the old-timers around town. It was an elaborate structure—Rudy was beginning to see why it would have been a tourist attraction—and it went up far more quickly than Rudy could have imagined, as if the ice came directly out of the pond prefitted, and each block helped its carrier find the perfect spot for its placement. Despite the often uneven surface of the ice, Rudy could barely make out the seams as the blocks were assembled into walls.

"It's beautiful!" a woman's voice said behind him. "It's just like I remember it!"

Rudy turned to face Emily Lorcaster, who gazed at the castle with tears in her eyes. Rudy thought to caution her against crying, to warn her that her tears might freeze, but talked himself out of the silly notion.

"Where's your husband?" he asked.

"Oh, he won't come *here.* He doesn't approve"—she gestured vaguely at the ice castle—"of all *this.*" Again, she seemed transfixed by her glimpse of the ice castle.

"And why's that?"

"He thinks I live too much in the past as it is. He thinks we all do, and that it isn't healthy. Besides, he never much cared for my grandfather."

No one did besides you, Emily, he thought.

"But from here . . . it's *so* magnificent!" she exclaimed.

"You can take a closer look," he said. Much to his surprise she grabbed his hand and pulled him along with her to the castle. She suddenly seemed like a young girl, and he began to wonder what it was she wanted from him.

She forced him to move too fast for the snow and icy slush that fronted the castle. Each stumble threatened to send them both face-first into the frozen ground. As they moved awkwardly around the shore of the pond he found he was amazed by its clarity. If the sky weren't so dark now he might be able to see all the way to its bottom. Gone were the shadows, the sense of something lurking just beneath the surface. The ice blocks of the castle varied in color from frothy white to near-transparent. *All the shades of purity,* he thought. Apparently, the ice harvest had done something to the essential quality of the ice.

"It's gorgeous!" she cried, leading him through the huge ice archway that formed the main entrance. Townspeople pushed past them laughing and singing, some of them even dancing, their hands stretched out, reaching, striving to form a massive daisy chain with everyone they passed. Even in their heavy winter garb, they moved with no awkwardness, no stiffness, as if they wore nothing at all.

He looked overhead as they entered the first big room. Icicles hung down in clusters like a series of elaborate chandeliers, the illusion made more perfect when they caught the last rays of the dying sun coming through the entranceway. The room was almost a perfect circle. Several ice tunnels led off to other parts of the castle.

"This is *incredible!*" he said. "It *is* a palace!" In fact, it reminded him more of the make-believe castles in fairy stories, or the way he'd imagined Spanish cities must be when he was a child: exquisite in their appearance and unfailingly comfortable. And it was the heaven his father had believed in as a child, but had been denied in the years after his release from the camps.

They wandered through a series of ice caves and larger chambers, passing more and more of the townspeople, some of whom laughed their way through, others shambling in silent awe. In some rooms were ice benches and chairs where people sat. If they remained there too long, would they be able to get up, or would their clothes be frozen to the ice? Now and then he thought he heard B.B.'s voice winding its way from some other part of the castle, but he never did see him.

Some of the townspeople stood in darkened corners of the structure, as if waiting for something. It bothered him. Everyone was watching him.

The castle was much bigger than it had first appeared from the outside. *They hadn't had enough time to build all this.* Again, he looked around nervously for B.B., to explain things to him. Fog swirled in some of the entrances and under some of the doors—condensation and sudden changes of temperature, he thought. Old men and women came in and out of the fog, but none said anything to him. When they came close he moved, afraid to have them touch him.

He came to see the townspeople as not simply other, but *other.* Their faces were gray and shadowed. *They were no longer human*. . . . Sometimes in distant halls he could hear a small girl's laughter.

Near the back of the castle they arrived at a short staircase of ice blocks. "This way," Emily whispered. "We can get away from all these people." Then she pushed him up the stairs.

The ice walls here were imperfectly formed, their surfaces streaked and cracked. In fact, a crevasse had formed on one wall, so large that Rudy feared for the safety of the entire structure. "I think we'd better warn . . ." he said, turning around, but Emily Lorcaster wasn't there.

The castle suddenly seemed very quiet. He turned back around and looked at the damaged walls. The outer layers of ice were shaving off and dropping onto the floor. Dark stains flowed down the walls as the ice began to melt. Black rivulets crisscrossed the ice floor.

Rotted chunks of ice fell from the castle roof, shattering into bone-shaped fragments at his feet.

In one corner of the room was a crib sculpted out of ice. He walked over to it. Black holes had melted into the bottom of the crib. He bent closer to peer inside: The holes seemed endless. Their edges melted together, widened, the dripping ice around those edges half-frozen into icicle teeth. Rudy stepped back. They looked like a nest of hungry mouths.

He turned away and stared at the slight shadows of countless children trapped within the crumbling ice walls. Their faces came closer to the surface. He could see that all their mouths were open. Their shadow hands came up to the surface of the ice, fingers outstretched, and then their emaciated arms and skeleton fingers thrust completely through the ice, begging, desperate to touch. Their porous skin hung like pale, damp tissue from their bones, as if they had been underwater for a very long time.

The ice walls began to split. They leaned precariously. In the distance he could hear other parts of the structure rumbling. Rudy could feel the closeness of a terrible cold.

In me, he thought. *The terrible cold in my heart and in Old Finney's heart is responsible for all this ice.*

The floor split open as the ice blocks beneath him slipped and faulted. Rudy fell past long curls of ice, broken white cornices, shattered pinnacles many feet tall, curtains of icicles and fragile accumulations of rime. *The pond is much bigger than it is.* Countless frozen hands tried to grab him, whether to hurt or help him he had no idea. *We all live in a cemetery, all of us—there's no escaping it.* He thought of concentration camps where the dead were stacked into huge freezers, then shipped into the German mountains by the thousands in order to cool the Führer's summer home. His arms and legs grew numb, his chest almost too cold to move the air through his lungs.

He could barely feel. *But isn't that what I've wanted?*

The sudden halt in his descent left him dizzy and unable to breathe. He was inside a huge bubble of ice it seemed, the only entrance or exit being the hole he'd torn through the ceiling during his descent. *I'm down inside the frozen pond. The pond has a basement.*

Around him lay hundreds of small hummocks of ice. Mounds of snow. The air was so cold that the warmth of his body, carried in his breath, created great stretches of white cloud across the chamber. Scattered about were larger pieces of ice, almost small bergs, with hollows and soft places, the ravaged ice skulls of a tribe of giants.

The coldness in my heart created this cemetery. He thought about Eva, sweet Julie, Marsha and their unborn child, his father dead of cancer ("I caught it in the camps. It sounds crazy but I swear—I know it's true."). His life had become a tombstone. His heart was a headstone of ice.

Thin hands with broken fingernails broke through the surface of the icy hummock beside him. The sounds of cracking and shifting ice filled the chamber, echoing back and forth from wall to wall until it overlapped his own thoughts and it was his thoughts cracking, his nerves splitting and thawing his emotions.

Across the chamber, hands and knees and feet and heads emerged from the ice, flesh tearing on the ragged edges of ice, bones breaking audibly. But there were no outcries. No blood. Pale faces tight against the bone. Slow shuffling gaits. Eyes straight ahead, uninterested in what lay around them. Mouths gaping, moving, hungry for something but not knowing what. All those Old Finney had murdered over the years and dumped into Ice House Pond rose up and began to walk.

The forces of memory set in motion, ready to devour the living. The pond was much much bigger. Once he'd set them in motion, Rudy could not avoid the moving walls of ice. The walls of ice crushed everything in their path.

The moving figures were multiplying with a perverse fecundity. The bodies—so many of them—pressed up against him, touching, rubbing, pushing him hard against the ice. Now and then one would reach out to hold him, and he'd feel guilty when he evaded its grasp.

Rudy was appalled to discover that there was more than one layer of bodies below the icy hummocks. After the first wave had passed and gone to the icy sides of the bubble where it futilely attempted to scale the walls, more pale hands and feet and heads appeared from the ragged holes. The dead staggered forth, their hands outstretched, clutching one another in a great, obscene daisy chain. Flesh rubbed against flesh until they began to meld.

And after these another wave, and then still another. All the Greystone dead rising up through the pond, through the doorway Old Finney's coldness had created and Rudy's own coldness had allowed to continue. They rubbed and joined until all these pasts were the same, all flesh the same, and Rudy was able to crawl his way out of the hole in the ceiling on top of this great mound of death.

Back on the shore, the ice castle was collapsing. He joined Emily and B.B. to watch the end. He thought about his family, his families, now long gone. *When they died, the world should have died. If the world doesn't die on its own, sometimes you have to murder it.* Obviously he hadn't been the first to feel that way. Old Finney knew. But now Rudy felt the freest he had in years. His families were gone forever. But he was still alive.

After a few days Rudy gave serious thought to what he would have to do to get back to the city and start his life over again. He thought it likely that Mr. Lorcaster would be eager to buy the place back from him, especially if Rudy had Mrs. Lorcaster on his side. Ice House Pond belonged to Greystone Bay—it was too dangerous to permit some outsider to live there. B.B. would help straighten up things around the place, board up the windows, shut off the furnace for good. And seal up all entrances to the ice house. B.B. had claimed to have achieved some peace after what he'd seen in the ice castle, although he never would tell Rudy exactly what he had seen.

But Rudy knew such plans were useless. He knew he wouldn't be leaving. Not anytime soon at least. When the next cold weather arrived in the Bay, pushing the fog into great pools that filled every depression, he was aware of the invisible hands on his body, seeking comfort and release.

* * *

Rudy's father used to read him a story from one of the big fairy-tale books in his study, an adaptation of one of the Norse myths, having to do with the end of the world. Rudy had read the story to Julie hundreds of times, from the time she was four years old. She had loved it very much. When she had curled up against his chest during those readings, his stronger breath seeming to support and drive hers, he had thought he was protecting her from all harm. He had believed he was insuring her a long and happy life. As far as he had been concerned, Julie was going to live forever.

When the end of the world finally came—and certainly few were surprised that it came, having seen it in their dreams for years, having seen it even in the faces of their newborn children—the seas, lakes, and rivers all frozen solid. The fish were all fixed in their places, their final sea-thoughts preserved for all time, so that looking through the ice the fisherman believed these fish had simply been painted on the underside of the ice, and they went home without their daily catch, waiting for death with their families.

When the gods died they began to dream, and those dreams took the form of snowfall. And the dead gods dreamed for a very long time. ("I guess they had nothing else better to do," his father had always remarked.) The snow piled up unendingly.

The winds screamed. There was no heat in the sun, which had become old and white, a blind eye.

The great wolf Skoll, who had pursued the sun through the heavens for millenia, finally caught up with it, leapt upon it, and devoured it. ("You can't escape the past," Rudy had told her, hugging her close against the cold, hoping she would remember this someday. "You just learn to live with its ghosts.")

The moon died in the night. The stars flickered and went out, leaving a darkness greater than any before.

Josie, In the Fog

by Charles L. Grant

GREYSTONE BAY DIED THAT YEAR, the year Josie came home. It wasn't a spectacular death, and the town did the best it could, but there was snow, and heat, and tides much too high for the jetties to contain; and when we met on the last day of the last spring, I could tell she was trying awfully hard not to cry. That was only one of the surprises I had had since she'd returned, not the least of which was that she had returned at all. She hated it all, both the Bay, and the bay. Never swam in it with the rest of us, never fished, never saw the beauty of the sun on white pebbles beneath the surface when the water was clear and the waves were low, could never hand-catch the small dark fish that tried to hide in the dark shallows. It wasn't that she was all that different; she just didn't like it.

I shifted, waited patiently, fussed with the laces of sneakers long since worn thin at the toe and around the heel. My mother had been trying forever to get me to buy a new pair, but I resisted. They were, I said, the ones I had hit my only home run in, how could I get rid of them and not jinx myself?

She wasn't impressed.

But then she had never seen me play either. She thought baseball, in or out of school, was a complete waste of time when there were so many good books to read, so many interesting places to visit, so many "nice young ladies" I could be bringing to the house, for lemonade or dinner or for a Sunday afternoon visit. Right. To the house. With my mother dropping hints like a World War II bomber, and my father belching beer in the backyard and complaining to the air and robins about how fast the shaved ice melted under his fish in the deli, we'll probably all starve before August.

Bring a girl around.

Right.

Ganner once suggested I pretend I was a monk; Craig said monks were no good, I'd have to pretend I was dead. At least until the summer began and all the girls in their bathing suits were back in on the beach and couldn't easily escape, like herds of ripe-for-plucking gazelle stalked by ravenous cheetah. Nobody thought it was funny. Besides, Ganner already had Hillie, and Craig had anyone he wanted.

I, on the other hand, was too tall, too many bones waiting vainly for flesh and muscle, a face too smooth to do anything with but pat gently on the cheek. Like Craig said, I could hit a home run but I damn well couldn't score. My Uncle Wayne had put it right, even though it had hurt: "Rick, god help you, right now you're every girl's big brother."

Except Josie.

And she had moved away four years ago, my junior year in high school, taking my adolescent heart with her in the bottom of her expensive luggage, someone mailing it back that first Christmas in a crumpled, soiled envelope marked "Addressee Unknown."

Jesus, how I had loved her.

A roll of my eyes and a silent groan at the image, at how stupid I had been, how my friends had teased, then laughed, then just avoided me until I had come to my senses and had seen, in one morning's mirror, the real jackass I had become. Some kind of dumbass raving Romeo or something, wilting like a poor fragile flower because its sun had been forever taken away. Jesus. Christ.

Then the Bay began to die.

And Josie Pastor came back home.

"Hell," she said, a husky voice that carried even when she whispered.

She had called last night.

I had just gotten out of the shower.

"Rick?"

A frown. "Yeah?"

"It's Josie."

My sister had come racing down the upstairs hall then, grabbed at the towel tucked loosely around my waist, and shrieked with laughter when it folded to the floor. By the time I had dropped the receiver, grabbed up the towel, rewrapped it, grabbed up the receiver again and gasped, "Josie, you still there?", she wasn't.

Just a dial tone.

But if she really was back, back from wherever, I knew where she would meet me. So I had gone out to a narrow stretch of sand too small to be a real beach, tucked between huge boulders near the base of North Hill.

When she finally came, scrambling agilely over the rocks as if she'd never been away, I amazed myself by not feeling much at all, just a slight surprise that she hadn't changed much, though I wasn't exactly sure what I expected; it wasn't as if she'd been away for fifty years—tall, complexion oddly dark for the shade of her red hair, a face people stared at without knowing they were, not because she was beautiful but because she had eyes so pale and blue they were sometimes disturbing, sometimes, and unnervingly, just not there.

She plucked a ragged broken shell from the sand, tossed it over the waves sliding past us toward the beach, then wiped a sleeve over her face and looked eastward in disgust at the ragged broken town. "I don't know how you stand it, Rick, honest to god I don't."

"Clean living," I said, deliberately misunderstanding her.

She turned her head so slowly I couldn't see it move; one minute she was in profile, freckled with shadow, the next she was looking at me with a teacher's sternly pursed lips, an exasperated mother's narrow eyes. "Jerk."

"Who? Me?"

She uncurled her legs, stood and stretched, and said, "Jerk," again before striding away. Paused before she was out of sight and looked over her shoulder. Hair across her face. One visible eye so pale it seemed white, seemed empty. Insubstantial and seductive, like a movie-screen image that would be coarse if I touched it, and so didn't touch it, didn't try. The image would serve.

She waited.

I watched, stomach hollow, willing myself to stay where I was, I was older now, she had to do more than just wink and purse her lips, crook her finger and beckon.

I didn't love her anymore.

Her photograph in my closet hadn't been taken out for over a year.

Not since I'd heard the news, and in hearing, didn't believe; and in not believing, lost my chance.

When she yelled, "Jerk!" a third time and left, artfully

flouncing, refusing a look over her shoulder, I didn't follow. Josie, in one of her moods, had always been something more than a royal pain in the ass, something less than a perfect candidate for murder. Besides, I didn't have the energy for it. And she wasn't going to leave the Bay anytime soon anyway.

Not until she killed me.

I grinned then—for the melodrama, for the setting there above the waves, for the way I picked up a stone myself and aimed it at a tide pool somewhat larger than my bed. It missed. I supposed I could have made something of it, but I didn't. It would have been too much. It would have meant slipping back into the melancholy I had almost forgotten. Instead I grunted to my feet, dusted off my jeans, and wondered what the hell I was going to do next.

I could always go back to the road, get in the car, return to town and tell the police there was a chance I was in danger. But the ones who were left would only look at me, shake their heads, and tell me to get lost. We're getting outta here, kid, they would say while they packed; what's the matter with you, are you blind as well as stupid?

Or I could go home to a fairly large house opposite the cemetery on Baylor Street, which would suit my mood as well as my future. An empty house now because the family had left this morning.

Or I could go after her.

Ridiculous.

Not unthinkable, of course; just ridiculous.

I didn't love her anymore; I just never forgot her.

So, faced with probably doing nothing at all, I slipped and slid my way across the rocks, ducked around slick brown boulders where barnacles clung in shadow, found the path we always used, and climbed to the top. The breeze was cooler there for whatever reason breezes are sometimes cooler when you're not near the water, and I put my face to it, let the sweat dry and my hair play a little, before leaning back against my car and looking down at where I lived.

I couldn't see any people.

The marina almost directly below me, Harbor Road, the shops and the hotels and the seawall and the beach—all of them were empty. Port Boulevard was a desert, nothing grew and nothing moved. All of it like a theater set whose paint had begun to peel away, chip away, the lighting not quite right and the curtain old and frayed.

And the actors . . . they never came.

I think my folks had known for weeks, maybe months, that the end was near. They had never gone on vacation before, you see. Dad was always too busy with the store and Mom was always too busy trying to be busy. But suddenly they were gone, off, they said, to New Hampshire, and they made me promise, made me swear, that as soon as I'd said my good-byes to my friends, I'd get on the next bus along.

A crow fat and old settled on what was left of a pine tree at the edge of the drop, watching me with what I was sure was great amusement.

I sneered at it.

It ruffled its wings, and settled with its back to the road, to me.

Little prick, I thought, and looked west toward the horizon, squinting in the wind.

There it was.

Sitting out there, erasing the horizon as far up and down the coast as you could see.

The story goes, as stories go, that Greystone Bay was born in a fog that hadn't been born for any natural reason. I don't know if that's right, it sounds pretty good, but if that fog bank out there ever decided to come in, I sure as hell knew how the hell the place would die. That thing was thick, and unlike others I'd known every spring since I'd been born, it didn't send bits and clouds of itself inland, as if testing the temperature of the land for survival. It was just there, and I had an uncomfortable feeling that if I took a boat, and touched it, my hand wouldn't go through.

The crow preened.

I sneered again, and grinned maliciously when the sputter and cough of a wheezing car made the crow lift into the air. But it didn't flee. It hung there. Black against blue. Riding the currents as if it were a gull.

I shivered, turned, saw a sedan that should have died in a junkyard years ago clank and smoke to a halt at the place where the unpaved road turned down off the hill. I waved, and as I did I frowned, because I could see suitcases and boxes piled in the backseat, and the trunk lid tied as far down as it could go over more boxes and cartons.

Ganner Durham slid red-faced out the passenger door, puffing and swearing; Hillie Bergman emerged from the back, holding her skirt against the wind; Craig Lamat took his own sweet time getting out from behind the wheel.

Jesus, I thought; they're really going to do it.

I didn't know whether to be angry or frightened.

Hillie came to me first, red curly hair grabbing for the breeze, eyes squinting, arms folded across her stomach and hands clasped around each elbow. "You playing Heathcliff today?" she said as she kissed my cheek, stared over my shoulder for a moment at the fog out there, waiting.

I shook my head. "No moors, sorry."

"No sympathy, either," she said flatly.

Ganner, round where Hillie was thin, rounder where she was round, slapped at his shirttails flapping around his waist. "Christ, this is nuts." He wore oversize sunglasses, undersize jeans, and wood sandals, bright red socks. He had no hair for the breeze to work with; that was his choice, and it made him look stupid, and twice as heavy. "We could have a great time, you know. Vagabonds, gypsies, midnight campfires, shit like that." He looked at me, but I couldn't see his eyes, only rectangles of the hazy sky. "You're out of your mind, Molleen. You're out of your goddamn mind."

Craig stayed by the car. Sunglasses there, too; silver. I couldn't see his eyes either, but I could his hands, and they were nervous.

"You have to come, Rick," Hillie said softly.

Ganner picked up a stone and threw it at the crow, still up there, still riding.

"I can't," I told her. "Josie would kill me."

"She'll kill you anyway," Ganner snapped. He stabbed a finger at his temple. "She's going to kill you because you know goddamn well—"

Hillie slapped his arm hard; he wasn't apologetic. Neither was she.

"I don't think so," I said when he didn't speak again. I didn't. I really didn't. She couldn't kill me because I didn't love her.

Ganner turned away, to the bay, the beach, the town. "Damn. All the money I used to make at the SeaHarp there, you know? Every summer I was in high school, dawn to dark every day. Tote that bag, lift that trunk, plant them guests in their rocking chair coffins, fetch for the drunks and flirt with the ladies, chase the damn kids out of the gardens." He laughed and scratched at the back of his head. "God, I made a fortune in tips and hated every minute of it. God."

"Listen," Hillie said to me, "I'm not going to let you ruin your life, okay? You're going to come with us if I have to drag you myself."

I was touched. I was angry. I was Rick, the stumble-around kid who needed a keeper when it came to women, to studies, to practically getting dressed in the morning. If it wasn't my mother, it was my aunts; if it wasn't my aunts, it was my friends, the female ones.

And it used to be that if it wasn't them, it was Josie.

The crow settled back on its tree and called to us.

Hillie shivered.

I knew why.

It sounded too much like a laugh.

Ganner threw more rocks down the slope, muttering to himself and shaking his head.

Craig reached into the car and blew the horn.

"Rick?"

"Hillie, look, I know what you all are thinking, and you're wrong. Not only that, you're nuts, okay? My folks are nuts. Everybody's nuts. Jesus." I swept an arm to cover the empty streets, the deserted beach. "There are terminals, tides, cold fronts, all kinds of shit to explain the damn fog. You guys are acting like it was the Millenium or something. You listen to those stupid preachers, you'd think it was the end of the goddamn world."

Hillie's eyes instantly rimmed with red.

"Don't," I warned her. "It isn't going to work."

Ganner came up behind her, touched her shoulder. "Let's go," he said, not looking at me.

She shook her head.

He grabbed her shoulder this time. "Damnit, let's go, Hillie. He's a jerk, okay? Or he's a goddamn hero. I don't give a damn, but I ain't walking all the way. Which I may have to if Craig leaves without us."

She shook her head.

I couldn't believe it, the way they were acting. A fog rolls partway in, hangs in there, quite naturally blocks boats and ships from coming in or going out, and the town goes wild. Revival meetings, experts from the universities, government people who think we're nuts too. Plenty of perfectly rational explanations that, for some bizarre reason, nobody believed. But what astonished me the most was the way Ganner, Hillie, and Craig had been behaving. First, it was party time, and there were plenty of them—boats sailing and motoring right up to the edge of the bank, music blaring, beer flowing, dancing, laughing, and not a little taunting.

That lasted about a week.

The second week saw the first of the fishermen creep around North Hill and Blind Point to other ports; the tourists who had come to see the fog left, and stayed away.

The third week brought empty stores and empty houses and empty schools and empty churches, as if Greystone Bay hadn't existed at all.

Amazing.

I had already started a book about it, a firsthand account of the birth of a ghost town. When this was over, when the wind finally drove the fog away, I was going to make a fortune. I already had more photographs than I needed, and a dozen commitments from a dozen magazines for articles and excerpts. My high school English teacher would have a heart attack if she knew; I planned to send her an autographed copy.

Craig blew the horn again.

Ganner insisted they leave, his face slowly reddening, and

Hillie finally surrendered with a sigh and a single tear. I could tell she wanted to say something to me, but Ganner wouldn't let her. He took her hand and led her away, released the hand and slipped the arm around her waist. She leaned against him. They didn't say good-bye.

And I didn't wave.

At that moment, watching their backs, I hated the three of them. All the years we had known each other, all the troubles we'd gotten into, gotten each other out of with friendship and outright lying through our teeth, all the times we ate and slept over and argued and parted and came together again and wept and laughed and did some pretty hilarious and stupid things . . . all that time.

All that time.

I stared out at the ocean, heard car doors slam, heard an engine fire and grumble, heard wheels roll over the dirt road. And stop.

Heard footsteps, running, and turned back just as Craig reached out to grab me.

"You idiot," he said, voice hoarse and low, lower lip not quite trembling. "You goddamn stupid son of a bitch, what the hell are you trying to prove?"

I blinked; I said nothing.

He punched my shoulder. "She's *dead,* you jackass."

I blinked; I said nothing.

His lips worked, his gaze tried to get inside me and find some answers, his hands became fists that opened and closed until he had to jam them into his pockets.

"Rick, for god's sake."

I blinked.

I said nothing.

He couldn't take it. He was either going to hit me again or

walk away, and I watched as he walked away. Ran away. Practically fell into the car and backed out of sight.

I didn't wave.

The crow talked to me again.

"Yeah, yeah, yeah," I muttered angrily. "Yeah, yeah, yeah, go to hell."

I walked around my car then, examining it as if I were in the market for its purchase. It was my first car. Rust here and there, dents and dings here and there; it was the most beautiful machine in the world, and I loved it. I patted its roof, dusted the outline of its trunk, looked in at the steering wheel and the sheepskin cover I'd put around it, god only knows why. Then I left it and walked to the headland, pushing aside brush that was stiff with dying—brittle and snagging—until I found a clearing not far from the edge.

I sat down, cross-legged, and picked at the earth.

That's when the chill began; that's when spring's warmth fled from North Hill and left me in shadow even though the sun still shone.

That's when I heard Craig say *she's dead, you jackass,* and that's when I saw the fog bank begin at last to shift and break. I grinned. I saw my books on the stands and my picture in the magazines, and saw a decidedly obscene number as my bank account balance.

The crow flapped over me, dove down toward the rocks I couldn't see from my position, and reappeared.

Riding the currents.

I stared at it for so long I finally had to rub my eyes to clear my vision, and that's when I realized that the fog bank wasn't breaking up at all; it was moving. Bits of it, clouds of it sneaking on ahead. Not a fog, not really, but a mist that had decided it had waited long enough.

* * *

Like the mist on the pond.

December, just after Christmas four years ago, and we were all there in Fletcher Park for a skating party one night. A low fire for hot dogs and coffee and warmth, snow for snowballs, the prolonged scrape and cut of blades on the rough ice. Calls in the dark, sharp in the sharp air. Music from a tape deck on the opposite bank where another fire burned, but the mist rising from the ice spread that light, diffused it, exaggerated its dance and the shadows both fires created.

Ganner, without his pencil-mustache and twenty pounds lighter, trying to get up a game of night hockey with some of the other skaters around the pond; Craig and his latest girl, skating with their arms about their waists, showing off and not doing very well; Hillie was there, bundled for weather a hundred degrees colder, not really a part of us yet but knowing she would be soon enough; me standing by myself on the bank, looking for Josie, who had disappeared a few minutes before. Aching for her. Practically yearning. Cursing myself viciously for telling her how I felt the day before, and nearly hysterical with anticipation because she hadn't laughed but had whispered that she had something special she wanted me to have. But later. After the party.

Laughter and squeals.

Blades on the ice, harsh and soft.

I hurt that I was alone. Tonight was supposed to have been different. Tonight, Josie had promised again by touch and look and what hadn't been said that she would tease me no more about being sweet sixteen and never been kissed. But when all the others arrived and the party began to jell, she had deliberately avoided me, skating arm-in-arm with Ganner, whispering with Hillie, only once in a while coming to me, smiling, trying to coax me out onto the ice.

I wouldn't go.

She was a champion, state and almost national, and seldom missed an opportunity to remind us all how terribly good she was, in this and other things; *my* efforts, in skates tied so tightly there was hardly any blood in my feet, barely got me to the other side in one piece where I'd have to rest for a minute before starting back. Less than a hundred yards. I was no good, never had been.

Skates rushing.

Figures gliding.

Craig, short and bulky and determinedly hatless, skating around Hillie, who twirled in place and fell, scrambled up and tried to trip him.

Fire snapping.

The mist breaking and reforming.

And Josie.

Suddenly Josie.

I saw her out there and hurried down the shallow bank to the edge of the ice. I had no skates on then, and my gloved hands were crammed tightly into my parka's pockets. And from where I stood I could see it all, in a world that had abruptly lost all its sound.

Figures dark and moving, untouched by the dim flickering light; bits of ice sailing in slow motion from charging blades; Hillie's mouth open as she raced after Craig right to left; Craig looking over his shoulder, mouth open in a mocking dare; Ganner speeding in from the left, a branch in hand to slap at a stone he was using as a puck.

Josie heading straight for me.

Arms behind her back, legs moving, firelight winking from

the firelight in her hair, head down, face up. Smiling. Grinning. Through the mist and gone, out of the mist and dark against the light behind her.

No sound.

Just the movement.

I blinked and tried to wave my arms, to cry a warning, but my arms wouldn't move fast enough and my throat wouldn't unlock, and all I could do was stand there and watch as Ganner collided with Hillie and knocked her backward.

while Josie came through the mist

and Craig tripped over Hillie's arm and spun, grabbed for Ganner, spun him, whipped him, and didn't release him

while Josie came through the mist

and I stepped helplessly onto the ice, face contorted when Ganner lost his balance and landed on his back, Craig on his stomach, and their arms and legs windmilled as they turned so slowly I was sure Josie would see them and swerve neatly out of their way

but Josie came through the mist

and they collided.

The silence broke, but there was no sound beyond the fire's spitting, a rush of air that might have been a breeze, and the tangled bodies thrashing over the ice toward where I stood. Slower. Slower. Until Ganner's mulelike laugh brought back the music and the steel on ice and Hillie's giggles and Craig's guffaws, and the worry on my face replaced by a grin I damn well knew was going to split my face in half.

Josie was nearly naked as she slid to a halt at my feet.

A hand grabbing blindly at her for help, the rough ice snagging and bunching her sweater, the sheer force of the collision . . . Nobody knew, and nobody asked.

Her ski pants were down around her ankles, her sweater was up around her armpits, and her breasts caught the light because she hadn't worn a bra.

The first thing I thought was that my god she had really meant it, and the second was that she was going to be royally pissed.

The wind had been knocked out of her, and she lay on her back, gasping, gulping, staring at me *for god's sake cover me up you shithead,* her arms flapping weakly at her sides.

I only stared.

The others stared.

What seemed like the whole town popping out of the mist and skating by, pointing, whooping, snickering, commenting, until Hillie finally arrived and stripped off her jacket, knelt and dropped it over Josie's chest. Only then was there a storm of offers to help, apologies, blushing, blaming everyone in sight, getting her to her feet where she stood in rigid anger while Hillie pulled up her pants, pulled down her sweater, dusted her off.

"Bastard," she said to me.

I couldn't answer.

She shook off all the hands and skated away.

Into the mist.

Like the mist across the bay.

The crow was gone.

The sun aimed squarely at the middle of my back.

It's funny about people like Josie Pastor. You can call them all kinds of names, play all kinds of stupid tricks, try to beat them in things they liked to consider their forte, which in Josie's case was just about everything you could mention. You can do all this stuff, and they hardly bat an eye.

Humiliate them, however, and their sanity switches off.

I don't get it; I never did.

She never spoke to me again, not after that night in Fletcher Park. Like the rest of us, she was off to college; unlike me, however, she had the money to stay there, to stay away. I had to take this semester off; the funds weren't available and I wasn't smart enough for a scholarship and my dad wasn't prosperous enough for a loan. It happens.

Like the car that went off the road in Colorado and killed Josie last year.

It was in the *Greystone Gazette,* of course, and we all sat around the Seven Sirens, and other watering holes, and muttered how sorry we were, what a hell of a way to die, when I die I want to go quick, not bleed to death the way the article said Josie did. In the dark. But they weren't really sincere. Ganner had always thought her an unbearable snob, Hillie thought her a bitch, Craig thought her a conquest he'd never made and never wanted. That's all. Which was why they barely tolerated my mentioning her now and then.

They didn't hate her; they just didn't care.

Her death, then, meant less to them than the death a week later of Hillie's ancient, crippled dog, who had been around since all of us, practically, had been alive. Not an accident; it just slipped away while it slept.

Funny thing, though.

Funny.

When Josie called last night, I wasn't surprised, and I never once believed it was some kind of hoax.

There are some things you know, and some things you don't; I knew that Josie would come back to get me.

Humiliation, you see.

It sounds silly, definitely petty, but people like Josie Pastor just never forgive. Not to the point of actual murder, of course, but definitely to the edge of what they like to call revenge in kind. And being the idiot I am, if you listen to my kid sister, I was curious to find out how Josie was going to humiliate me. When she was alive, it probably would have been easy; now that she was dead, and the Bay was empty, it made for fascinating speculation.

A hell of an ending for my book.

I know what Hillie had wanted to say to me back there; it was clear in her eyes, the words already at her lips: *You're crazy, she's dead.*

I don't know. Maybe I am. Right now, I don't think it matters.

I picked up a stone and flipped it over the edge.

A gust of salty wind blasted into my face and I twisted away from it, just in time to hear an explosion. Faint. Distant. I scrambled awkwardly to my feet, shaded my eyes, and looked down at Harbor Road.

There was fire there, and smoke, in the middle of the street, at the Port Boulevard intersection. Colored helpless things fluttered over the sidewalk, the seawall, and it took me a moment to realize they were clothes. Some of them were burning, most of them were not. The dense smoke cleared for a moment, and something burst out of the flames that had erupted from the car. Someone. I don't know who. Waving arms, smoking, stumbling to the seawall and, finally, toppling over to the beach to lie there and let the fire do its job.

I couldn't breathe.

A white shirt—a T-shirt, a winter nightgown, I don't know—somehow made it beyond the breakers where the wind released it, and it bobbed gently with the waves, not quite reaching the sand, not quite riding out to sea, not quite fully visible through the mist that had reached the shore. I watched it with mouth open, watched until it sank.

That's when something decided it was time to run, it was time to get the hell out because revenge is one thing, and vengeance is something else.

Two steps, maybe three, was all I managed before I saw Josie coming through the brush.

She wasn't angry; she wasn't gloating; she wasn't smiling; she was beautiful.

She didn't touch me. She sat, drew her legs up, and hugged her knees as she watched the fog. "You're a bastard, you know that?"

I sat. "It's part of my charm."

Christ, I'm a liar:

I loved her then; I love her now.

"If you're so damn smart, Molleen, do you know why you're such a bastard?"

I had a dozen quips, a few wisecracks, and some snappy repartee to counter the question. I looked at her, saw her face, and shook my head.

Her chin settled on her knees. "Because," she said, "I never forgot you."

I didn't know how to respond, or how she meant it.

"They were laughing," she said; a lift of her shoulders better than a sigh. "You weren't. You wanted to, I could see it, but you didn't. You didn't laugh." She turned her head, one eye squinting. "But you didn't help me, either. You didn't help me, Rick."

"For Christ's sake," I said, my temper fraying as my nerves began to quit, "it was only a damn party, remember? And there was an accident, so what?"

I knew what.

She knew it too.

There are some kinds of people . . .

Something occurred to me then, and the chill returned,

much stronger, hunching my shoulders briefly and tightening my jaw. "You didn't . . . I mean, this wasn't . . ." I jerked a thumb toward town.

"No."

But she didn't mean Craig's car.

I rubbed my arms to warm them, rubbed the tops of my thighs. It didn't work. The wind had stopped, but the chill remained, and the fog kept drifting inland.

My kid sister teases me all the time, not because I'm her brother and a perfectly natural target because I don't dare hit back; it's because I'm famous, or infamous, for being the dense one in the family. Not stupid necessarily; not gullible, either, but something close enough for kin. I'm perfect for practical jokes; it takes me forever to understand what people are saying when they don't say it straight out, and I've never been able to figure people out unless I've known them forever. Partly, I suppose, it's because I haven't yet put together all the experiences I've had, as limited as they are, into something that might, someday, be the foundation of the kind of wisdom that simply comes with age.

I just didn't *know*.

So when I looked at Josie, and was digging for the courage to ask her what she planned to do with me, or to me, or if I was going to be haunted by her for the rest of my life, I was shocked to see the way she was looking at me in turn.

Jesus, I thought.

She looked away.

Jesus, I think she loves me.

I stood up quickly, put my back to the sea, and swallowed a cry when I saw the fog finally crawl over the seawall. It wasn't a mist now. It was grey, and it was thick, and it rolled up the Boulevard, and Birch Street, and Hull Street, up Nightbird and Accaro, over the SeaHarp Hotel, over the

Atlantic and the Ocean Arms, over the marina, over the shops and houses, not in a wall like a tidal wave rolls, but in slow motion billows and great humps tumbling over each other as though the fog were made of large and small grey things that couldn't wait to find their place at the head of the line.

The crow flew over it, circled it, dove into it, reappeared and rode the currents. Like a gull, I thought again, and realized with a start that the gulls weren't around, and they hadn't been for weeks.

Josie stood, dusted her legs, and moved to my side; she didn't touch me.

"You didn't do this," I said.

"No."

I believed her.

We watched then as the fog reached the park and swallowed it and the famous pond, reached the hospital and consumed it, reached the cemetery and buried it, reached the Plaza and took it, reached my house and I looked away.

"It had its chance, you know," she said, and this time she took my hand. I flinched without thinking, but she didn't pull away; she was patient, and I relaxed. I had to. Her flesh was warm, her skin was soft. A thread of hair reached out and drifted across my cheek. "The Bay had its chance, a couple of hundred years. But sometimes there just isn't enough around to keep a place going. You can call it energy, you can call it power, you can call it a life force, you can call it God or the Devil; I wouldn't know."

The fog began to climb the cliffs. Billowing. Rolling.

Waves against the boulders at the bottom of the cliff.

She had to raise her voice; but just a little, not a lot. "Holy men build a place, and . . ." She shrugged. "All you can find now are ruins."

The crow flew toward Blind Point, but I couldn't see the place anymore, and soon I couldn't see the bird.

"Sometimes, men that aren't so holy build a place, and maybe you don't even find the ruins."

Twilight took the rest of town, drawing the fog inside it and turning it grey to black.

"That isn't always true, though," I said.

"That's right. It's not."

My father still thinks I'm a kid, my mother still thinks I'm her baby, my kid sister thinks I'm something closer to a brain-dead mule.

Jesus God, I'm going to miss them.

"And sometimes," Josie said, taking my other hand, tugging gently, turning me to face her, "some people just never learn to give up."

At my feet now, and touches of it drifting to my face like the kiss of a passing ghost.

She looked so sad, and so angry, that I wanted to embrace her, hold her as tightly as I could, kiss her where before I'd only kissed her in my dreams.

At my waist, and it was cold.

Dusk now, and there were no streetlamps to bring the light, no neon, no headlamps, or lamps in windows. The theaters were dark, the trees were gone, the valley beyond the town invisible in the grey.

The slow dying sun, weak below the horizon, mottled her face with shifting shadow, made her figure insubstantial, made her sad and angry smile nothing more than a flare of white.

The crow called out once.

I heard the tide explode and roar.

She squeezed my hands.

Her skin was warm; her flesh was soft.

And then, without a word, she was gone.

I didn't move. I didn't call her name. I put my palms to my cheeks and smelled her, and felt her, and I think I let her go. I can't be sure, you see, because, like my sister says, I'm pretty dense at lots of things.

I let her go, I think I did; but if I did, it wasn't soon enough.

Slow learner, I guess.

But I do, sooner or later, learn.

And I felt then the fear come in with the tide, I felt the emptiness of the air; I felt the ground, and through it felt the rumbling vibrations of the waves; I felt the little boy trying so damn hard to be a man.

And I saw Greystone Bay die, taken back by the fog that despite the ocean's voice was done in total quiet. Not a scream. Not a sob. Not a single plea for mercy.

It was gone.

But without knowing why, or how—and not even caring, not now—I also knew that it wouldn't be long before the fog would change its mind and bring it back. Someplace else; some other time. Another part of the coast, maybe, or another country, in a valley, on a plain. It wasn't gone for good. It would be back. Just like the fog.

I won't be with it, though.

I'll still be here. Standing on the headland, listening to the sea.

Waiting for the crow.

I have no choice.

I let her go, I let her leave me, but she's still out there, and she won't let me go at all.

She loves me, you see.

I wasn't wrong.
After all this time, she still loves me.
In the sea.
And in the fog.

The Final Chroniclers

ELIZABETH ENGSTROM lives in Oregon, and is the author of the extraordinary, ground-breaking *BLACK AMBROSIA,* and *LIZZY,* a chilling and fascinating novel about Lizzy Borden.

CRAIG SHAW GARDNER lives in Cambridge, Massachusetts. His latest project, among many, is a trilogy with the over-title, THE OTHER SINBAD. He's a Godzilla devotee, and collects cowboy songs to which he knows every blessed word.

KATHRYN PTACEK lives in New Jersey, and her latest novel is *THE HUNTED.* She is also the editor of the critically acclaimed WOMEN OF DARKNESS series, publisher of *THE GILA QUEEN'S GUIDE TO MARKETS,* and, in her copious spare time, teaches her cats how to break dance.

CHELSEA QUINN YARBRO is the creator not only of the exquisite vampire, St. Germain, but also of Charlie Moon, attorney-crime solver, whose latest mystery is *POISON FRUIT.* She lives in Berkeley, and when she isn't writing, she's butting wills with a horse named Magic.

NANCY HOLDER lives in San Diego where she raises bees in the walls of her home. Her highly acclaimed and decidedly unique stories have appeared in virtually every major market in the U.S. and UK, and her first horror/thriller novel is *DEAD IN THE WATER.*

STEVE RASNIC TEM, from Denver, has more computers than IBM in his house, is the author of *EXCAVATIONS,* and his stories are consistently among the best published anywhere, in any genre.

CHARLES L. GRANT, from New Jersey, uses his home state as a setting for most of his novels, the latest of which are *STUNTS* (paperbound) and *RAVEN* (hardbound). Among his pseudonyms is Lionel Fenn, the creator of the Kent Montana novels of B-movie adventures.